ADVANCE PRAISE FOR HAVE YOU SEEN HER

"In this clever, breathless thriller, the talented Catherine McKenzie explores deep themes of trauma and revenge against the dangerous, atmospheric backdrop of Yosemite National Park. Full-throttle action mingles with dark secrets and hidden agendas in a gripping thrill ride full of hairpin turns and jaw-dropping twists. You'll devour this in one sitting—I know I did!"

—LISA UNGER, *New York Times* bestselling author
of *Secluded Cabin Sleeps Six*

"I love that each book Catherine McKenzie writes is completely unique. *Have You Seen Her* is no exception. McKenzie immediately hooks us with a wonderfully flawed, layered protagonist trying to unravel her past by returning to the scene of one of her greatest traumas. With the incredibly vivid setting of Yosemite National Park, captivating characters, and superbly executed twists, this thriller is mesmerizing from beginning to end. I absolutely devoured it!"

—SAMANTHA M. BAILEY, author of *Woman on the Edge*
and *Watch Out for Her*

"*Have You Seen Her* is a delicious mix of the physical dangers of the Yosemite wilderness and the secret lives of the humans who visit. McKenzie's latest illuminates that we are, none of us, who we seem, nor can anyone predict what we're capable of when pushed to the limit. A smart, twisty thriller that will have readers glued to the page until the final, explosive chapter, *Have You Seen Her* belongs at the top of your reading list."

—DANIELLE GIRARD, *USA Today* bestselling author of *Up Close*

"The dangers Cassie Peters encounters while working search and rescue in Yosemite National Park can't compete with those she left behind. *Have You Seen Her* is a story of secrets and survival, told with breathless urgency by one of today's leading thriller writers. A skillfully constructed stunner of a novel."

—TESSA WEGERT, author of *The Kind to Kill*

"*Have You Seen Her* is an edge-of-your-seat ride through the world of search and rescue where some of the characters have even more to lose than it appears. Cassie is a protagonist worth rooting for in this high-stakes thriller that gives a whole new meaning to the term 'cliff-hanger.'"

—JESSA MAXWELL, author of *The Golden Spoon*

HAVE YOU SEEN HER

A NOVEL

CATHERINE McKENZIE

ATRIA BOOKS

New York   London   Toronto   Sydney   New Delhi

ATRIA
BOOKS

An Imprint of Simon & Schuster, Inc.
1230 Avenue of the Americas
New York, NY 10020

Copyright © 2023 by Catherine McKenzie

First Atria Books hardcover edition June 2023

ATRIA BOOKS and colophon are trademarks of Simon & Schuster, Inc.

For information about special discounts for bulk purchases, please contact Simon & Schuster Special Sales at 1-866-506-1949 or business@simonandschuster.com.

The Simon & Schuster Speakers Bureau can bring authors to your live event. For more information or to book an event, contact the Simon & Schuster Speakers Bureau at 1-866-248-3049 or visit our website at www.simonspeakers.com.

Interior design by Esther Paradelo

Manufactured in the United States of America

1   3   5   7   9   10   8   6   4   2

Library of Congress Cataloging-in-Publication Data is available.

ISBN 978-1-6680-1111-9
ISBN 978-1-6680-1113-3 (ebook)

In Memory of Those Who Are Lost, But Not Yet Found

CHAPTER 1

PUMPKIN HOUR

Now

We're losing light!" Ben yells over the whir of the blades. "We need to go!"

I turn to look out over the field to the tree line, taking in the scene of the crime. The dark green conifers, with their exposed lower limbs. The trampled grass. A wrapper from a protein bar tumbling over and over like a gymnast. A dark patch in the dirt that looks like it's tinged by rust.

I can't hear anything but the helicopter's whine, but the screams are still caught in my thoughts—sharp, terrified, then cut out, cut off.

"Cassie!" Ben yells next to me. "Move it!"

The fear in his voice unsticks my feet. I turn away, following Ben to the Huey. He goes up first, and I put my foot on the landing gear, careful to keep my head bent as I was taught, conscious of the blade spinning above me. Ben crouches in the opening and reaches out his rough hand. I grab it and let him haul me into the helo's belly. I stumble, then right myself, still bent over.

"You got this?"

I nod and he lets me go. I shuffle to one side and sit in an empty seat, facing Ben and Gareth. As I strap myself in, I try not to think of the body that rests on the floor between us, zipped into a thin black bag by Ben and Gareth after they found me. But the space is so tight that I can't put my feet on the floor without resting them on it. That possibility brings bile to my throat, so I raise my legs in front of me. They protest; I won't be able to keep this position for long.

The pilot checks us over his shoulder. He, like Ben and Gareth, is wearing a dark helmet, a microphone by his mouth. The pilot points to a helmet hanging on a hook next to my head. I grab it and put it on, adjusting the volume with a wheel on the side. It's tight and uncomfortable, edging into the headache that's been building since yesterday.

The pilot's voice is tinny and distant. "We have ten minutes till pumpkin hour."

Ben gives him a thumbs-up, and I feel a moment of confusion until the meaning of the term thunks into place. The helicopter can't fly safely after dark in this mountainous terrain. They call it pumpkin hour, and there won't be a fairy-tale ending if we flirt too hard with that deadline. I know this, I *knew* this, but the shock of everything that's happened has affected more than my motor skills—I can feel it eroding my memory, like a thick fog descending that I must find my way out of before it's too late.

"Everyone strapped in?" the pilot asks as he does his final checks.

"Ready!" Ben says, giving a thumbs-up again. Gareth does the same, and then it's my turn.

I pop my thumb up in a gesture that feels more positive than possible. But I do have some things to be grateful for.

That they found me before it was too late.

That I'm alive.

That there's only one body in a bag at my feet.

The pilot turns away, and then the engine changes gear. The blades above us spin harder, faster, louder as we lift slowly from the ground. It's deep twilight now, the world fading like a watercolor left in the sun, and I cling to the straps holding me in place, petrified of the open door, and that I'll never be able to erase what I saw. What I did.

The Huey banks, heading back to the Heli Base at Crane Flat, circling over the small field we just left.

I don't want to look down, but I can't help but throw a last glance at the scene below. And maybe it's a trick of the fading light, but I swear I can see the faint outline of someone waiting at the edge of the tree line, watching to make sure we fly away.

CHAPTER 2

I SHOT A MAN IN RENO

Then

May

The Reno airport is different than I remember it.

I thought it was as seedy as the rest of that town, the walls caked with cigarette smoke stains, the air fetid from sad people with dried-out hopes, their skin pale in the blinking neon lights. I could envision the shapeless men and women sitting at slot machines with buckets of change in their laps, and a row of bounty hunters skulking at the bar, checking passengers' faces against the images of their prey.

But memory is a fluid thing—I know that better than most. Some memories are so clear and stark that you can recall the smell in the air and the music playing and the dialogue exchanged like it's a movie in your head. Others get painted over by life, or merged with other experiences, or changed entirely because remembering the sights, smells, and sounds is too much to process.

We don't get to choose which our brain keeps, amends, or discards. We just live with the consequences.

Either way, I'm wrong about the airport. It's modern, with

arched ceilings and hotel carpeting. And though there are slot machines, skylights above let in the sunlight and the bar has three thirtysomething women sitting at it, well-dressed and giggling over large glasses of chardonnay. The one in the middle is wearing a bright pink BRIDE T-shirt and a large diamond ring.

I rub at the empty spot on my corresponding finger and breathe a sigh of relief that it's still empty. That this is real, and not some dream I'm pursuing over too many hours.

Someone jostles me from behind. I stumble to the left, then stop just outside my gate. I widen my stance and adjust my pack, unused to the weight and how it affects my balance. At almost fifty pounds, it's a whole procedure to even get it on.

It's been ten years since I moved through the world with everything I own on my back.

I slip my thumbs under the straps, pulling them up and away from my shoulders to get some relief, then walk toward the exit, my steps slow and slumberous. I forgot how hard it is to walk gracefully with this much holding you down. Each step feels like one of those dreams where you try to run for a flight, but your legs are lead and you miss it.

I feel like that all the time now, whether I'm sleeping or not.

Dreams like those are never about something literal, and this feels like that, too. I thought I'd shed it when I got on the plane in New Jersey, but it's followed me through the sunlit sky.

I can change my location, but I've brought myself with me.

"Good luck, Cassie," the woman I sat next to says as she passes me at a brisk clip, her frizzy gray hair held in place by a tennis visor. I don't usually talk to strangers when I'm traveling, but Janice wouldn't be denied. I heard all about how she's in town visiting her daughter and grandchildren and everything they're going to do for the next twelve days.

"Thanks, Janice. Have a good time with your grandbabies."

She flaps a hand in goodbye and strides away, hopefully forgetting all about me. Out of context, I have one of those bland faces—washed-out blue eyes, dark blond hair, regular features. I look like a thousand other women, something that used to annoy me, but it has its uses.

I watch Janice's confident stride. In a moment she's lost in the crowd, and I regret that I didn't take her up on her offer of a nice family meal. Because now I feel truly alone. I don't know anyone here, and there's no one coming to greet me unless I've made a grave miscalculation.

Get to Bishop, Ben had said, *and I'll pick you up.*

There's no flight from Reno to Bishop at this time of year, so my next stop is the bus. But I have one more thing to do before it arrives.

I adjust the straps on my pack again, then continue along the hallway, looking for the right kind of store. I find it near the end of the terminal—a convenience store that sells electronics, including prepaid phones, a *burner* if you're a drug dealer. Something that can't be traced back to me.

I wait behind a stressed-out mother buying a chocolate bar for her wailing kid, then ask the cashier for a phone, pointing to the wall above his head. The pimply eighteen-year-old hands it to me, and when I ask, shows me the pared-down features—how to make a call, how to text, how to block my number.

It isn't hard to be anonymous. All it takes is a couple hundred dollars in cash. I pay for it and add in some snacks for the bus ride. Crackers and cheese, a package of maple-flavored beef jerky, and a Coke. It's almost four hours to Bishop, and the last thing I ate was a bad bagel with cream cheese at Newark at five in the morning.

I leave the store and exit the terminal. The air is warm and dry, the sun high in the sky. I shade my eyes, looking for a bench.

I find one to the right. I put my pack on it and feel around in the top pocket until I find my old phone. I stare at it for a moment, its cherry-red case, the stickers on the back that I collected over time. A daisy. A peace sign. A band logo. This phone has been my lifeline, everything good coming from it—this trip, this job, this change. But now, like so many things, it's time to let it go.

I should've left it in New York, but I couldn't bring myself to do it. If something unexpected came up, I needed a way to communicate. And I should put it in the trash right now without looking back, but I have trouble doing that, too. I want to check in one last time, like that half bottle of wine you swore you wouldn't drink. You know you should pour it out, but one more glass can't hurt, can it?

My hands shake like an alcoholic as I turn it on, wondering how many texts there'll be. It takes a minute for it to connect to the airport's Wi-Fi. Then it shudders and pings as the messages load. In the end, there are five. Four texts and an email for good measure, all saying the same thing.

Where the fuck are you?

My heart starts racing, and my armpits fill with sweat. My fingers hover over the screen, years of reflexes pushing me to answer, to assuage, to diffuse. But I don't do that anymore. I don't have to answer; I'm not going to.

Instead, I control my breathing, then google my old name: *Cassandra Adams*. A few articles load, along with tags in friends' social media posts. I scan the list quickly, but there's nothing new. I try another search: *Cassandra Biggs missing*. Again nothing. And then one more: *Cassie Peters missing*.

Did you mean Cameron Mack missing? Google asks. Below is a link to an article headed with a ten-year-old poster of Cameron Mack and the phrase HAVE YOU SEEN HER? underneath her gap-toothed smile. I stare at her innocent eyes, feeling a mixture of sadness and kinship. Cameron isn't missing anymore, and I don't seem to be either.

I close the browser and take photographs of my important contacts, and the texts, too, in case I need them. When I'm done, I pull the SIM card from my iPhone, then crush it beneath my heel and toss it and the phone into a nearby trash can, watching it disappear below cast-off ice cream cones and soda cans.

That's how easy it is to throw your life way.

On the ride to Bishop, I can't help feeling like one of the men sitting on the bus is watching me. He has that bounty hunter look I was expecting to see at the airport—bulky arms filled with faded, menacing tattoos and a vigilante expression, his aviators covering his eyes. He gives me a hard stare as he walks down the aisle. I stare him down and he looks away, and I tell myself I'm being paranoid. I didn't escape from Guantanamo. There's no crack commando team trying to locate me, just one angry man who doesn't have my number anymore.

I rest my head against the window and watch the scenery. The faded, round hills full of scrub bushes that surround Reno. The blue lakes and bleached-out sky, the sun hot through the window. Small tourist towns that seem to spring up out of nowhere. I've forgotten how everything is so spread out here compared to New York, the years in Manhattan painting over my life before, when I was Cassie Peters, and still thought good things happened to good people.

I drift off for a while, and at some point, we cross into California. When I wake up, the view is made up of large conifers spread out on hillsides with the High Sierras peeking out behind them. My stomach feels empty, hollowed out. I eat the snacks I bought at the airport, wishing I could dig into a healthy meal. The last fresh thing I had was the orange juice I made at the apartment four days ago before I moved into a decrepit motel in Jersey near the airport to let the dust settle before I took my flight.

It was an odd, suspended feeling, being there. Starting at noises outside. Keeping the blinds shut. Only venturing out when I had to, a hat pulled low, my hoodie zipped up to my chin. I slept poorly and my muscles started to hurt from lack of exercise. But when it was finally time to go, I was nervous. I wasn't safe in that motel, but it was a fear I knew. What lay ahead was filled with uncertainties. I left anyway, taking a cab to the airport, and passing through security with my eyes roving over the other travelers. When no one stopped me or pulled me aside, I breathed a sigh of relief that I'd passed the first of many hurdles.

I do that now as I rinse out my mouth from the jerky, the salt clinging to my tongue.

When we arrive in Bishop, it's after six and my hunger is palpable despite the snacks. I'm meeting Ben at Schat's, a local bakery chain that's famous in these parts. It's a short walk from the grocery store parking lot where the bus drops me off, but I have an errand to run first.

The man in the aviators gives me that hard stare again, like he's memorizing me, and I give him my best New York glare back, the one I've learned to use to dissuade catcalls from construction workers. He turns away, and I watch him walk into the arms of a petite woman who he picks up and swings around like a child.

I dismiss him and struggle with my pack. The air is dry and thinner than in Reno. Bishop's at four thousand feet—enough altitude to feel it, especially if you're carrying fifty pounds.

I set off for the post office, and the back of my T-shirt is sweaty within minutes. The buildings look familiar, the memories sharp. I grew up forty miles from here in Mammoth Lakes, and Bishop was where we'd go for supplies and doctors' appointments when my mother remembered to make them. Nothing much seems to have changed in the intervening years.

A car passes me and slows. It's a man driving, his burly arm resting on the windowsill and covered in blurred tattoos. I give him a friendly smile and wave him away. A ride with a male stranger is the last thing I need right now.

I pass a lot full of RVs and trailers protected by a chain-link fence topped with barbed wire. Three people stand near the entrance—an older white woman who's tanned like leather, with short, spiked gray hair; a man in his mid-thirties with a protruding belly; and a younger woman in her mid-twenties with light brown skin and hair that's almost white blond in a thick braid down her back. They appear to be having an animated discussion.

I watch them as I walk past. The older woman seems to be haggling over something. Then the younger woman puts her hand on her arm and says her name distinctly enough that I can hear it. *Sandy.* I know the tone; it's one I've used more times than I care to remember when I want to calm down someone who's being unreasonable. To soothe them right before they explode.

Sandy, she says again, and Sandy finally hears her. She changes her stance, smiles, and she's charming. The man relaxes, says something—a number, maybe?—and then Sandy smiles again and extends her hand to shake. The younger woman releases a slow breath. A deal's been made, everyone's happy, the tension I could sense even across the road evaporating like a desert rain.

I smile too, feeling relief at a crisis averted.

Finally, I arrive at the post office. It's a low, white building with one red and one blue strip running parallel above block chrome lettering. I go inside and search the row of P.O. Boxes until I find mine. The key to it arrived a week before I left, and I put it on the chain around my neck, next to the medallion I wear.

There's a package waiting for me inside, and I take it out, then lock the box back up again. I shove it into the bottom compartment of my pack, groaning at the thought of the extra weight. Then I exit back into the day, my steps a little slower, but feeling more secure.

I arrive at Schat's. It's a Cape Cod–style storefront with a line out the door even though it's seven p.m., the sun settling into the horizon. The smells emanating from inside are incredible—butter, flour, coffee, cream. I still have half an hour before I'm supposed to meet Ben, so I get in the line and wait my turn.

I step into the store, and it's heaven. Shelves piled high with confections in cellophane wrappers and homemade jams glowing like red and orange jewels in glass jars. The sugary smell hanging in the air almost overwhelms me. I've always had a sweet tooth, and I want one of everything. I can't afford that, though, and I've been on a strict diet, dropping ten pounds of city weight while I gained the muscle I need to do my new job. That much sugar and fat would probably fell me.

But I do deserve a treat, so I order a chocolate croissant and a freshly squeezed orange juice. The prices are shocking, even to someone who's used to Manhattan, but when I get back outside and sink my teeth into the *chocolatine*, I don't care what I paid. In this anonymous town, I can groan out my pleasure. No one knows me here anymore, and no one's going to judge.

"Cassie?" a man's voice says, startling me. My head jerks up and panic sets in.

Because despite all my precautions, maybe I've been found out after all.

PHOTOGRAPH—A couple in their early twenties—she's Black, petite, smiling; he's white, all-American, satisfied with himself— with their arms around each other in front of a classic Airstream camper

Liked by **mamajada** and **23 others**

@JadaJohnsonInsta We were supposed to leave at *8* in the AM and now it's after *8* in the PM!!—but it happened, doubters! Jim and I are FINALLY saying adios to Cincinnati and are #ontheroad. That's right, bitches! Finals are DONE, #summer is here (almost, it's hot, whatevs), and it's #YOSEMITE or bust! One hot man and his boo in his daddy's Airstream for the summer! #WhatCouldGoWrong? LOL.

Follow along for all the FEELS, REELS, and STORIES, and drop your hashtag suggestions in the comments. It's getting all Kerouac up in here! Let's goooooo!

#JadaandJimForever #LongHaulSummer #AirstreamLiving #HopeWeDontBustBeforeWeGetThere

mamajada Drive carefully!

theyfreedBritney Squeeee! Wish I was with u! #JadaandJimSittingInAnAirstream

jimislivingthedream @mamajada thanks for the snacks!

bellasgram #BetterYouThanMe

JadaJohnsonInsta @bellasgram ha!

MAY 22

CHAPTER 3

THE BEST BURRITO

Then
May

I did three things in the lead-up to leaving Manhattan: started skimming 20 percent of my gallery salary to save money; enrolled in a wilderness first-responder course to requalify to work in search and rescue; and went to the climbing gym every morning where they also offered a self-defense class. The training and flip takedowns coupled with a strict diet heavy on protein and low on carbs made me feel strong, and reminded me that I could hold my own when I wanted to.

So as this man towers over me outside Schat's, knowing my name and looking like he expected to find me here, my brain immediately tries to decide if I use a choke hold on him or if I just kick him in the nuts and run.

But then he says, "I'm Ben."

Ben, my ride. Ben Cowell, the man I'm supposed to meet here, not the one I'm afraid might find me.

"Oh," I say, hoping my voice is steady, but knowing it isn't. "Hi."

"Sorry to scare you."

"That's all right." I shade my eyes from the setting sun. Ben is outlined like a shadow. He's a few inches taller than me, maybe five ten, has sandy hair, a tanned face, and eyes that are either hazel or green. His body is typical climber: wide shoulders and thinner legs, and he's wearing stone-colored tech pants and a plaid shirt I recognize from too many hours browsing REI online.

"You enjoy your Schat's?" he asks with a knowing smile. His voice is deep and a little slow in its cadence, but pleasant. I'd put his age around thirty, like me, though he could be five years on either side of that.

I look down. The front of my gray sweatshirt is covered in flakes of pastry. I brush them off, blushing with embarrassment. "It was pretty great."

"Sometimes I dream about it, to be honest." I smile as he bends to pick up my pack. He lifts it easily. "This all you got?"

"Yep."

"My truck's just over here."

I follow him to a dark blue Ford pickup. He puts my bag in the back and we climb in. When he turns on the engine, some song by the Grateful Dead blares from the speakers. He reaches over and turns it down. "Sorry about that."

"No worries," I say. "Listen to what you like."

He puts the truck in gear and pulls out, turning north on 395, which will take us to the Lee Vining turnoff to Yosemite. Once in the park, we'll head to Tuolumne Meadows, where we'll be staying for the summer as part of the search and rescue team.

"How was your flight?" he asks.

I'd told him only that I was flying from the East Coast. "Long. And then a bus ride. This day already feels like a thousand years. Where are you coming from?"

Ben's hands are loose on the wheel. "LA."

"You live there?"

"My parents do. In Malibu." He glances at me to gauge my reaction. He comes from money, he's telling me, which can be a touchy thing in climbing culture.

"It's pretty there. Great surfing."

"Indeed." He smiles, the moment passing.

Up ahead, the Sierras loom large in front of us, the last of the sun glinting off the broad, rounded peaks, still half covered in snow. It's cooling off fast as we gain altitude, and I wish I'd pulled my puffy from my pack.

"Do you mind if I turn on the heat?"

"Suit yourself."

I reach for the controls. A hot breeze puffs out of the vents, and I settle in, watching the scenery. I haven't been here in ten years, and it's both familiar and new. Same road, different houses, or old ones with a fresh coat of paint. The mountains never change, though, and I forgot how much I love this view.

"First year on SAR?" Ben asks.

He means search and rescue. "I did a summer ten years ago. You?"

"Fifth year."

"Last one, then?" The park has a policy about how long you can be on the team. Five years is the limit, then you have to move on unless you become a ranger.

"Guess so." He smiles, his face crinkling around his eyes and mouth. "Maybe I'll find a way around that, like Brian."

"Bri's still here?" I say, laughing. Though no one would ever confirm it, Brian was probably the reason for the rule. He came to the park every summer to be part of the team, then couch surfed for the rest of the year, living off his network of climbing buddies and women who found him charming for a few months at a time. The last time I'd seen Bri, he'd been doing naked yoga as the sun rose, giving me a full salutation as a goodbye.

"He's dying in the valley if he can manage it," Ben says.

"So he always said." I shake my head. "Some things never change."

"You spend a lot of time in the park?"

"I grew up in Mammoth. It was our backyard."

"That's cool. How come you only did one summer?"

I shiver despite the heat. "I decided to go to college." That was part of the truth, but if he hadn't heard the whole story, I didn't need to tell it.

We pass the turnoff for Mammoth, and this all suddenly feels more real. My mother still lives there—another person I left behind. I turn the heat up a notch. The valley we're traveling through is wide-open, the purple-streaked sky impossibly high, the massive mountains a darkening outline against it.

Ben glances at me. "Nervous about coming back?"

"A bit. It's been a minute since I worked in a wilderness setting."

"How'd you get the job, then?"

"I reached out to Jenny. We worked together ten years ago." Jenny Evans is the emergency services coordinator, in charge of the search and rescue teams and their staffing. "Someone dropped out last minute, and I was available."

"Gotcha. She's a good boss. What'd you do after college?"

I quell the voice in my head telling me not to answer. His questions are normal, not probing. We're going to spend the summer together. I need to get used to sharing some details. "I moved to Manhattan."

"What made you want to come back?"

I laugh. "Have you been to Manhattan?"

"No, ma'am."

"Too many people, too much ambition, too much of everything."

He nods slowly. "Sounds horrible."

"It has its good parts, but . . . it was time to go."

"Now that, I get."

Time to go, I'd said, and it was time. Past time.

"What do you do in the off-season?" I ask.

"Vegas."

"As a rigger?" Lots of climbers work in Vegas in the winter, doing the rope work needed to mount conventions and Cirque du Soleil shows.

"Yep."

I was in Vegas once years ago for a bachelorette party. I remember the smoky hotel casino lobbies filled with blinking lights and pumped-in air, the impossibly long strip where people handed out playing cards advertising strip clubs and brothels, and the people wandering onto the hotel elevator drunk at nine in the morning. "You must hate it there."

"It's not that bad. Plus, there's great climbing up at Charleston and Red Rock."

"I've heard that. Never made it up there."

"You a climber?"

"Isn't everyone on the team?"

He smiles at me. "Where do you get to climb in Manhattan?"

"Mostly in the gym these days. I'm looking forward to getting back on some real rock."

"Hear, hear."

We crest a hill. On Ben's side of the road, there's a collection of trailer homes and RVs that I don't remember huddled between the asphalt shoulder and the mountainside. Most of the houses we've passed since we left Bishop have been large, meant to impress, sitting on the tops of hillocks, with massive windows pointing toward the Sierras. In contrast, this place has a down-on-its-luck air to it, with rusted-out cars and cement blocks in haphazard piles between the dwellings.

"You hungry?" Ben asks.

"You mean, after I scarfed down that chocolate thing at Schat's?"

He grins. "You want to stop at the Mobil?"

"Do they still have the best tacos?"

"Oh yes. Also mango margaritas." He slows the truck as we approach a Mobil gas station that contains the Whoa Nellie Deli.

Memories crash into me as we drive up the hill. Laughing over drinks and food with Jenny. Dinners with Bri. Looking at the message board fluttering with posters of Cameron's face, begging for information on whereabouts of her and her boyfriend, Chris, who went missing along with her. "Shouldn't we be checking into the park?"

"Doesn't matter what time we arrive tonight. So long as we're at roll call tomorrow morning. Plus . . . did you get supplies in Bishop?"

"No." I'd meant to, but it had taken longer than planned to get to the post office.

"There's not much to be had at the Meadows, in case you don't remember."

"Right. Good idea."

He gives me that grin again—the one I'm sure has gotten him out of a lot of trouble—and parks the car. It's nice to have a man smile at me like that: interested but not predatory.

The light is almost gone now, just a sliver on the horizon, and I shiver when we get out of the truck. I pop into the back and grab my puffy along with a beanie, then follow Ben inside.

The Mobil sells T-shirts and the usual gas station supplies, including a couple of aisles of groceries. There's also a food counter where you can order tacos and sandwiches and yes, margaritas. The last time I was here, I'd had three of them, the second one giving me a brain freeze that felt like it was splitting my head in two.

I'd left Yosemite a week later and gone to college in Colorado, trying to leave the guilt I'd been attempting to blot out behind.

"Why don't you pick up what you need for the next week, and I'll grab dinner?" Ben says. "Carnitas okay, or are you veggie?"

"Not veggie. That sounds good. And thanks."

He walks to the counter, and I take a basket and wander the aisles, checking prices as I go. One of the odd things about my new job is that I'll only get paid if I go out on a rescue. I'll have a camping spot and unlimited access to the park, but that's it. I've budgeted fifty dollars a week for food, which isn't going to get me anything that's fresh or healthy, certainly not in a gas station. I fill my basket with mac and cheese and ramen noodles, spaghetti, and canned sauce.

In Manhattan, I never checked the price of anything, just tipped whatever I wanted into my cart without a care. When I think of some of the things I've left behind—clothes with the tags still on, shoes I never felt comfortable in, the thousand-dollar phone I threw in the trash—I feel ashamed. But that life's gone now, so I can spend a week eating like a college student and hope that next week's shop will be healthier.

I pay at the register—forty-seven dollars and thirty-two cents—pocket the change and go to find Ben. He's picking up our tray filled with fish tacos and two cocktails in plastic cups with paper straws.

"What do I owe you?"

"Nah, it's on me."

I think about protesting, but paying Ben back is out of the

budget, so instead I thank him, and we head out onto the back patio and sit under a heat lamp. The tacos are as good as I remember, and the sweet margarita, too. We eat in silence as the stars come out above us, filling the darkening sky with pinpoints of light. Across the road is Mono Lake, a saline soda body of water that has a high alkaline content, which used to be the water supply for Los Angeles, until a conservation group sued to stop it.

I take the last bite of my second taco as an old RV turns off the road and pulls my focus. It parks cautiously next to Ben's truck. It's the women from Bishop—Sandy and the younger, striking one, who looks like she could be her daughter. But when she comes around the corner of the RV, Sandy reaches out her hand. The young woman takes it, smiling in a way that's not familial. She's got a large daisy tattooed on the back of her hand, a trail of petals blowing off it. They stop, and Sandy pulls her in for a deep kiss.

A man behind us whoops and they break apart. Sandy's face registers annoyance. She's fierce, protective. It's an expression I recognize and fear.

"People are jerks," Ben says.

"Understatement."

Sandy pulls the young woman toward the entrance, her defiance clear. "Come on, Petal."

Petal follows in her wake. As they pass us, Petal's eyes slide toward mine. Her face is kind, open, innocent, but her eyes tell a different story.

Petal is afraid.

"Ready to say your goodbyes?" Ben asks.

I tear my eyes away from Petal's and Sandy's retreating backs. "What?"

"To civilization."

"Oh, ha. Yes, I guess so."

"Don't worry, I'm happy to bring you into 'town' whenever you need something."

"That's nice of you to offer."

He stands and gives me a slightly devastating smile. "We're teammates, right?"

"Right."

We clear our places and I steal one last glance back into the Mobil. Petal and Sandy are wandering the aisles, picking items off the shelves. They catch stares from the other patrons, a guy in a trucker hat with a Confederate logo on the brim, and a young couple dressed in ski jackets that I guess are heading to Mammoth for the last skiing of the season.

I turn and follow Ben out to his truck. On the drive up to the Tioga Pass entrance, the road is dark, and empty, a dome of stars above. It's a steady climb, gaining over another three thousand feet in elevation to what we climbed between Bishop and Lee Vining, and near the entrance my ears pop. This entrance only opens to regular visitors in four days for Memorial Day weekend, but the ranger lets us through when Ben explains who we are.

Once we're through the barrier, we start to pass familiar landmarks. Mono Dome. Tioga Peak. Mount Dana. Eventually, we arrive at Tuolumne Meadows, where the SAR site is located in the middle of the campground. We'll be part of the "T-SAR." There's another SAR site on the valley floor an hour away—the team there is called YOSAR—but this is the one I'd asked Jenny to assign me to. Tuolumne is where I'd grown up roaming, the place I was the most familiar with. It felt more manageable for my first summer back, away from the hustle and bustle of Half Dome and El Cap.

Ben checks in with the head law enforcement ranger, who I'll meet in the morning, and points me toward a tent, one of eight set in a circle in the middle of the wooded site.

"Thank you so much for everything," I say, feeling shy and tired as we linger near the truck. It's past ten, but I'm still thinking in Manhattan time, automatically calculating that it's one a.m. tomorrow.

"No trouble at all," Ben says, his eyes soft and warm. "Get some rest. Orientation in the morning." He pulls my bag from the truck bed and brings it to the entrance to my tent, then puts it down gently. He rests his hand on my shoulder and squeezes. Its warmth feels nice, like his smiles. "Goodnight."

" 'Night, Ben."

I zip open the door and lug my pack inside. I take my camp lamp out and turn it on.

The tent is eight-by-eight. It's high enough at the peak to stand in, sloping down to the sides. On one side, there's a small platform for an air mattress, on the other, a makeshift set of shelves made of old boards and cinder blocks, and that's it. It smells musty, and like it might be the last resting place of a mouse. I grimace, then prop the tent flap open to clear the air out.

I used to live in a two-thousand-square-foot apartment on the Upper West Side with a doorman and empty rooms that were meant for children I didn't have. I had friends whose apartments were triple the size and the only place they worked up a sweat was in their Peloton classes. If they could see me now, they'd laugh their asses off.

If *he* could, it would be a different story.

I shiver and take out my new phone. It has service, though Ben warned me that it was still intermittent in the park, depending on location. I tap in one of the numbers I photographed off my old phone at the airport.

This is Cassie. Arrived safely, I type, waiting for the text to send.

The response comes quickly. *Good. Everything go smoothly?*
I think so.
Call if you need to. This number is secure.
I will.

I put the phone down, then turn it off. It's been odd not having messages to check. I can't think of the last time I spent an entire day without electronic communication. I miss my phone, that constant buzz of someone reaching out. It feels pathetic, given everything, but I can't help it.

I reach inside my shirt and pull out the chain with the key to the post box and my medallion. It's got a butterfly stamped on it, emerging from its chrysalis. I trace my fingers over the form, thinking about its meaning. How you can start off as one thing and become another. How that can happen through biology but also through will. That's what I'm doing here. Changing myself.

My shoulders slump. I'm exhausted, but finally, the edge of fear I've been living with has loosened its grip. I could sleep standing up, but I need to unpack first.

I tuck the medallion away and empty my pack. I blow up my air mattress, then cover it with my sleeping bag. I add a travel pillow in a pillowcase, fluffing it up with some warmer clothes. I create a nightstand by hauling the bookshelf over and fill it with the clothes I've brought. Climbing gear and trekking pants. Long shirts and T-shirts. A warm thermal layer. I have two of everything, and seven pairs of underpants, my life edited down to the essentials.

I put a flashlight and a GPS tracker next to my toiletry bag, not quite ready to find the facilities on the other side of the campground. Instead, I change out of my travel clothes, slipping into a warm pair of sweatpants and my top thermal layer. I put my puffy back on, zipping it to the chin, and keep my beanie in place.

Then I sit on the edge of my makeshift bed and reach into my pack for the last item that I picked up at the post office earlier.

It's encased in a cloth, wrapped over and over so it's shapeless. I unwind it carefully, feeling its weight, the metal cold in my hand once I free it from the binding.

A gun.

May 20—Lee Vining RV Park

We got it! The PERFECT trailer. Sandy negotiated the best deal in Bishop, and now we'll have a REAL home, not some nasty pop-up where we're always on top of each other. Not that I don't love to be on top of Sandy. Ha! Can you believe Daddy asked me that when I told him I was leaving with her?? Fucking perv. Whatever. He can keep his Lord and his Fox News and his Sunday Night Football! I'm FREEEE.

Maybe if Mama were still around things would be different. I mean, being dropped off with Daddy wasn't a picnic, not gonna lie, but she couldn't take me to all those places she sent me postcards from, could she? Bali and Bengali. The Andes and the Rockies. The last one I got was from right here, Bishop, California, though I guess the closer address would be NAMELESS COMMUNITY NEXT TO LEE VINING. Ha! Sandy says I have a knack for sarcasm. I think that's what she loves most about me.

But oh! I'm supposed to be using this to work on my writing. Journaling, that writer lady called it in that one class I took at the community college, right before I met Sandy. Write every day, she also said, though that seems like a lot. If I practice describing what I see as often as possible, eventually I'll have the chops to write something worth a damn, apparently.

Here goes: Tonight at the Mobil—it was full of rednecks from out of state and this one couple who looked so in love, only they were in love with skiing. Mammoth THIS and Mammoth THAT I heard them saying in their rich East Coast accents. I tried to imagine what it was that they loved so much. Why they felt the need to ride a mechanical chair and strap on expensive plastic to enjoy the outdoors. Was it the fancy jackets they got to wear? The helmets? I saw the label on the woman's jacket, and I recognized it from that Patagonia store Sandy and I window-shopped at in LA before we came up here a month ago. It was seven hundred dollars! I've never had that much money in my life, though Sandy handed over much more than that to the man at the RV place, so I guess we do have that much money. Sandy pulled that big wad of cash out of the mattress. Not under, but out of.

I asked Sandy about it, and she says there's a lot more where that came from, only we shouldn't talk about it, and sometimes I feel like she's saying that because she's testing me. Wondering if I'm with her for the money, even though I didn't know she had it. Like I might've been able to smell it on her through the patchouli oil and vape. But I'm with her for love. If she hadn't come along, I was leaving anyway. I was going to get my own life. Maybe I'd follow those postcards from Mama until I found her.

"She can't replace your mother, you know." That's another thing Daddy had to say. Like he couldn't understand why I'd be attracted to someone old enough to be his old lady, even though my "aunts" have been getting younger by the year, like some science experiment or that Dorian Gray portrait Mr. James made us read about in the eleventh grade before I dropped out.

Whatever.

I guess that isn't very literary. People in the fancy books Sandy reads don't say "whatever." They speak in song lyrics, and go on about trees, or how a rosebush has all these white flowers except a few that are starting to rot. These books are so boring they make me want to SCREAM.

Sandy says they're good for me. But I don't want to write like that. I want to write FREE, like the feeling I had when we drove away from Daddy's musty shack in Cape Cod, how the sand flew up under our wheels and we were AWAY, no looking back.

Like that other woman I saw in the Mobil tonight, the one with the hot guy who kept looking at her like she was a Christmas present.

"Cassie," I heard him call her.

She had this look on her face like she's scared someone might catch up to her. Like in those horror movies right before the bad man pops up right in front of you in the woods.

—Petal

CHAPTER 4

WELCOME, DIRTBAGS

Then

May

My radio crackles next to me. "This is Victor 1." Eric Moser, the head law enforcement officer, is calling. His call sign is Victor 1. "We have a W call on Lembert Dome."

I've spent the last two days in orientation and training, refamiliarizing myself with the park, going over rope protocols, learning call signs and strategies and passing my "pack" test, where each member of the team has to complete a three-mile course with forty-five pounds on their back. We've each been assigned a pager and a radio, and it takes a little getting used to, waiting for that crackling sound and the jolt at your waist. I'd forgotten how it sets my heart beating, how the adrenaline rushes through my bloodstream when a call comes in. It's a thrill, but it's exhausting, too—like a high, there's a comedown afterwards that can leave you feeling strung out and weak.

Lembert Dome is nearby, just up the road from the campground. I pick up my radio. "Victor 1, this is SAR Peters. Responding to the W call on Lembert Dome."

"Copy that, SAR Peters."

I sigh as I stand up from the battered picnic table where I've just finished a late breakfast. I was up early to climb a nearby wall, my first day back on the rock. It felt good to be out there, but I kept it short so I didn't tire myself out. It's not even Memorial Day weekend yet, and already the distress calls are coming in fast and furious.

It's been all minor calls so far—people who are found before I get there, someone who dropped their keys on the trail, an annoyed and entitled man who thought he could ask us to bring him water. And then there are the W calls—our code word for "wimp." Out-of-shape people who hike themselves into the wilderness and can't get out, clutching their chests, claiming heart attacks that turn out to be panic attacks. Depending on the nature of the injury and whether it's real or imagined, they may get charged for their rescue by the Park Service.

Not that all the calls are unserious. There are real heart attacks and strokes, injuries where a climber has to be littered out or removed by airlift. Those are the truly stressful calls, where it's your skill and speed that will mean the difference between life and death. Innocent mistakes can turn serious quickly in the wilderness. A tired hiker can die of exposure if they aren't found fast enough, particularly in the spring. The park is alluring, but dangerous, and that's why we're here—to help visitors focus on the positive and not end up on the wrong side of their enthusiasm.

"You want company?" Ben asks, coming out of his tent. It's a cool day, and he's dressed for it in long pants, a fleece top, and a puffy jacket, the yellow of his Yosemite search and rescue shirt poking out at the collar. I'm wearing the same shirt over a long-sleeved thermal layer under my own red puffy.

"Sure."

Ben grabs his rescue pack and puts his radio harness on, the radio diagonal across his chest so that it's easy to access. Then we go to the SAR cache and take one of the park vehicles for the short drive up the road to the base of Lembert Dome. It's around ten, and the morning mist has burned off the meadow, though the dew is still clinging to the grass. The sky is light blue and clear— by the afternoon, it might feel like summer is coming.

I turn the vehicle into the parking lot. It's full of cars, and there's a line for the bathroom.

"Must be one of the school groups," Ben says, pointing to a collection of yellow buses on the far side of the lot. They come into the park in all weather, but this is a peak time, right before the end of the semester.

"Likely." I park the vehicle, and we grab our gear and walk to the trailhead. I hesitate at the beginning of the trail, memories flooding back to me. This is where I started my last rescue ten years ago.

"You okay?" Ben asks, resting a hand on my shoulder.

"Yeah," I say. "First week jitters; it's nothing."

"It'll be fine."

"Of course. Let's head up. Which way should we go?"

Lembert is a sloping dome of granite that's about nine hundred feet of vertical, which springs up from the surrounding meadow like it was dropped there from outer space. There's a three-mile loop trail that goes around the back, or you can climb up the steeper slope to the top. That way is bare and looks intimidating, though it's an easy climb with the right gear.

"Hold on." Ben checks in with the dispatcher. The call came from near the top, but on the trail. "Let's take the trail. That way we can run up and get there sooner."

Ben's not kidding about running up. It's what part of all my training was for, to get myself in that kind of shape. One where running up a mountain doesn't leave me hobbling the next day. There's been a lot of that these last couple of days, and every part of my body hurts.

We take off at a quick pace. The trail is full of teenagers, talking loudly and breaking branches off the passing trees. We weave through them and issue warnings about preserving the wilderness. About a mile in, our radio crackles.

"SAR Peters, this is SAR Smith." It's our teammate Gareth calling.

I use my radio. "SAR Peters, go ahead."

"This situation is deteriorating. Where are you?"

My heart accelerates. "Half a mile."

"Pick up the pace."

"Will do, over."

"That's not good," Ben says. "If Gareth's worried . . ."

I nod in agreement. In the short time I've known Gareth, I've never seen him stressed. And judging by Ben's expression, neither has he.

I met Gareth and his girlfriend, Mia, on the first day of orientation. They're an odd pairing who've been working SAR for a couple of years. He's a big, overconfident bear of a man who likes to laugh no matter the circumstances, while she's petite, Asian, and quietly self-assured. I'd heard of her before I got here because she's a sponsored climber who often appears in climbing magazines. She's earned her reputation free soloing some of the hardest pitches in the world and sending new routes up El Cap and Half Dome. Gareth's specialty is bouldering, a strongman activity that involves climbing up boulders with no ropes or other protection.

"We'd better get up there," I say.

"Agreed."

We increase our pace, pressing up the hill. My calves protest, and my mind starts to cycle over the possibilities of what we'll find.

We clear the forest path, and now we're on the smooth, rocky part of the trail. There's a small cluster of people up ahead, off the trail marked by cairns on the bare rock. A woman is lying prone, and Gareth and Mia are hovering over her along with a small circle of lookie-loos.

Accidents always draw a crowd.

My breath is ragged but I'm focused, going through my mental checklist of what to do. Her right leg is lying at an odd angle and already I'm thinking it's a break and we're going to have to carry her down, an arduous procedure depending on the person's weight, where they're strapped to a litter and then walked or rolled down the mountain. This woman appears slender, fit. Hopefully it won't be too bad.

"Mia," I say, and she turns to me.

Her dark hair is hidden by a knit cap, and her brown eyes are bright and kind. She smiles, but it's not relaxed. "You made it."

"Assessment?"

"Woman, early thirties, suspected ankle fracture."

I crouch down to examine the ankle. Gareth is blocking the view of the woman's face in front of me. "Gareth," I say to get his attention. He steps aside and then starts to shake. Is he in shock? And why is everyone looking at me like that?

"Cassie," a voice says, and my eyes trail away from the woman's ankle to her face. It's Jenny Evans, the emergency services coordinator, and she's smiling.

Gareth starts to laugh loudly, clutching his sides as he shouts a phrase I've already become too familiar with. "Welcome, dirtbags!"

Dirtbag. That's me.

"So," I say to Jenny twenty minutes later. "Did I pass?"

We're hiking back down Lembert Dome, completing the loop around it. Jenny's ankle is fine. The call was a sort of hazing, a prank, one I'm surprised Jenny would agree to participate in, frankly. Gareth, on the other hand, had laughed his ass off, and said, over and over, "You should've seen your face!"

"I told you already, you made the team," Jenny says in her clipped voice.

I learned a long time ago not to take her tone personally; it's the way she speaks, as if she's always in a hurry, which she generally is. People often told us we looked like sisters, but the resemblance is superficial—two bland blondes with light blue eyes and Waspish features. She's shorter than me and tougher, her forearms thick and strong, the planes of her face hard and chiseled. "Why the hazing, then? I thought you weren't into that kind of stuff?"

"Truth?"

"Yeah."

She glances over her shoulder. Gareth and Mia got called away to another rescue, and Ben is talking to a group of hikers about fifty feet behind us. We're alone. "I wanted to see how you'd react."

"Because of when we found Cameron?"

"Of course because of when we found Cameron."

"That was a long time ago."

"Sure, but you haven't been in the scene since then." Jenny stops and puts her hands on her hips. "I took a risk in hiring you, okay? Called in some favors. I can't have you falling apart on me like you did that day."

"That's not how I remember it." What I remember is that we

were both a mess. Nothing, *nothing*, prepares you for the sight of a dead body. It's grisly even when you don't know them and didn't have anything to do with their disappearance.

We were both exhausted and sick at the sight of her, but Jenny was the one who went into shock while I had to clean up our mistakes.

In the aftermath, we'd each reacted differently. I'd thrown in the towel and tried to put it behind me, while Jenny had dived right back in and eventually became management.

"Be that as it may," Jenny says, "I need to know I can rely on my team."

"Me, you mean?"

"Yes."

"And? Can you?"

Jenny turns and starts to walk at a brisk pace. I follow her, catching up, matching her quick, sure strides. "Ben tells me you're smart, responsive, and have good instincts with people. He thinks you're a bit guarded and secretive, but he's happy to have you on the team."

My stomach drops. "Ben told you that?"

"He's been assessing you."

This stops me in my tracks. I look back at Ben, who's almost caught up to us. He gives me a friendly smile and I return it with a fake one, thinking about the fact that he's been spying on me since we met. I thought we were building a team, but he was reporting on me this whole time. The thought of it makes my blood boil.

I hate to be watched more than anything.

"Would've been nice to know," I say to Jenny.

"Frankly, I'm surprised you didn't. Isn't it what you'd do in my position? You contact me out of nowhere after ten years of radio silence . . ."

"I needed a job."

"So you said. And I gave you one, but that's all I owe you, Cassie. Nothing more. Whatever happened out there . . . This pays my debt."

I start to protest, to say that I hadn't been calling in any favors, but that isn't true. I knew exactly what I was doing when I called Jenny. When I'd filed my report about our rescue, I'd made her the hero. I knew she was ambitious, and I helped her along the path I didn't want. "Fair enough. And I'm sorry about the radio silence."

"Thanks for saying that," Jenny says. "Friend hat?"

"Friend hat."

"Sometimes it's hard to be the boss."

"I get it."

"I want you to succeed here."

"Thank you."

"But I'm not quite sure what to do with you. What to make of all this. What were you doing, all this time?"

"Just . . . living my life."

Once I'd left SAR and gone to college, I drew a hard line with my past. I learned quickly never to talk about that summer. At first it was because every time I mentioned it, someone brought up Cameron. Her case had garnered national attention—when a beautiful, white nineteen-year-old goes missing, the media takes notice. While we were searching for her, there'd been wild speculation about what had happened. Was there a killer on the loose? Had she been kidnapped? Was her boyfriend to blame? And even after we found her, that speculation persisted. Somehow the truth didn't spread as far and wide as the rumors.

Either way, I didn't like everyone's ghoulish fascination with something I was trying to forget, so it was easier not to mention Yosemite, or T-SAR or any of it. Eventually, the whole place faded into my background, which proved useful when I needed a place where *I* could disappear.

"I really do appreciate everything you're doing for me, Jenny."

"I'm happy to help. Just don't make me look bad, okay?"

Ben catches up with us and punches me lightly in the shoulder. "On a scale of one to ten, how mad would you be if I told you there's video of your reaction back there?"

"What?"

"It's priceless, I promise."

I try to keep my voice calm. "What are you planning on doing with this video?"

"I thought TikTok?"

"Can you not?"

He frowns. "What's the big deal?"

"I hate all that social media stuff."

"Sure, no problem."

"Thanks."

The cloud lifts, and Ben is back to his sunny self. "How about I show you Wild Willy's Hot Springs to make it up to you?"

Jenny laughs. "She knows Wild Willy's."

"Oh, right. I keep forgetting you're from here."

"No worries. That does sound great though, thanks, Ben."

He rubs his hands together. "Perfect. I'll invite Gareth and Mia too, yeah?"

"Sure."

The radio at Jenny's hip crackles. "Sierra 1, this is Victor 1."

She raises her radio to her mouth. "Sierra 1, over."

"We have a wet rescue at Tenaya Lake."

Jenny looks at us. "You got this?"

"On it," I say.

Jenny clicks her radio on. "SAR Peters and SAR Cowell are assigned."

"Copy that."

Jenny gives me an encouraging pat, as if to hurry us along, and I let Ben take the lead, falling into rhythm behind him, my heart rate inching back up. A wet rescue can mean anything from hypothermia to a drowning. Either way, this one is real.

It's time to prove to myself, and Jenny, that I belong.

PHOTOGRAPH—Indian Museum of Art

Liked by **mamajada** and **35 others**

@JadaJohnsonInsta Three days in! Or is it four? Time flies when you're #ontheroad! We're not on a schedule, stopping where we feel like it. So now it's time for a #photodump!

This is us in #Indiana #Missouri #Oklahoma. The #indianmuseumofart was AWESOME! Check out this funky building—doesn't it look like a spaceship?

Next up was the #GatewayArch. Oh yes, we're doing ALL THE THINGS! Jim was DYING to see this cowboy museum, so here we are—check out Jim's hat! Giddy-up!

Next up, we try to figure out how to #pumpanddump this Airstream. Yuck! @jimislivingthedream will be bringing that to you live! Check out our #reels.

Laters, bitches!

#JadaandJimForever #LongHaulSummer #AirstreamLiving #HopeWeDontBustBeforeWeGetThere

mamajada Are you eating three meals a day, honey? You know you get cranky when you skip your food.

theyfreedBritney What the hell is a pump and dump?

jimislivingthedream @mamajada don't worry Mrs. Johnson! I'm feeding her on the regular.

bellasgram @theyfreedBritney Do NOT google it.

Papajim @jimislivingthedream call us when you get to the pumping station, and we'll talk you through it.

MAY 25

May 25—Lee Vining RV Park

We're solid in the new RV now. We spent a day cleaning it out from top to bottom—it took twelve hours because that place was FILTHY.

Found: three dead mice, moldy cereal, one USED condom, six old newspapers, a container of matches from a bar, and forty dollars in change. The change was EVERYWHERE, under every pillow we lifted, every corner we checked, like the dude who owned it before had thrown a cupful of it up in the air as if he was making it rain in a casino.

Sandy said I could keep the forty dollars and buy myself a treat, like she was my mama or something, which I did NOT appreciate. We had a fight about it, but then we got to make up, which was pretty awesome. If I'm serious about this writing thing, I'd try to put down how she makes me feel when she kisses me DOWN THERE, but I feel shy about it, like I'm writing one of those romance novels Mama abandoned in our trailer when she ran away.

Once the trailer was clean, we were disgusting. The shower in the RV isn't working well yet, so Sandy suggested we check out one of the hot springs out Mammoth way called Wild Willy's, a kind of natural bath, and she was right, like she always is about everything.

I don't know who did it—a lot of people, I guess?—but there's this pool made of concrete, full of water that comes out of the springs just out in the open in a field. It has taps for hot and cold water so you can adjust the temperature just like a bath! I'd always thought a hot spring would be a pool in the woods, something you'd happen on and sink into in relief. But this one is in a place that's more like a moonscape, with steam rising from the rock. When you sit in it, you have this awesome view of the High Sierras and rolling, grassy meadows and the sky, the sky, the sky.

I was so dirty the water clouded after I got in, and the other couple who were already in it looked annoyed and got out. We didn't care, though. That meant we had it to ourselves.

We've gone back every night. It's a forty-five-minute drive each way, but I like it. The hum of the road, the way Sandy sings along with the radio. She has a good voice, and she regrets not becoming a singer, she says, though I'm not sure her voice is THAT good. But it's just nice, you know, us driving somewhere, like we were in the beginning, before we settled down in the RV park full of crusty permanent residents that remind me of Daddy, and through-travelers that Sandy calls "itinerants." Like that's not who we are. Like we also don't have an itinerary.

I'm not sure why she's so judgey, but I guess it's because we're here to stay now, at least for the summer and maybe longer than that. Not that this was a decision we took together. Sandy said it the other night over our SpaghettiOs and looked at me in this way she has when she's waiting for me to agree.

I learned a long time ago that it's easier to go along with it when she gets like that. Daddy's like that too.

Tonight, we had Wild Willy's all to ourselves for a while until this group arrived from the park. Search and rescue workers, they said, only they called it "SAR," like I'd know what that was. I recognized the one couple from the Mobil the other night, only I'm not sure they're a couple. The girl is Cassie, and the cute guy is Ben.

They were quiet, mostly because this other guy, Gareth, who was so big he created this, like, WAVE, when he got in the water, talked a lot. His girlfriend—Mia—seemed sweet. She's very pretty, and I could tell Sandy was checking her out in her bathing suit. She has one of those tight bodies, with muscles in her stomach like a man. I wasn't jealous, exactly, but I'm never going to look like that.

Whatever.

There's that word again. It drives Sandy nuts, so maybe that's why I use it. Ha!

I'm curious about the girl, though. Not Mia, I get her. She'll stay with Loud Gareth a couple years, then she'll move on to someone else. But Cassie. She reminds me of someone. Maybe it's her expression, how watchful she is. Maybe it's how even when she laughed when Ben splashed her, there was a second before it happened, and in that one moment that maybe only I saw, she looked like Mama used to look right before Daddy hit her.

—Petal

CHAPTER 5

FLOAT LIKE A BUTTERFLY

Now

Twilight ends like someone snapped off the light. I can see the worried expression on Ben's face and the outline of the pilot's set jaw, his hands tight on the controls. We left too late, and now we're in the air when we should be on the ground.

It's pumpkin hour, but we'll be okay. There's still an orange glow on the horizon, and we don't have far to go. Fifteen miles over ground. The ride out will be ten minutes, even though it took me two days to hike there. The contrast takes my breath away, the time a fault line in my life.

On the way in, I still had hope that this would all work out. Now it's gone.

I turn away from what we left behind, catching Venus setting through the ombre sky. It's bright, steady, close, like the North Star, though it rises in the east.

I pull my focus back into the Huey, steadily avoiding the dark form under my hovering feet as my legs start to shake from the effort. I can't think about it—*him*—or I'll fall apart. I hug myself to stop my shivering, my body's temperature slowly returning to normal. My legs are starting to itch under my mud-caked trek pants, like they used to in winter when I'd run in Central Park.

Another life. Another fault line.

My stomach is empty, my mind full of questions I cannot answer. How am I ever going to explain any of this? How can I even begin?

I sense movement and meet Ben's eyes—they're still clouded with worry. He looks away and out at the fading sky. I can see more stars now, ones I don't know the names of. He clenches his hands against his knees.

"We're almost there," I yell to Ben to calm him.

Ben starts to speak, then stops himself. He takes off his helmet, fiddles with something on the side, then puts up two fingers. He wants me to change channels so we can speak privately. I glance at Gareth. His head is resting back on the seat, his eyes closed—he's likely sleeping; he's famous for doing that anywhere, anytime. But the pilot can hear us, so I take off my helmet and find the channel wheel next to the volume. I change it to two, then put it back on, the loud whir of the engine dimming when the helmet settles back over my ears.

"What happened out there?" Ben says. It's odd to watch his mouth move and have the sound reach my ears at a different speed, like a movie whose soundtrack is slightly off the beat.

"He found me," I say. "I don't know how."

"*He* found *you*?"

I thought Ben might understand, that I'd told him enough over the course of the summer, but my head is still cloudy, and my headache has a tight grip. I reach my hand back to the lump at the base of my skull. When I touch it, I feel queasy. The hit was harder than I thought.

"He was too strong," I say, trying to explain. "He . . . He was so angry."

Ben's face is in a deep frown, like my words aren't reaching him. Maybe I'm not talking loudly enough despite the microphone hovering above my mouth. But then Ben glances down and nudges the black body bag with his foot.

"Who is it?" he asks distinctly, and for a moment, I'm not sure what he's saying. Didn't he see who it was when they put him inside? But no, I forgot what happened to his face. I tried not to see it, knowing I'll never be able to erase it, but I didn't look away fast enough.

"Cassie?" Ben says, again with that delay between his lips and the sound in my ears. "Who's in there?"

I try to find the words, but my tongue feels thick. I can't get the name out.

"Cassie!" Ben's voice is sharp now, a command. "Who is it?"

My mind forms the name. It gets stuck in my throat, and then, finally, my mouth complies, releasing it like an obscenity. "It's Kevin."

Ben pushes back and away from me, recoiling into his seat as the Huey circles over the landing zone, settling down in the dark night. I watch the ground get closer, closer, and then we land as gently as a butterfly on a leaf and the pilot cuts the engine. As the blades above us rotate lazily, four members of the SAR team sprint toward the Huey with a stretcher like it's an episode of M*A*S*H.

Gareth stirs, the first time he's moved since we got into the chopper, and he and Ben help the team take the body out. It's stiff and difficult to maneuver, and I try not to think about why that is. How long he's been dead, and what that might mean.

"You going to help here?" Gareth asks me, annoyed, but I just sit in my seat, my harness still on, and shake my head.

"Leave it, Gar," Ben says, and I'm grateful.

Gareth mutters something under his breath, cursing me, and

then the body is outside and their footsteps thunder away, and it's quiet as the pilot goes through his postflight checks. I know I need to stand, to leave the Huey, to follow my teammates inside, but I can't make myself move. I'll just stay here, I think, until someone comes looking for me.

I don't have long to wait. Jenny pokes her head inside. "Cassie?"

My head lolls to the side, all my energy gone. "Hi, Jenny."

"Are you okay?"

"Honestly?"

"Let's get you out of here." She steps in and crouches in front of me. She unclips my harness, then helps me up. My legs wobble and I rest on her arm to walk around the place where the body rested.

The body.

Is that how I'll always think of him now?

"Careful stepping out," Jenny says as she jumps off the edge and lands lightly on the ground, flexing her knees. She turns and waits for me, ready to help.

I contemplate jumping, but my legs are shaking, so I sit on my bum and slip out, then raise up. It takes me a minute to orient myself to where we are. It's the Heli Base at Crane Flat, twenty-five miles from Tuolumne Meadows. I can hear the insects in the trees, the snap and crackle of the woods, and there's a sharp wind on my face. The half-moon is partially obscured by passing clouds, black outlines against the bright white.

"Cassie?" Jenny says. She's buttoned up against the night, her dark jacket and pants a contrast to the light braids of her hair that are hanging down over her shoulders.

"Yes?"

"I spoke to Ben . . . What's going on?"

"I tried to find them."

"Alone?"

"I know, it was stupid . . . I . . . I made a mistake."

"Who's that in there, though?" I follow her pointing finger to the building where the team disappeared. It's a log cabin structure, darkened wood with a green door. "Who is he, Cassie? Who is Kevin?"

I drag my eyes away from the building. They're filling with tears, blurring the world, blurring my life. Each time I hear his name, it's like a blow. And the fact that he's dead doesn't bring me any comfort at all.

"My husband," I say. "He's my husband."

CHAPTER 6

SHAKE IT OFF

Then
May

Memorial Day weekend is a beast. The weather is perfect and everyone within a thousand miles seems to have come to the park. The line to get in is hours long, the parking lots are full, and cars start to park haphazardly along the side of the road, causing traffic jams and frustrated motorists. The air fills with honking horns and an occasional yahoo yelling out their window, and half the SAR team is put on traffic duty.

It passes in a blur. A group of hikers doing the Pacific Crest Trail somehow wander off, and it takes us a day to find them. A woman goes into labor a month early and delivers in the first aid station. A busted ankle, a busted arm, three people stranded on El Cap for two days, a crowd huddled below, shooting videos on their phones and posting them to social media with hashtags like #ElCapMorons and #CappedOut.

By the end of the weekend we're all exhausted, and we watch in relief as the families pack up their cars and drive out of the park. No one lost their life during the first long test of the season, and now the place will settle into its summer schedule, a steadier flow during the week and busy on the weekends, but manageable until July 4.

In the meantime, we're having a cookout. It was Ben's idea, a way to wind down and celebrate. Gareth and Mia are here, along with Sam and George—the two other members of the T-SAR team. Brian and Jenny are coming, and even Eric Moser, the head law enforcement officer, might stop by.

We've all contributed something. Ben's making burgers and sausages, and I made a batch of cornbread in a cast-iron skillet that Jenny loaned me. Mia mixed a large salad in a bowl shaped out of a solid piece of wood, and Gareth's in charge of drinks. There's a cooler of beer and cider sitting under one of the aspens, shaded from the sun.

We gather in the common area between the SAR tents, around the picnic tables and the barbecue. Before the cookout started, I took the best shower I've had since I got here, timing the hot water right, finally feeling clean for the first time in days. Then I changed into a pair of sweatpants and a fleece sweater and covered my wet hair with a beanie.

"Cassie!" Brian says, grabbing me from behind and picking me up off the ground.

"Bri!"

He drops me with a laugh, and I hug him properly. No one knows exactly how old Bri is, but my best guess is sixty-seven. He's tall and thin, his face permanently tanned and etched like wood. His blue eyes are always twinkling, and though his teeth are crooked and one of them is missing, he has a great smile, warm and inviting. I've never heard him say anything negative about anyone, ever, which is a quality I wish I had.

He holds me away from him, inspecting me. "Cassie, girl, where have you been?"

"Around."

"Not here."

"Not here."

"I was stoked when Jenny told me you were coming back."

"I'm sorry I didn't stay in touch."

He lets me go and takes a swig of his beer, a High Sierra IPA with a green label. "No worries."

"I should have."

We let that rest between us. The truth is that I left Brian behind just like I left everything in the park and Mammoth too. He'd been a stand-in father for me growing up, teaching me how to send (a climber's term for "ascending") and helping me explore the outdoors. It was because of him that I joined SAR in the first place.

"What are you drinking?" he asks, like he can see my thoughts and wants to displace them.

"Not sure yet. How are you?"

"I'm good . . . yah."

"You staying in the valley?"

He rocks back and forth on his heels. His jeans are loose on him and stained at the knees, like he's been kneeling in the mud. "I got my camp. I suppose you heard they finally cut me off from SAR?"

"I'm sorry."

"Nah, it's fine. The scene was getting old anyway, you know? I'm not missing having to litter out some four-hundred-pound dude once a week."

I laugh. "Haven't had one of those yet."

"You wait."

"So, you're just climbing?"

"Just."

"Sorry. Habit from my old life."

He leans toward me, his breath musty from the beer. "Which was?"

"Nothing to write home about."

"Gotcha. You seen your mom yet?"

I look down at the ground. "Not yet."

"I saw her a couple weeks ago."

"Oh yeah? How'd she look?"

"You know she always looks good. You should go see her."

"Maybe."

Laughter on the other side of the camp pulls my focus. Ben and Gareth are standing at the grill. Ben is slapping hamburgers onto the grate. Flames leap up from the grease.

"About Cameron—"

I turn back to him. "You ever reach your goal, Bri?"

His concentration shifts. Bri's always been a little too fond of weed, and it's affected his ability to focus in casual conversation. "What's that, now?"

"Your lifetime pass? The holy grail?"

He smiles slowly. "You remember that?"

"You only talked about it *all the time*."

"I got it last year. Retirement present, they called it." He shoves his hand into his pocket and pulls out a battered leather wallet. He flips it open and there it is: a lifetime park pass, something he'd lusted over since he learned of its almost mythical existence. He had all kinds of schemes to get one, each one shadier than the last, but in the end, all he'd had to do was stick around long enough that people wanted to reward him for leaving SAR.

"Better than a gold watch."

"You betcha." He lifts his bottle. "I'm empty."

"And I'm hungry."

"Let's eat."

After I've eaten two hamburgers and a sausage and enough salad to fulfill my roughage quotient for a week, I sit next to Ben on a camp chair by the fire ring. Later in the summer, it will be too dry and risky to have a fire, but it's been a wet spring, so for now we can enjoy the flames. It's still cold at night, and I shiver inside my jacket, stretching my feet toward the fire. I'm wearing heavy socks in flip-flops, and the heat sinks into my toes.

I look up at the fairy lights that someone strung up between the trees and attached to a small solar panel. They're pretty up there, and they give a backyard feel to our makeshift courtyard. "What a week."

"Yeah, the first holiday weekend is always a bear."

"I'd forgotten."

"Regrets?" Ben says.

"Many."

Something about his tone flits my mind back to the other night at the hot spring. It had been fun at first. Driving out of the park in a caravan with Gareth and Mia, we'd talked about lighter things during the hour-long drive. How he'd surfed when he was younger but got sick of the culture. The first time he came to Yosemite with his parents, standing at the base of El Cap and watching someone make an attempt on the Nose. He'd started climbing the year after I left, but we knew a lot of the same people from back then. It was nice and comfortable, and my anger at the fact that he'd been spying on me seeped away.

But when we got to the hot spring and got undressed to get in, I could tell he was checking me out. His stare felt hot on my skin, and I sank into the foaming water in relief. I wasn't comfortable with another man's attention. It felt dangerous.

Ben's interest shifted the air between us, a feeling that was exacerbated by the fact that Sandy and Petal were also in the pool, cuddled up together in the corner. Petal was friendly, but Sandy was guarded. Then Gareth started making waves—with his bulk and his personality—and they left.

I watched them go. Sandy was sturdy, but Petal looked like a strong wind could blow her away. She had a deep bruise across her back, long and cylindrical in shape, which she touched briefly, as if she was checking that it was still there, before she pulled her T-shirt down to cover it. She must've felt me staring, because when she turned around, her eyes had gone from curious to cold.

I turned away, my cheeks hot. We stayed another half hour, then stopped at the Mobil for dinner before driving back to the park. Gareth was entertaining, and Ben was smart and thoughtful, but I couldn't shake the feeling that getting close to him, or any of them, was a bad idea. Since then, I'd tried to keep my distance, but that's hard to do when you're on a six-person team and live in a tent ten feet away.

"What do you regret?" Ben asks in a gentle tone.

"Everyone has regrets, don't they?"

Gareth sits across from us, a guitar slung over his back, and I'm happy for the distraction. He pulls it around to his lap and starts strumming. I was expecting the intro to "Stairway to Heaven," but instead, he plays something classical and delicate.

"Free Bird!" Sam yells from the picnic table, where he and George are playing quarters.

They're both on the shorter side with dark hair and beards. They're the youngest on the team, in their second year, and only twenty-two. They drink a case of beer between them every night, but are sober as a judge in the morning. That young metabolism. I'm already worried my three beers tonight are going to be regrets tomorrow.

"Any other requests?" Gareth asks. "Like, from this century?"

"Taylor!" I yell, and Ben laughs next to me.

"Yeah, show us your sensitive side!" Ben adds.

"You got it, dirtbag," Gareth says to me.

I grit my teeth. *Dirtbags* is a common self-term for climbers, one I've used myself. But somehow, ever since my hazing on Lambert Dome, Gareth has started calling me *dirtbag*, singular. I keep meaning to tell him to cut it out, but it feels like if I make a big deal about it, it'll egg him on.

"Just play the song, asshole," Ben says.

Gareth throws him a finger, then starts to play the chords for "Shake It Off." He has a great voice, his falsetto doing a close mimic of the original.

"Who knew Gareth could sing?" I say. "Like a girl?"

"Hidden depths." Ben holds his beer in his lap. "I can talk to him, if you like."

"Who?"

"Gareth. I know you don't like it when he calls you that."

"No, it's fine."

"It's not, though."

My throat feels tight. I'm not used to this, someone caring how I take the impact of words, and it's making me emotional. I look across the fire at Gareth. Mia's sitting next to him, singing along, shaking her hands during the chorus, free and happy. Ben's foot is tapping the ground next to me in time to the music, but I feel removed. A part of this, but not.

"I'm going to head to bed. See you tomorrow." I stand and walk toward my tent, but I'm not entirely sure where I'm going.

"Hey, Cassie, hold up."

I stop in the dark. Gareth has switched to another song, something by Pearl Jam, I think.

"Did I say something?" Ben says, standing in front of me.

"No, it's not you . . ."

"It's you?"

"What?"

Ben smiles. "That's the other side of that, right? 'It's not you, it's me.' "

"Right."

"What's going on?"

"I'm sorry. I can't explain it."

He puts his hand on my forearm. I flinch, and he drops it. "I didn't mean . . ."

"No, you're right, Ben. It is me. I can't . . . I can't do this."

"We're not doing anything."

"Okay."

"I mean, I like you."

"I like you too. But I can't. I can't get involved with anyone."

"Why?"

I don't owe him an explanation. My refusal should be enough. But we have the summer together, and if I'm going to put up this barrier, I might as well put it up right. "I'm married."

Ben takes a step back at this, like the information is a blow. It can only be a small one though, because nothing has happened here, not to him, only to me.

PHOTOGRAPH—Rain pelting down a window

♥ ◯ ◁   ⬚

Liked by **mamajada** and **49 others**

@JadaJohnsonInsta Hold up, hold up. How come no one ever told me how depressing an Airstream was in the rain? Or how COLD?

It's been raining for days, and it's biblical out there. #Climatechange is real, y'all. We're still moving, though, rollin' through this U.S. of A., state by state.

Jim is a BEAST, driving in all weather, a state a day, no matter what. And now I can almost see it. CA-LI-FOR-NI-AY. The #SunshineState. Or is that Florida? I DO know it's in some massive drought rn. Is it wrong to be happy about that? Yeah, yeah, I know.

Okay! Enough whining. Jim told me that the weather report for tomorrow is clear skies and WARM. I feel better already.

#YosemiteHereWeCome #JadaandJimForever #LongHaulSummer #AirstreamLiving #HopeWeDontBustBeforeWeGetThere

mamajada Make sure you dress warm, baby! I know how much you hate to be cold.

bellasgram You better call me back, bitch!

theyfreedBritney Hate to say I told you so, but . . .

Papajim @JadaJohnsonInsta Don't be believing all that stuff you read on the internet. Climate change is FAKE NEWS! The weather isn't any different now than when I was a boy. I'll email you some articles.

YosemiteBot Promote it on www.superxxx.com

Papajim @YosemiteBot I went to that site and it's disgusting. You ought to be ashamed of yourself.

MAY 29

CHAPTER 7

A ROSE BY ANY OTHER NAME

Then

June

The day I met Kevin was the day I changed my name for the first time.

I was about to move to Manhattan. I'd graduated from college with a degree in art history and spent a year interning in an art gallery in Denver. The job and the city felt like a dead end, like I was moving backwards. I knew too many people, or they knew me, or thought they did. Too many times, a customer would squint at me and say that I looked "awfully familiar." And even though it was probably nothing, I didn't want to be Cassie Peters anymore. I wanted to be someone fresh, someone new.

Peters is my mother's last name. She'd given it to me in a fit of anger at my father, who'd disappeared to Alaska when she was six months pregnant. But he was right there on my birth certificate—Albert Biggs. He'd show up occasionally when I was a kid. I remember ice cream cones I wasn't supposed to tell my mother about, and once, an ill-fated camping trip at June Lake. He wasn't a big presence in my life other than the rants my mother would go on about how he never paid his fair share for me, like I was some object that had been put on layaway, or a credit card that was being paid off.

But then I told my mother I wanted to leave Colorado, and I asked her for a loan. Instead of the terms I expected, she told me I was cut off. I'd already run away from her once when I'd left Mammoth for college; she wasn't going to help me get even farther away from her.

I didn't know what to do. I didn't have enough saved up to move to New York. I needed help.

Then someone at the gallery said, "Why don't you just ask your dad?" It got me thinking. Why didn't I ask him? I wasn't even sure I had a valid number, but I called the last number I had. He answered it and was glad to hear from me, even offered up some money, said it was back child support that he always meant to pay. "You're a Biggs," he said. "I don't want you to forget it."

We didn't hug it out. Nothing fundamental changed between us. But when I met Kevin Adams in the first-class lounge three days later—my father had insisted on using his points to book my flight—and he asked me, over a glass of free wine that he'd brought to my table, what my name was, I'd said, "Cassandra Biggs." Like I'd left Cassie Peters at the security checkpoint. Like I was stepping into my new life even though I hadn't yet left the state.

Like I had something to hide.

Because Brian is right, I take the following Friday off, borrow Jenny's car, and drive to Mammoth to see my mother for the first time since I went away to college.

She came to visit me once, in my first year in Boulder. I'd been distant, she'd flirted with a man at a bar, and I'd left in a huff. She didn't come back after that, and it was a slow decline between us until she'd cut me off.

After I'd moved to New York and settled in, I'd call her occasionally and update her about my life, but that was it. I didn't invite her to anything—not my first curated gallery show, not my engagement party, not even my wedding.

The wedding was small—just me and Kevin and two witnesses at the courthouse. I filled out the forms to change my name to Cassandra Adams at the same time, because it was important to Kevin that we present a united front, and what did I care? When I'd arrived in New York, I'd legally changed my name from Peters to Biggs to match the name I'd given Kevin at the airport. Kevin was going to be my family now, the family I'd always wanted, the family I never had. Our last name was a symbol of that, so I was happy to do it, proud, even.

Peters, Biggs, Adams . . . I could be anyone I wanted to be. I could change my location and my life with the stroke of a pen. Sign me up.

When I called a few weeks later to tell my mother that I'd gotten married, she was apoplectic. *How could you do that to me? Get married without me, your own mother? And was your father there? I bet he was there! Are you trying to kill me? You must be trying to kill me; it's the only explanation.*

I hung up, and we didn't speak for two years. I kept trying every couple of months out of an odd sense of loyalty, and eventually she took my call. We never spoke of the marriage, her disappointment, my *betrayal*. Instead, I gave her the Instagram version of my life, what I was willing to share with acquaintances and strangers. I never knew how much of it she absorbed. My mother wasn't someone who thought much about other people, least of all me.

But she is a creature of habit. So, after I drive to town on a bright, sunny day, memories on a loop, I don't go to her house, which is located in Aspen Creek. Instead, I head for the tennis courts at Snow Creek, where she spends most of her time in the summer, running her real estate business from the wide brown deck off the back of the athletic club and taking lessons from Rich, the long-standing club pro who spends his winters surfing in Malibu.

I walk through the entrance, into the gloomy lobby and up to the check-in desk. "Hey, Tonya, is Andrea Peters out there?"

The sixtysomething receptionist nods without looking up. The club hasn't been updated since I was last here, and it still smells the same. Sweat and chlorine from the pool mixed in with the conifers that surround a lot of the buildings in Mammoth, like the minimum amount of trees had been removed to insert whatever building you were in.

I walk through the turnstile as memories assault me. The sound of the trampoline squeaking as I learned to flip during training sessions; the murmur of the cocktail hour on the deck; my first kiss at fourteen in the pool with Dave Mack, Cameron's older brother. And Cameron, her red braids flying behind her as she charged around the court, chasing after balls as they came off the pro's racquet.

I shake all that away and walk outside. I spot my mother on the court, wearing a pink-and-white tennis dress and a red visor. She's playing doubles with a group of women her age, all fit and savage at the net. She had me at eighteen, so she's not even fifty yet, and it's a point of pride with her that people think she's still in her thirties. No one ever mistook us for sisters—our coloring is completely different, and she's barely five feet—but by the time I reached ten, I never felt an age difference between us.

I watch the game for a few minutes, checking the time. It's a few minutes to three; regardless of the score, they'll have to finish soon. I watch my mom go to the service line and throw the ball up to serve. It's a laser out wide, and her opponent barely returns it. She smiles and claps racquets with her teammate, and that's when she sees me.

"Cassie?" Her voice floats into the air, breathy and high-pitched.

I walk closer to the green chain-link fence. "Hi, Mom."

She glances back at the other women on the court. "We're in the middle of a game."

"I'm not going anywhere."

She frowns at that but turns away and gets ready for her next serve.

"Who's that?" I hear her teammate say, looking at me over her shoulder.

I can't hear what my mother says, but my mind fills in the blank—*no one.*

When she's done with tennis, we go for an early dinner at the Tamarack Lodge. It's a small, expensive restaurant with a view of Twin Lakes, and totally in keeping with my mom's vibe.

She's changed into a linen pantsuit and her dark hair is perfect despite the tennis.

I feel out of place in this elegant restaurant with white table-cloths. Not because I'm a stranger to fine dining. It was a staple in New York, something Kevin found important. But I'm dressed in the only clothes I have—clothes appropriate for Yosemite, and I can't get the dirt out from underneath my fingernails no matter how hard I try.

My thoughts are scattered. My mother always does this to me.

"To what do I owe this honor?" she says over her appetizer of beef carpaccio. Until now, she's spoken only of her tennis game, giving me a point-by-point analysis of her teammate and opponents as if she'd just played the U.S. Open.

"What?"

"You visiting after all this time . . ."

I look down at my plate. I got a salad because it seemed simple and greens have been in short supply in my diet. But I don't feel hungry. "I'm working in Yosemite."

"I heard."

I stab at the lettuce. Bri must've told her. "Yet, you didn't reach out."

"Was I supposed to? You've made it perfectly clear you don't want me in your life."

I check her face. With anyone else, you'd expect to find emotion, tears. But not her. And not just because it's Botoxed into submission. "I needed to leave."

"Yes, you said."

"I had to build my own life."

"And how has that worked out for you?" She raises an oversized white wineglass. "Ten years away and back where you started."

She's always known how to go for my jugular. "It's complicated."

"You think I didn't have challenges?" She waves her glass around. We're alone in here but for the waiter. Most people don't eat dinner at four. "That I didn't have circumstances to overcome? A baby at eighteen, your father abandoning me."

"I know."

"You had *everything*. Why do I get punished for mistakes you made in your life?"

"I don't know, Mom. I'm sorry."

She takes a swallow of her wine. Her neck is not as taut as it used to be, and there's a hint of jowls along her jaw. "Is that what you came to say?"

"No . . . I . . . maybe. Bri said I should come."

"Brian is a good man."

"He is."

"Not like your father."

"Okay, Mom."

She folds a piece of carpaccio into a square with her fork. "I'll never understand why you took his name. Never."

"I've tried to explain it to you."

"Well, you failed. Honoring him like that when he never did anything . . ."

"He did pay off my student loans. And help me move."

"That was the bare minimum he could do."

"Mom, I . . . I had to leave. After Cameron . . ."

Now there are tears in her eyes. Cameron's mother, Julie, is one of my mother's best friends. "What happened to that poor girl is tragic. Julie's still broken. But you're alive, Cassie. You didn't die out there in the woods. You came back."

I finally put a piece of lettuce dripping with rich olive oil in my mouth. What can I say to my mother in this moment? That part of me *did* die out there in the woods with Cameron? That those two days looking for her made me shed myself like a snake, and when I emerged, I didn't recognize myself? She wouldn't understand. She wouldn't say anything that would help. And even to myself, it doesn't make sense. "I did what I did to heal."

"Run away."

"Yes. But I'm back, okay? I'm back. And I'm trying to . . . I'm trying to fix my life."

"By replaying it?"

"Yes, maybe."

"Life isn't a horse, Cassie. It's not just something you can climb back on."

We stare at each other, in a standoff. I've never understood her, and she's never understood me. It's probably too late to change that. "What do you want me to say?"

"I want you to acknowledge what you did to me. Leaving like that. Calling me a few times a year. Not inviting me to your wedding. Never introducing me to your husband. It was like you were dead. But I couldn't mourn you because you were still out there. And for a while I thought—maybe she'll come back. Maybe she'll realize what she's done. But you didn't. So I did mourn. I moved on as best I could, yes. I can't feel guilty for that."

"Come on, Mom. You always knew where I was. How to get in touch with me."

"You don't know . . . You weren't here. *What did she do?* everyone thinks. *How terrible was she that her daughter never visits?*"

Guilt crashes down around me. "I'm sorry."

"You said."

"Well, I am. And I'm here. Near here, anyway."

"For how long?"

"I don't know. The summer at least."

The waiter approaches to see if we're done with our appetizers. My mother puts on her ingratiating face, the one that sells multimillion-dollar homes and makes her a favorite of the waitstaff at every restaurant in town. I nod silently, even though I've barely touched mine. I don't remember what I ordered for the next course, and I'm regretting my decision to forego wine.

"Well, then," my mother says when the waiter has left with our plates. "What do you think of this place?"

"What?"

"The restaurant. It's quite nice, isn't it? Maybe not up to your standards in New York . . ."

"It's fine, Mom. It's good."

She raises her newly full glass and sips at it. The wine is burnished gold in the sunlight. "You were wrong, you know."

"About?"

"I did call you when Brian told me that you were in Yosemite. That last number I had for you. I called that. But a man answered."

June 2—Lee Vining RV Park

It's June, winter finally behind us. It's something in the air, a feeling I can't describe. But there isn't any frost on the lawn in the morning, only drops of water that shine bright in the sunlight.

Frost on the LAWN—ha! Such a fancy word to describe some weeds poking out of the dirt. Everything is turning green around us, flowers unraveling, reaching out to the sun, but in this RV park, time stands still. Where the plants are concerned, anyway. And maybe also where the people are.

For me, it's like time goes backwards. I've been dreaming about Daddy. That I'm still back in HIS trailer, that I have to listen to the night sounds to make sure I'm not about to get HIT out of my sleep. Daddy could be real vicious when he was drinking, and it didn't matter about staying out of his way. He'd come and find you so he could give you the beating HE deserved, taking out his own disappointment on me and Mama before she left.

I don't blame her. I only wish she'd taken me with her.

Maybe I've said that before? I don't want to look back and check. Things shouldn't be repeating themselves this early in my life, but they are, they are.

I've asked around about her. Mama. Down in Bishop, and in Mammoth with its expensive outdoor stores and restaurants with wild game plates. She sent me a postcard from here—I think I've said that before too—but as far as I can tell, she didn't stop here for long. Not long enough for anyone to recognize her in the crumpled photograph I have or remember her name when I've said it out loud.

Maybe she changed it. Not that Daddy went looking for her, but I'd understand if she wanted to leave Josephine Fernandez behind her like so much dust spitting up from the wheels of her beat-up Honda. Or was it a Ford? Some things are so clear, and others are hard to hold on to. I didn't use to have trouble remembering things. It must be this place.

Maybe that's why Mama didn't stay.

But here WE stay, for how long, Sandy won't say. She's got a part-time job at one of those sports stores, waiting on rich people, helping them find the right "fit" for their three-hundred-dollar hiking shoes that they'll use once. She says I should apply too, but I don't want to work in that store, or any store. I didn't come here to do that. I'm supposed to be soaking up experiences so I can write. That's what that teacher said. You need to live before the stories come. You need to know something about people who aren't like you.

Understanding human nature. That's my job now.

I didn't apply at the store. Instead, I roam the RV park, the Mobil, and Yosemite with my notebook, looking for stories.

Like the couple that arrived here yesterday in their shiny Airstream. Jada and Jim are shiny too. Young, fresh, and excited. Posing in front of their camper so they can post to social media. Reducing their life to hashtags. I found her on Instagram, traced their route on a map. Yosemite is their destination, but they ended up here, in the Lee Vining trailer park instead.

THAT's a story. One they were fighting about tonight, after the fake story was posted and liked. I could hear them clearly as I crouched beneath their window in the dark.

That sounds like I was CREEPING. I was just going to say hey, maybe see if they wanted to potluck or something, if they were staying long. Jada was so friendly when they pulled in, asking Sandy to help with their hookup. Come over anytime, she said. It's been so long since I had a friend, someone just for me. And so I did.

But I could hear them yelling as I got close, so I stepped up slowly, quiet-like, because I didn't want them to know I heard. I'm always so embarrassed when people hear Sandy and me fighting.

I want to go home, she said. And, don't do that!

Then there was a noise, a BANG!, and what sounded like a slap.

But maybe I heard it wrong. Noises at night are hard to tell—what direction, what destination, what origin.

I backed away just as quiet as I came.

Later, at the washstand, I found her crying, a dark streak of mascara on her cheek. I tried to memorize what everything looked like. The way she tilted her head away so I wouldn't see her tears. The brave smile she put on, a friendly public face, like a mask. The bright white light above us that the bugs were plinking into, struggling against something that was going to kill them.

Then Jim called for her to come back to the camper, and the moment was gone.

I hope I got it down right.

—Petal

CHAPTER 8

SMOKEY THE BEAR

Then

June

When I get back to the park after visiting my mother, it's dark.

My mood is dark, too. Under cross-examination, my mother said she hung up the phone when a man answered, only realizing afterwards that it might be Kevin. The man didn't call back and she let it go. *But where is Kevin?* she asked. Had we broken up or was she *finally* going to meet him?

I told her the minimum, then changed the topic and gave her my new number. We ate the rest of the meal under the weight of her chatter about people I didn't know or care about in Mammoth.

Eventually, my heart rate returned to normal. While I wasn't listening to her, I reviewed the facts. Kevin thinks I'm from Colorado because that's where he met me, and it didn't seem important to correct him. He wasn't one for asking many questions about my past. His parents are long dead, so it's not a topic he likes to talk about. He knows I have a terrible relationship with my mother and that I speak to her infrequently. The last place anyone would look for me is anywhere near her. But that doesn't keep me from frantically searching my memory to figure out if I ever told him that she lived in Mammoth, or what her last name was. I kept so many things from everyone, the details I did let slip through are hard to hold on to.

What I'm certain of is that Kevin and my mother have never truly spoken, not more than a quick hello when he took the phone from me once, teasingly, when I called her on her birthday. After that, I made sure he was out of the house when I called her.

But none of that answers the crucial question of who the man was who answered the phone. When my mother checked at my insistence, it turned out she'd called an old number, one I'd abandoned years ago. It must've been reassigned. That's the only plausible explanation.

I'm still safe. I'm still *gone*. No one is looking for me.

But I can't help feeling paranoid. It was a mistake to leave my old phone in the trash so close to my destination. To turn it on at the airport—that was especially stupid. Someone who knew what they were doing could trace me to Reno, at least, because of that. I should've dumped it in New York or at the motel near the airport. I shouldn't have been so sentimental about a piece of technology that—

"You hear about the bear?" Mia says as I come out of the Park Service building where I've just returned the keys to Jenny. It's after six, and there are a couple of rangers sitting at a picnic table in their dark green Park Service jackets. One of them smiles at us as we pass.

"What's that?" I say.

"In the campground. They're calling him Smokey."

"That's not good."

"Right? You walking back to the site?"

"Yeah, I'm beat."

She nods in recognition. Her dark hair is tucked up into a rainbow beanie, her face a bit windburned. It's cold tonight, and I pull the zipper up on my puffy and slip my hands inside the sleeves.

"Everything go okay in Mammoth?"

I didn't tell Mia where I was going, but news travels fast around here. "I was visiting my mom. Haven't seen her in a while."

"I know how that is."

"Yeah." We turn onto the path that will take us to the campground. "What's the bear doing?"

"He's been getting into bear boxes. I think he even opened a car door. Not so unusual, except today he took food right out of this girl's hand."

"Shit."

"She was feeding him, I think. Like on purpose? And her boyfriend was filming it for some live feed or some shit like that."

"People are morons."

"Agree," Mia says. "Only now, we have a bear that thinks people will give him food."

"Is he tagged?"

"They know who it is. He's never been a problem before, but . . . I don't know, the biologist was looking stressed."

Yosemite has a bear mitigation program that tracks problematic bears and imposes strict protocols on visitors to reduce their interactions with humans. The biggest issue is if they get accustomed to viewing people as a source of food. Once that happens, simply relocating a bear doesn't usually work. Those DON'T FEED THE BEARS signs are there for a reason.

We pass under a stand of pines, the branches reaching out and casting shadows. "What's the procedure now? Is there still bear court?" "Bear court" is our term for the proceeding that determines whether they're going to euthanize a problematic bear.

"Yeah, that's still a thing. Hopefully we can keep it under the radar."

"How so?"

Mia rolls her eyes. "All these social media types . . . Last year, we had an issue in the valley with two young bears. One of them swiped at a *kid*. So the bear was going to be euthanized, right? But then some tender heart got wind of it and started posting about it and it blew up. There was some petition that got a hundred thousand signatures to save the bear. It got out of hand."

"What happened?"

"The judge ruled against the bear, of course. It's a matter of public safety. It sucks, but . . ."

"I get it." I sigh. "It was put to sleep?"

"They relocated one of them—even though that almost never works—but yeah, the one who hurt the kid? Sayonara."

I shiver inside my coat. "Ugh."

"Man versus beast. Beast is going to lose, especially if it hurts a kid."

"Hopefully it won't come to that with Smokey."

Mia turns to me in disbelief. "Girl, you did not just use that bear's name."

"Sorry."

We arrive at the SAR site. The fairy lights are on, and a fire is burning in the firepit. I just want to hide in my tent and close my mind on this day, but Ben and Gareth are sitting at the picnic table, and they're quick to wave us over. I could ignore the invite, but things have been weird between Ben and me all week, ever since I dropped the "I'm married" news. Walking away now seems like the wrong call.

"Have you eaten?" Mia says.

"In town. But come to think of it, I didn't really."

She laughs and we walk to the picnic table. There's a large

pot of stew in the middle—a kind of stone soup version that gets made around camp, where everyone contributes something they have lying around. I can see pieces of beef, carrots, beans, potatoes, and a thick rich sauce that smells like bouillon and red wine.

I sit down next to Ben while Gareth smacks a loud kiss on Mia. She laughs and swats at him. I wonder how they met, though I never remember to ask.

"How was Mammoth?" Ben asks.

"It was fine. Family stuff."

"My parents still talk to me like I'm fourteen."

"Me too," Gareth says. "Hey, dirt—Hey, Cassie."

Ben stiffens beside me. He must've talked to him.

I choose to ignore it. "Hey, Gareth. This smells great."

"Everything stew is always the best." Gareth quickly serves up four large plates of stew and rice. When he places mine in front of me, I realize how hungry I am. I barely ate anything at lunch, my stomach roiling with worry about that stupid phone call.

"Thank you." I pick up my fork and dig in. The dish is rich and satisfying and I can feel the tension leaving my body as I eat half my plate quickly. "Mia was telling me about the bear."

"Smokey?" Ben says with a twinkle in his eye.

"We probably shouldn't use its name, given what's going to happen to it."

Ben lifts his beer. "Maybe he'll get off with a light sentence."

"Mia said he'd already been collared."

"Yeah, that's not good . . . But they do try to save the bear now."

I take another bite of my food. "That's good. Stupid tourists."

"They were doing it for Instagram," Gareth says. "So dumb. Like, major dumb. Pretty girl, though."

Mia leans into Gareth. "Her boyfriend's hot too."

"Young, hot, and beautiful," Ben says. "Sounds about right."

"*Your* post is blowing up, by the way, Cassie," Gareth says, his cheeks red from the wine.

"What post?"

"Your hazing. It's hilarious."

I go very still. "I asked you not to do that, Ben."

"I didn't . . . What the fuck, dude?"

Gareth grabs the bottle of wine and refills his cup. "If you didn't want me to post it, you shouldn't have texted it to me."

I put down my fork. "Where did you put this?"

"On TikTok. All the SAR guys are on this hashtag on there. What's the matter?"

"I don't do social media."

"Ah, lighten up. It's funny. And two days from now, something else will be in there and everyone will forget about it."

I push my plate away. Gareth is probably right, but I feel sick just the same. "Don't do it again, okay?"

"Sooo sensitive. Can't call you 'dirtbag,' can't put you online. You need to get with the program."

"And what program is that, exactly?"

He waves his cup around. "Life, dude. Living. Enjoying the great fucking outdoors. Isn't that what we're all here to do?"

"I'm not your dude."

"Gareth." Mia puts her hand on his arm.

"No, seriously. You know how many people want this job? And you just walked into it because you're tight with Jenny and shit. And then all you do is moan about it."

"I haven't been moaning."

"He's drunk," Mia says. "He doesn't mean it."

"It's fine." I stand. "I'm going to go to bed. Thanks for dinner."

I walk away quickly, hoping Ben doesn't follow me, but he does.

"Cassie . . ."

I turn around. "I want to be alone, Ben."

"I wanted to apologize. I never should've sent him that video."

"Why did you?"

"I don't know. It was stupid."

"Yeah."

He shoves his hands in his pockets. "Do you not want that out there . . . Is it something to do with your husband?"

"It's not about him, it's about me."

"But you're separated, right? I mean, it's kind of obvious . . ."

"Yes."

"Does he know you're here?"

"That's none of your business." My voice is harsher than I meant it to be.

"We can be friends. You can talk to me."

"It's not something I want to talk about."

We stand in a beat of silence.

"I'll see you tomorrow?" I say.

"Sure. And again, sorry for all of that. Won't happen again."

"Thank you." I feel like a jerk. Ben isn't the enemy. He's trying to be my friend. "I was thinking of climbing Tenaya tomorrow morning. You want to join?"

His face breaks into a wide grin. "Yeah, I'd like that a lot."

"Alpine start?"

"Alpine start."

" 'Night."

I enter my tent and zip the door closed. It's gloomy in here, the walls casting a low light. I turn on the lamp and sit down. If I still had my iPhone, I'd put on the Calm app and spend ten minutes meditating to reduce my stress. Maybe I can put something like that on this phone?

I take it out. There's a text from a number I know, and one

I don't recognize. My thumb hesitates over it. I feel like I know what it will be, even though I don't. But I'll never know if I don't check.

The words slam against me like a punch.

I WILL find you. Just you wait.

CHAPTER 9
HELI BASE

Now

As the helo's blades stop spinning, Jenny pulls me into the Heli Base, a brown, square building, and finds a corner for me to sit in. The base is up on a hill, the heli pad looking out over the valley. At seven thousand feet, it's integrated with the Crane Flat Fire Lookout, which has eight firefighters and EMTs stationed there. Its purpose is right there in the description—to search for fires and keep them from spreading.

Jenny gets me a warmer blanket and leaves me alone for a few minutes as I watch the swirl of activity around me. Ben and Gareth are talking to the EMTs, telling them, presumably, that the body was beyond saving, beyond recognition. They keep glancing over at me, but I don't look away, just let the gray scratchy blanket warm me slowly.

When I worked in the park ten years ago, I did a stint in this lookout, spending my days in the glass-boxed room above, staring out into the vast forest and watching for a wisp of white that wasn't supposed to be there. It was both meditative and stressful, and at night, as I tried to sleep, my thoughts would be invaded by hints of fire. The smell of the smudge. A slight catch in my throat as if I'd been caught in the middle of it. As if I'd set it and hadn't escaped in time.

That's how I feel now—like I'm caught in the middle of something I set on fire. The body—I can't think of him as Kevin, I *can't* because it's too much, it's too hard—is waiting for the ambulance to arrive and take it to the morgue.

The immediate cause of Kevin's death will be obvious, the shots fired unmistakable. But the root cause, the reason that the gun went off in the first place . . . I'm the only one who's going to be able to explain that. They're going to want to speak to me, they're going to *have* to speak to me. A flood of questions is coming.

What was I doing out there? What happened? Where did he come from?

I'm cross-examining myself in preparation. But I'm having trouble concentrating, the words I need to hold on to like those wisps of smoke I used to search for.

"Here, drink this," Jenny says, handing me a steaming mug of coffee in a dark green insulated cup.

I take it from her carefully and bring it to my lips. The aroma is overwhelming, fresh beans and a strong brew. It's too hot to drink, but I do it anyway, feeling it scald my tongue and the back of my throat. It doesn't matter. The burn is nothing compared to everything else I've been through. The feelings I've been keeping at bay that are going to catch up with me.

"Better?" Jenny says.

"A bit."

She drags a chair toward me, its metal feet scraping across the floor in a high-pitched whine. "What happened out there?"

I meet her eyes for a second, then look down into my cup. "Is Eric coming?"

"Yes, I think so."

"Shouldn't I wait till he gets here?"

"If that's how you want to play it."

I put the cup down on the floor, then wrap my arms around myself, feeling the hard metal of my medallion under my shirt. "I'm not . . . I just don't want to have to tell the story over and over again."

"I'm not sure you quite understand what's going on. You're most definitely going to have to tell it more than once."

Tears swim in my eyes. "I can't right now, okay, Jenny? Remember Cameron? What happened out there . . . it was ten times worse. I know I have to talk to Eric, to help the officers figure everything out, and I'll do my best. But right now, all I want to do is sleep."

"I don't think that's an option."

I lean back against the wood wall. It's gloomy in here, faded light coming down from the glass structure above, and it feels damp, the air almost wet.

Jenny's radio crackles and she walks away to answer it. I breathe in and out slowly, trying to still my mind and put the pieces together in a way that might make sense to someone else. Where are they going to want to start? What's the first question going to be?

When's the last time you saw the victim? That's what they always ask on TV.

The last time I talked to Kevin was in our New York apartment. He was late for a meeting, rushing around, lifting couch cushions and magazines on the coffee table. He couldn't find his phone, and right when he was about to lose it, I reached between the back of an armchair and its cushion and pulled it out. His handsome face eased in relief, the anger rushing away like a cloud in the wind, and he'd plucked it from my hand and kissed me on the forehead.

"See you for dinner," he said.

"See you for dinner."

But I wasn't there for dinner. In my place was a partially empty closet and a note.

Don't look for me, it said. *You know why I'm leaving.*

I tried to imagine him reading that, the days I waited in the airport motel, staring at the stained ceiling, searching TV channels obsessively for news that I was gone. I'd wondered if he was shocked. Was he going to let me go, or was he or someone he hired going to knock on my door and haul me back to my life?

I'd left several days earlier than planned because I couldn't take the waiting anymore. I felt like everything I said to him was suspicious, and if I made one wrong move, he was going to figure it out. So I'd bolted and hid in a cheap motel until it was time for my flight.

I should've known that wouldn't be the last of it. Of him.

How could you? he'd said out there in the woods.

Why? He'd asked that, too.

Then that terrible *BOOM!*

I want to put my hands over my ears, to block out the sounds. Maybe it will block out the memory of his face disappearing in a bloom of blood. I can tell those details to Jenny, to Eric, to anyone, but it won't explain anything.

Jenny comes back to her chair. "That was Eric."

"Okay."

"Do you want a lawyer?"

I try to focus. "What?"

"A lawyer. Someone to represent you. If you do, you have to say that to Eric right away, when he starts the interview. And then you can't answer any questions until the lawyer comes."

"What do you think I should do?"

"It would take a while for a lawyer to get here." She sits in a metal chair and scoots it closer to me, that scraping sound like fingernails on a chalkboard. "It would give you some time to sleep, probably."

"Here?"

"We could take you to the lockup."

I pull the blanket tighter against me. "I'm being arrested?"

"No, just . . . So there are no questions tonight. I thought that might be a solution. It will show that you want to cooperate, but you need a bit of time, a bit of advice."

I think it over slowly. A lawyer. Someone who'll tell me not to answer their questions, who'll run interference for me, who'll want to know the truth when we're alone.

"Everyone will think I have something to hide."

Jenny leans back. "Well, don't you?"

PHOTOGRAPH—Climbing rope curled up on a picnic bench

Liked by **mamajada** and **72 others**

@JadaJohnsonInsta We have ARRIVED!

After a small diversion at a trailer park because SOMEONE forgot to get our reservation for the park, we're now installed in the #TuolumneMeadows campground for the foreseeable future.

The rock here is SICK, my friends. Like I thought I knew what I was doing in the climbing gym, but this shit is real. We'll get the hang of it, though. Jim is RARING (sp?) to go. So today we SEND our first pitch of granite.

He wants to #FREESOLO but we'll see! I'm bringing this rope just in case.

By the way, y'alls comments on that #smokeythebear video Jim live streamed were real extra. He was gentle and sweet and hungry. No need to lecture me about bear safety and whatnot. The ranger was plenty mad!

I love my life!

#YosemiteWeAreHere #JadaandJimForever #LongHaulSummer #AirstreamLiving

mamajada Oh don't tell me before you do one of those climbs! I'll be worried till you text me you're okay.

BearsAreMammalsToo Bear safety isn't a joke. Your video was totally inappropriate.

theyfreedBritney @BearsAreMammalsToo—get a life, my dude. Like, seriously.

bellasgram You got this!

Papajim Please check all of your equipment carefully and use those knots I taught Jim. Safety first.

Papajim @BearsAreMammalsToo People like you are what's wrong with this country.

JUNE 3

CHAPTER 10

FREE SOLO

Then

June

Tenaya's the first pitch I soloed. I was fifteen, full of confidence, and I did it without telling anyone. I ascended the northwest buttress, going up one of the easier pitches with little ventures over to the harder pitches when I felt like I could handle them. It was both terrifying and thrilling. When I got to the top, I whooped loud and long, took a couple of pictures, then started the scramble down. That's the thing about climbing—hiking, too. All that effort for a few minutes of view, of accomplishment. It's the effort that's the point, not the peak.

Because it's there, a famous alpinist once said about Everest. And that's true of every climb. We do it because it's there.

I guess that's true about a lot of things. Like that message on my phone. I read it over and over again because it's there. The sender blocked their number so I couldn't respond even if I wanted to, even if I knew what I wanted to say, or who, precisely, I was writing to.

I thought about ditching my burner phone right then and there, about running away again, but where would I go? If it's *him* somehow, and not some spam text sent to a million people, he doesn't know where I am. All he said is that he *would* find me. But Kevin was always full of false bravado, and I'm feeling that, too. I put a continent between us. This is my territory, not his. Let him come. Then he'll see.

But see what? I didn't know. Last night, I took my gun from its hiding place and put it under my pillow. It felt easier to sleep with its hard shape below me. But was I really going to use it? Could I ever do that, even to someone who'd made my life a misery?

I didn't want to find out.

If it *was* Kevin, then he must've gotten my number from my mother, I decided in the night as I turned my medallion over and over in my hand like a rosary. I gave it to her, and a few hours later, there was a message. I'd specifically told her not to tell him where I was, but I guess she couldn't help herself.

But when I called her in the early morning, she swore that she didn't give my number to anyone, that she'd never betray *me* like that. I believe her. She's a lot of things, but not, generally, a liar.

I shoved the fear away with so many other things and got dressed.

There was nothing I could do about it now.

It's just after sunrise when Ben and I pull into the Tenaya Lake parking lot. The sky is streaked with orange and a few high clouds, and there are already several cars in the lot, along with an Airstream.

We get out and I look up at the dome of granite beyond the crystal-blue waters of the lake. There are ten other climbers on the pitch, at various stages of their climbs, some taking the gentle scramble route up the ridge, and others on the more difficult pitches, some roped, others soloing.

"What do you think?" Ben says, opening the back of his truck and pulling out his climbing shoes.

"A bit crowded to free climb. Why don't we see how it goes?"

"Sure."

He sits on the tailgate, and I join him. Our breath forms clouds around us, and I rub my hands together before I put my shoes on. This is always the moment that's hardest for me. Putting on my climbing shoes, so tight they make my feet cramp. Chalking up my hands, that rough dryness sending chills down my spine. Thinking about the route I'm going to take. Even though I've done plenty of climbs much harder than this one, I have to show each one respect.

We finish putting on our climbing gear and grab our packs. Tenaya is shaped like a half circle—it has a rounded slope up its left side and a sheer face on the right. Its base feeds into Tenaya Lake, which warms in the summer, but for now is still glacier cold.

We check each other's equipment, then start down the trail to the base of the climb. On the way, we pass a woman sitting at one of the picnic tables. She's got a journaling notebook and she's looking up at some climbers taking one of the harder routes. She's wearing a stained dark green puffy jacket and a knitted cap with holes in it, but I'd recognize that hair anywhere. It's Petal. I haven't seen her since Wild Willy's, and this is the first time I've seen her without Sandy.

"Morning," I say, and Ben says it too.

"Hey," Petal says, looking up. The page in front of her is scrawled with a messy cursive and a good line drawing of a young couple preparing to go up the rock. He looks determined, she looks tense, their bodies in alignment.

"That's good," I say. "Your drawing."

"It's Jada and Jim," she says, using her pen to indicate the couple above. "I'd watch out for them."

"How come?" Ben says.

"Didn't look like they knew what they were doing."

I sigh. "Wouldn't be the first time."

She smiles. She has a small gap in her front teeth that I hadn't noticed before. "I guess."

"You going to climb?"

Petal blinks her dark eyes slowly. "No, I've never done it."

I feel a rush of something for her. Empathy, sympathy. There's something about her that reminds me of me. I want to know her better, this person that keeps turning up in my life. "I could show you sometime, if you're interested."

"Sure, maybe."

"Come look for me at the SAR site in the Meadows campground if you want a lesson."

"Okay." She looks away, and I can sense Ben's impatience to start the climb.

"Have a good one," I say.

"You too."

We leave her and walk down the trail, soon coming to the wall of granite.

"That was nice of you to offer," Ben says.

"She seems a little lost."

"There's a lot of that around here."

"True."

"You want to lead?"

"Yes." I like leading a pitch. That way I can choose my own pace and rely on myself. I don't have to arrest anyone if they fall. "Let's go up the left side and avoid those two."

"Agree," Ben says.

I put my hands on the cold rock, find a hold, and push myself up. It's a short pitch to the route below the spine of the mountain, where it will be more of a scramble than a climb, and that's fine with me. I put my feet on two holds and move up to the next one. A few more and I'm up the pitch, on more solid ground. I check Ben below me. He's an elegant climber, moving at a steady pace like he knows exactly where the holds are going to be. He reaches up for the last one and pushes himself up to the ridge I'm on.

"This was a good idea," he says, grinning.

I smile back. "Always nice to start the day on a climb."

He looks down. Petal is still sketching below, but maybe this time it's us. "She's a strange duck."

"I wonder what her story is."

"I saw her partner, Sandy, in Mammoth the other day when I went to get some gear."

I rest my hands on the rock to start the next pitch. "Interesting age difference."

"Right?"

"But then I think—would I say the same thing if it was a dude and a girl?"

"Hell yeah, I would," Ben says.

I laugh, then climb the next pitch quickly. Ben does the same, and when he reaches level with me, he pulls his shades down from the top of his head as the sun crests the ridge. We're half-way up now, keeping a good pace, and we've passed the climbers Petal was worried about. They're below us and to the left on the steeper pitch, moving slowly.

"That's the girl from the bear video," Ben says.

"You're right." Jada was the one Mia was talking about the night before, the one who Instagrammed herself feeding Smokey, putting them both in jeopardy.

I watch her and her partner, Jim, for a minute. She's sending the pitch, but her moves are tentative, while he rests below her, playing out rope.

"She shouldn't have posted it," Ben says. "I checked this morning and it has over a hundred thousand views."

So many, so quickly? That wasn't good. "Ugh."

Ben sighed. "I doubt she knew it would get the attention that it did. None of her other posts have many likes."

"You checked her out?"

"I wanted to see how bad the video was. Stupid influencers—"

"Too tight!" Jada says, her voice floating over the rock. "Give me some slack!"

I can't hear Jim's response, but the rope loosens and Jada puts her left hand up slowly to the next hold.

"Not that way," Ben says. "Shit."

"Let her see if she can find it."

He meets my eyes as Jada corrects her course and finds the right hold. "I'm getting sympathetic vertigo."

"I never could watch *Free Solo* because of that."

"Alex does some sick shit." He means Alex Honnold, a famous climber who'd put up some crazy solo routes without using rope. He was careful and methodical, planning his routes for years, but the problem was, when someone did something big like that, it encouraged others to do it too, whether they were capable or not. The documentary won an Oscar, and the stupid things people did climbing where they shouldn't had increased exponentially.

"You see him in the valley this year?" I ask.

"Not yet. But he'll be here."

"I'm sure." I point to Jada and Jim. "They seem to be okay. Should we continue?"

"Yeah, but let's keep an eye out."

"Good idea."

I start on the next pitch, and we climb in silence until we reach the peak. It doesn't take us long, our rhythm good, the route easy. We get to the top and I get my moment—the three-sixty view breathtaking, no matter how many times I've seen it. It's a gorgeous day, and we're alone up here, a rare thing in Yosemite.

"I never get sick of this," Ben says, spinning in a slow circle.

"Me either."

"Can't believe you stayed away for ten years."

"I went to school in Colorado for a while," I say slowly. "Great peaks there, too."

"Oh yeah, whereabouts?"

"University of Colorado. In Boulder."

"That's a nice spot."

"It is."

"And then New York."

"Yep."

"What were you doing there?"

"I worked in an art gallery—" We both turn our heads at the shouts, clear and loud. We rush to the edge and look down. It's Jim and Jada, both of them yelling for help.

"Shit." Ben reaches for the radio slung across his chest. "Dispatch, this is SAR Cowell. I'm on Tenaya Peak, and there's a climber in distress on the pitch below me."

"This is Dispatch. Do they need medical attention?"

"SAR Peters and I are going to assess."

"Copy."

"Stay still," I yell down. "We're coming."

Jada looks up at me slowly, her dark brown eyes wide with fear. She's hanging by her rope, while Jim is arresting her below. I didn't see it happen, but I can guess that she lost her hold and swung into the rock on her fall. She's holding her left arm against her chest.

"How's your arm?"

"It hurts."

"Do you think it's broken?"

"I don't know."

"I'm going to build an anchor," Ben says to me, taking off his pack.

"Can you hold her?" I yell down to Jim. His forearms are muscled and strong, straining on the rope. "It'll be a minute."

"I got it," he yells back. "But hurry, please."

"I'm going to downclimb to her," I say to Ben. "I'm not sure he can hold her long enough."

"Be safe."

"Always."

I search the top of the ridge till I find what I'm looking for. An old piece of protection, a bolt that's been there a while. I test it. It seems secure. I clip in and start to downclimb, not putting weight on the rope if I can help it, in case the protection doesn't hold. Jada's about two hundred feet below me, just above a ledge.

"I'll be to you in a minute, Jada. Just hold still."

I inhale a slow breath, then release it. Downclimbing is counter-intuitive, moving your feet and hands below you instead of up, and for me, it takes an extra level of concentration. I find the holds I need, and in a few minutes I'm on the ledge just below her.

I reach up to steady her. Her eyes are wide with fear and un-focused. "Hi, Jada, I'm Cassie. And up there is Ben. I'm going to need you to trust me and to bring yourself down half a body length so we can give your guy a rest, okay?"

"I can't do it."

"Yes you can. Jim is holding on to you. He's your boyfriend, right?"

"Yes."

"Great. Can you look at me, Jada?"

Jada moves her head slowly to the side so that we make eye contact. "Cassie?"

"That's right. I'm here. There's a ledge just below you. It's big enough to stand on. I'm going to ask Jim to lower you slowly so you can stand on it, okay?"

She nods weakly.

"Jim? Can you hear me?"

He looks up at me. I can see that his hands are trembling on the rope. "Yeah?"

"Can you lower Jada about a foot? Slowly?"

"Okay."

"Are you anchored in?"

"Yeah."

"Okay, slowly now." I hold on to Jada as Jim lowers her down. When her feet hit the ledge, they collapse under her, and I wedge her against the rock. "Tighten the rope, Jim. Do you have any protection there?"

"There's a bolt."

"Anchor the rope there."

"Okay."

I hold Jada against the rock while her whole body trembles. "Ben?"

"I'm coming down."

I watch as Ben rappels slowly off the ledge on the other side of Jada. He's got a harness around his neck, ready to put it on her. He's on the ledge on the other side of her in a minute.

"I think it makes more sense to take her up than down," Ben says.

"Agree." I rub Jada's back. "Jada? We're going to put this harness on you. That way we can haul you up to the top."

"Okay."

"Ben will help you. You'll raise one foot and then the other, okay?"

"Yes."

I look down again. "Jim, you all right down there?"

"I think so."

"Can you go laterally? It's less steep over there to the left, and you should be able to scramble up."

"Will do."

Ben helps Jada into the harness, and when she's secure, he unclips her from Jim's rope and clips her into the anchor rope. "I'll climb up?"

"Yes."

He does it quickly, while I hold Jada steady and give her encouragement. I check in on Jim's progress toward the easier slope. He moves methodically, his skills not bad. But not good enough to be up here on this pitch. I feel angry at him, assuming, perhaps wrongly, that it's his fault that they're here. Man-ing Jada into it, his ego on display. I can only hope that he learns a lesson from this. That they both do.

"Jada?" Ben says. "I'm going to start lifting you up, okay?"

"Okay."

"Ascending."

"Ascending," I say as I let Jada go and Ben pulls her up through the anchored rope. I toggle my radio. "Dispatch, this is SAR Peters. The climber is secured. No visible injuries, but we'll reassess once we get her on solid ground."

"Roger that, SAR Peters."

I wait for Jada to disappear over the cliff. Then I start to climb up, my arms weary, but there's only a short way to go. I reach the top at the same time as Jim. I make sure he's secure, then unclip myself and go to where Ben has Jada on the ground, moving his hands over her limbs to see where she's injured. When Ben presses his hand to her forearm, she winces. He starts to pull her sleeve up, revealing a bruise the size of a man's thumb. Jada pulls away and tugs her sleeve down.

"Doesn't seem broken," Ben says.

"Are you okay, Jada?" I ask. "Can you move your arm?"

She nods, holding her arm out and flexing it slowly. "Only I feel stupid."

"It's fine, don't—"

"Jada, baby. Are you okay?" Jim hustles up and grabs Jada into his arms. She resists for a moment, then dissolves into tears. "It's okay, baby. I'm here." He pats her on the back while Ben and I share a glance over them.

I pry Jim gently from Jada. "We haven't finished assessing her injuries."

"Oh, okay, sorry."

Jim backs up and Ben resumes moving his hands over Jada's arms and legs, asking her if she's in pain. Jim's face is set in a jealous mask.

"Ouch," Jada says as Ben touches her shoulder. "That hurts."

"Is that where you hit the rock?"

She nods.

He probes it gently. "Probably not broken, just bruised. You might want to get an X-ray in town."

"Is that covered by insurance?" Jim says.

"Depends on your plan."

"It's her mom's."

"You ask her, then," Ben says, talking to Jada. "But you should get it looked at."

"I will," Jada says.

Ben finishes his inspection. "You'll probably have some bumps and bruises. You need to take it easy for a few days. And we're going to need some info from you. For our report."

Jim frowns. "Why?"

"It's standard operating procedure."

"Are we in trouble?"

"No," I say. "We just need your name, address, that sort of thing, for our statistics."

"Am I going to have to pay for this?"

If we forced everyone who did something stupid out here to pay for it, the Park Service would have to spend most of its time chasing bad debts. "The service is free, but I suggest you keep to easier pitches in the future."

"I'm not the . . ." He trails off when he sees my expression. "Yeah, okay, of course."

"You don't want anyone to get hurt."

"No." He looks around. "How do we get down?"

"There's an easy hiking trail that way," I say, pointing to where it starts. "You go down that slowly, and you'll be fine. Stop often. It's not a race."

"Okay, thanks."

"Sure enough." I take their information quickly: name, ages, address, phone number, where they're staying in the park. "You should head down now. Make sure Jada gets something to eat and some rest. The shock's going to catch up to her."

He nods, then reaches down and helps her up. We watch them start down the trail, and though my plan was to rappel and get to the bottom quickly, I make a snap decision that it's a better idea to follow them in a few minutes to make sure they get down safely.

"What do you think is going on there?" Ben asks.

"Not sure. But nothing good."

CHAPTER 11

FOLLOW UP

Then

June

The next morning, I go to check on Jada to make sure her injuries remained mild. It's a common practice when the injured party is still around. Too often, something that can seem innocuous can turn serious, like so many things in the park. Others don't heed the advice they're given for treatment.

So, here I am, knocking on the door of their Airstream in the Tuolumne campground, listening to the morning sounds—people packing up, children running around escaping their parents, the rattle of dishes being washed, and car doors being slammed. It's shaded under the trees and the air is dry, augmenting the smell of the earth and dead pine needles underneath my hiking boots.

The door opens and Jada pokes her head out. She's wearing a long-sleeved maroon shirt and black hiking shorts that hit the tops of her knees. She looks pretty and well-rested, none of yesterday's distress lingering.

"Oh, it's you," she says. "I thought Jim had forgotten something."

"He's out climbing?"

"Yeah."

I glance around. There's a couple packing up in the campground across the dirt road, within earshot. "I'm glad you're resting. How's the arm?"

Jada touches it gently, then flexes out and folds it back up. "Seems to be fine."

"Mind if I take a look?"

"Why?"

"It's standard procedure. Just to make sure we assessed your injury properly."

"Oh, okay." She steps out of the Airstream and walks to the picnic table. She waves to the couple across the road. She's only been here a few days, but she seems to make friends quickly.

I follow her to the table. "This is a nice site."

Jada looks around and smiles. "Yeah, we were lucky to get it. Jim forgot to make a reservation." She rolls her eyes.

Our eyes meet as a laugh escapes. We sit. "Hold out your arm."

She does and I pull up her sleeve. The bruise from yesterday is larger, less defined, but I can tell from the coloration that it's not that deep. I touch it gently, feeling for heat and swelling, but it's minor. "Seems like you'll live."

"That's good."

A kid rides by on his bicycle, the front wheel wavering. He waves to Jada. "I saw Smokey!"

We both tense. "You did?" Jada says, as I say, "Where?"

He stops pedaling, his feet barely touching the ground. He's six, maybe, or seven. He points over his shoulder. "Back there by those big garbage bins!"

Jada starts to rise. I put a hand on her shoulder to stop her while I speak to the kid. "Don't go near the bear . . . What's your name?"

"Timmy!"

"Timmy, don't go near the bear, okay? It's dangerous."

"He's cute!"

"Cute can still be dangerous. You should go back to your campsite. Just peddle back slowly."

He looks disappointed. "Okay."

I detach my radio. "This is SAR Peters. There's been a sighting of the bear known as 'Smokey' near the Tuolumne garbage bins."

"Roger, SAR Peters. Dispatching now."

I breathe a sigh of relief as I put my radio away.

"Why did you do that?" Jada asks, pulling down her sleeve.

"Because bears are dangerous."

"He's just living his life."

I stand up and walk to the road, checking that Timmy is in fact riding back to his campsite. He's moving slowly, like I told him to. He stops a few sites up and turns in.

"Probably not anymore," I say.

"What does that mean?"

I turn toward her. She's crossed her arms over her chest, striking a defiant pose.

"That was a mistake," I say, "feeding him. Posting that video. A lot of people saw that."

"How was I supposed to know? Usually it's just my friends on my Insta."

"There are signs everywhere saying not to feed the animals."

"I won't, then."

"No, it's too late. It's gone viral. And now something's going to have to be done."

"Why?"

"Because he ate out of your hand, Jada. That's super dangerous."

Her face falls and her arms follow. She looks young, vulnerable, like she did yesterday on the rock. "I didn't . . . I didn't realize . . . What's going to happen to him?"

"Nothing good."

Tears start to well in her eyes. "Is it my fault?"

"I . . . I'm sure he's been getting bolder for a while. But stay away from him, okay? Keep a low profile. You don't want to exacerbate the situation."

"What situation?" Jim says, coming up behind me.

Jada freezes for a moment, then rushes into his arms. "I got Smokey into trouble."

I watch him comfort her, his arms tender but his expression steely when he looks at me. "Did you need anything else?"

"I was checking on Jada. After yesterday."

"She's got me to do that," he says. "That's all she needs."

When I get back to the SAR site, I borrow Mia's phone and check out Jada's Instagram posts. Jim and Jada's history is set out there like a storybook. I flip through it backwards, like starting with the end of a book and working your way to the beginning.

They'd driven cross-country over the last couple of weeks and intend to spend the summer in Yosemite, climbing and exploring as so many have done before them, including me. Based on her posts, she and Jim started dating a few years earlier after meeting in college, and they took up climbing together. They mostly climbed in the gym like I'd been doing in New York, but there was some good rock near them in Kentucky and they'd made trips there, sending easier routes, improving their skills. There were lots of pictures of them on top of mountains, their Patagonia gear shiny and new, their arms wrapped around each other. Another of Jada on graduation day, throwing her cap in the air with her proud mother standing behind her, their eyes tipped up to the sky. One or two posts with her group of girlfriends, but mostly the feed was Jim.

The last post was about her fall yesterday, painting Jim as the hero who'd arrested her from tumbling to the ground. She also mentioned the AWESOME SAR TEAM who rescued them, but didn't use our names.

Her most popular post by far is her video of Smokey that Jim shot soon after they arrived in the park. In it, she's holding out dried fruit cupped in her hand, and the bear is eating from it. There's a still shot too, whose composition is amazing. It's a little blurry, with the bear in portrait focus and her laughing in the background like she's being tickled. It has thousands of likes and comments, which is bad news for the park because Smokey has been seen again in camp. Something has to be done about it.

I x out of Instagram, ready to return Mia's phone. But something stops me. My new phone is rudimentary, without access to the internet, and it's been a while since I've checked in on myself. I do a quick Google search for my names like I did in Reno: *Cassandra Adams, Cassandra Biggs, Cassie Peters*. Nothing new comes up, just the same posts about my old life. Then I google Kevin. The top hit is his LinkedIn page, which is fitting because that's what Kevin cared about the most—his career selling complex insurance products to high-net-worth individuals.

He hadn't been happy with the photo that the office had taken, so he'd gotten me to find a professional portrait photographer and we'd both had head shots done. I thought it was silly at the time, but Kevin was deadly serious. He made us salon appointments, hired a stylist and makeup artist, the whole nine. I remember looking at us in the studio mirror, when we stood next to each other for the couple shots Kevin also insisted we take, in dark jeans and bare feet and crisp white shirts. It felt like my transformation away from Cassie was complete, and I wondered if I even was playing a part anymore. I'd become Cassandra Adams, a polished woman who worked in an art gallery and got her nails done and knew how to blow out her hair almost as well as the salon. A woman who looked good on a man's arm, whose life revolved around him and his friends. A woman old before her time.

Then Kevin had smiled at me and smacked me playfully on my bum and said something about us looking too stuffy. He'd picked me up and we'd both started laughing and that was the shot that we got framed and put up on the wall. Us happy, playful, carefree. I could see Cassie *and* Cassandra in that photo. And I could see Kevin, too, the man who'd swept me off my feet, who didn't care where I came from, who wanted to be with me forever, he said, who loved me so much it was scary.

I close the browser with a slow exhale as my own phone pings in my pocket.

I take it out and stare at the text floating on the screen.

Did you think I wouldn't look for you?

I shudder as I read it, and I can't help but wonder—could he sense me thinking about him, even this far way, or was there something else at play?

June 14—Lee Vining

It's been a minute.

I haven't been keeping up with my writing, but tonight I felt the itch, so I found a quiet spot near the road and told Sandy I was going for a walk.

I can't write in the RV. Maybe it's the stale air or the weird mold stain in the corner. Or maybe it's having someone else watch me while I do it. Sandy is super encouraging of my writing IN THEORY, but when I actually do it . . . I don't know, she gets this weird expression on her face, like I'm taking something from her. She asks all kinds of questions, and when she goes quiet and I look at her, she's just staring at me in this kind of creepy way.

I'm sure it's just my OVERACTIVE IMAGINATION, as Daddy always used to call it, but that's why I'm sitting on this tree stump with the purple sky above, rubbing my fingers against my palms to keep them warm. One day, I hope, it will be summer at night here, but not yet.

So, I'll start. But what IS that start? How do you know what the thing is that starts a rock rolling downhill?

Okay, okay. Big metaphors. Or is it a simile? Moving on.

I guess it started when I talked to Jada that night at the washstand when she was crying . . .

No, that's not right. That's how WE started, but not IT.

IT started when she posted that photo of her feeding Smokey. That happened before the washstand, because I brought it up that night. I told her it was cool. Mainly I said it to stop her crying because I've noticed that the easiest way to get someone to turn their emotions around is to compliment them. So I told her it was cool, and she wiped her tears away and she told me how much she loves animals and how she might want to be a photographer eventually, maybe a wildlife photographer. Later. When she's grown and whatnot, even though she studied science in college because that's what her parents wanted her to do. But now she's graduated and here for the summer and there is SO MUCH BEAUTY—her words—and she's all inspired and shit, and being young is for making mistakes, isn't it? So you don't have regrets?

I don't know about that. I don't think it's possible to live your life without regrets. Mine are stacked up like cordwood.

But Jada didn't seem interested in debating that point, so we talked a bit about photography and other things and then, the next morning, they left—her and Jim—to go to Yosemite, which had been their destination all along.

Lee Vining was a mistake, she said, and I couldn't agree more.

We didn't trade numbers. When you cry with a stranger, it's usually best not to keep that connection. I thought that would be the end of it. Or if I saw her again, it would just be in one of my stories.

But then, two days later, I went to Yosemite.

I wasn't looking for her. I was just . . . feeling ITCHY, so I borrowed this terrible loud car from one of the other owners—one of those older guys who's always staring at me like those men used to in Daddy's trailer park—and I'm sure he expects something in return, or that's what Sandy said anyway.

She wasn't too happy that I'd borrowed it, but I have to have SOME freedom, I said. There aren't enough stories in the trailer park. Not enough scope for the imagination, as that stupid redhead says in that book Sandy loves because it reminds her of when she was a kid and felt free.

Whatever.

I drove that car to the park, using some dollars I scrounged from around the RV to get in—the change never stops turning up, like beach glass—and I found Jada right where she said she was going to be. I'm not sure why I did it, only once I got in the park, it seemed big, and I felt like I needed someone to guide me. I know that doesn't make sense, but feelings don't have to.

And Jada was SO NICE to me that day. SO HAPPY to see me, she said, and then she gave me a hug and pulled away, shy and grinning. She showed me all around Tuolumne Meadows and we got along like a house on fire, as Daddy used to say, the way two people who are different on the outside but feel the same on the inside sometimes do.

The campground where Jada and Jim are staying is sure nicer than the RV park! I tried to convince Sandy to move us there, but it's too far from work, she says, plus the cost of the permit, when she'd already paid six months for our currrent spot. I thought about mentioning all that money in the mattress, that it would set us up right for the summer near a beautiful lake, with clear air and no creepy old men, but I realized it was probably a bad idea to bring up the money because she'd said we weren't supposed to talk about it.

So, I swallowed that thought down like bitter medicine and decided I wouldn't tell Sandy so much about what I did every day anymore.

I'm writing stories; I can tell her stories too.

But one good thing did happen from all of it—Sandy bought me a car, an old beater someone in town was selling for next to nothing. She said it was to give me my freedom, but I know it was because she was worried about what I'd have to do with that guy if I kept borrowing HIS car. It doesn't matter, though. It was thoughtful and kind and that IS Sandy most of the time.

No one's perfect.

Anyway . . . Jada. Yeah. Once I got the car, we started hanging out. Not every day, but sometimes. I'd watch her and Jim climb, and we'd all go swimming in Tenaya Lake, though it's fucking FREEZING, like a slap in the face when you jump in.

Sometimes we'd go looking for the bear. She named him Smokey, which isn't very original, but don't say that to Jada! She's, like, OBSESSED with that bear, always taking pictures and videos and posting them online even though she shouldn't. It's weird to me, but it makes her happy, I guess.

Sandy doesn't like that I'm spending time with Jada. Making myself memorable, she says, when I should be staying in the shadows, like her. When I ask her why, she won't say. Just that it's better to keep a low profile. Better to keep to ourselves and not make friends. She should be enough for me, she says, and then she goes off all day to work.

What am I supposed to do, I want to know? Sit around and wait for her? Make a nice meal like a housewife? Be like Mama used to be, her whole world spinning around Daddy and his moods?

I didn't sign up for that.

I don't do what Sandy says, even if I'm going to get punished for it. I've been punished before and survived. I'm all GROWN. I can do what I want.

Today, Jada and I went for a hike and we found Smokey's cave. It was her idea, because I don't care that much about that bear. I'm not sure why she does, only I think she feels guilty for bringing attention to him. The SAR is worried about Smokey. I've heard them talking on their radios about him, and that's how I knew where the cave was. When I mentioned it to Jada, she was hot to trot, even though I said it might be dangerous. If I'm being honest, I think that's maybe why she wanted to go.

It was just the two of us. When I asked her where Jim was, she touched a spot on her arm that was covered by her sleeve and said he'd gone climbing with some dirtbags he'd met at the campsite. Then I asked her what she meant by "dirtbags," and she said that's what climbers call themselves, but that seems like a funny name to give to yourself. She laughed and said that sometimes words could have lots of meanings, that sometimes you have to call yourself what others call you to take ownership of it, and she had this LOOK in her eye that I didn't quite understand. I didn't ask anything else after that. I just accepted her excuses about Jim like she accepts mine about Sandy.

Smokey's cave was about three miles from the parking lot on the trail and then another half mile in the woods. It was hot out, and by the time we got to the cutoff, my water was already low. I have to pay better attention to things like that. How quickly something like water can disappear.

We found his cave was up against a cliff. And it was only when we got real close to it that Jada decided she was scared. "What if he's in there?" she said, like that wasn't always a possibility.

I should've been scared but I wasn't. I just told her we'd be ALERT, and we walked toward the opening slowly, making lots of noise, because bears don't like noise, right?

But then I remembered this one comedian Daddy used to like, saying that different kinds of bears liked different kinds of things and you were supposed to lie still for one and make noise for another, and how was I supposed to remember which was which? Was Smokey a black bear or a brown bear or something in between? Jada told me, but I don't retain that kind of information.

I just remember thinking, when that comedian was HAHAHA-ing at his own joke, that bears sounded like men, always keeping you on your toes, never clear about what they want, and how are we supposed to know? Too much drama.

It didn't matter, though. The cave was empty. It smelled strong, like bear piss, I guess, and God knows what else. We went inside for a minute and it was peaceful in there. Hidden back from the trail, the entrance partially covered by moss. It was bigger than I thought it'd be, too. The ceiling high enough in the middle to stand up in.

Jada and I had to squeeze in tight together, and I could feel her trembling. I asked her why she was afraid, and she said she wasn't. She was just in awe, she said. That's a feeling of reverential respect mixed with fear or wonder, according to the dictionary. Like what you're supposed to feel *in church, I guess. Like the way you're supposed to treat the person you love. Fear, wonder, respect.*

You could hide in here forever, Jada said, and no one would know you were even there.

I wonder if that's true?

—Petal

CHAPTER 12

ARREST THAT BEAR

Then
June

Days pass. I don't get any more texts, other than from my mother, asking when I'm coming back to town. I put her off and go to sleep, trying not to dream, hoping to rest. Each day feels the same, then different, then the same again. New people coming in and out of the park who look just like the people before them. Those there for the summer, like Jim and Jada and others staying in the campground, becoming part of the background.

I work and I sleep and I wait, because the job is waiting, and my life is too.

And then, in the third week of June, Jenny gathers the SAR team together at the picnic tables at lunchtime, along with one of the park biologists. I'm sitting next to Ben; Mia and Gareth are across from me. It's a hot day, the sun beating on my neck, sweat trickling down my back. It's been a busy couple of weeks as traffic picks up in the park, increasing the number of rescue calls exponentially. We're all tired, this meeting unwelcome.

"We need to take the bear into custody," Jenny says, standing before us like a schoolteacher delivering bad news. She's got her hair in pigtails, but her tone is deadly serious.

"Oh no," Mia says. "Not Smokey."

Gareth rubs Mia's back. Even though she chastised me for calling the bear that in the beginning, she's succumbed to his charms. A five-year-old black bear with a medium-brown coat, Smokey has deep brown eyes that remind me of a cocker spaniel and a gentle manner about him even though he's a wild animal who could easily hurt any one of us. We've all seen him up close by now, shooing him away from our camp with pots and pans and making sure the bear-proof box is closed up tight.

"He's been seen one too many times in the campground. He's now approaching people for food," Katie the biologist says.

"It's that girl's fault," Sam says. He's sitting at the other table with George, the two of them always gravitating toward each other whether it be for rescues or parties.

"That stupid video," George agrees. "There's some TikTok challenge where people have to try to replicate the shot of her feeding it."

"Oh, God," I say. "Really?"

"What's a TikTok challenge?" Ben asks.

"Dude, even I know what that shit is," Gareth says.

"The point is," Katie says, "we can't keep the bear around."

"So what, then?" Mia asks.

"We'll take it into custody, and then the bear court will decide."

"If that gets out, it's going to be a circus."

"I agree. That's why we need to do this quietly, if at all possible. The bear has a tracker on it. We know the route it takes and where it spends the night. We'll go early tomorrow morning and sedate it. Then we'll bring it into custody and the magistrate can decide."

"Does the bear get an advocate?" Mia asks.

"Yes, of course."

"She wants to do it," Gareth says. "Right, Mia?"

"No . . . I'd feel so guilty if I didn't do a good job."

"We can address that later," Katie says. "For now, we need volunteers to bring the bear out. It will be at least three miles of carrying it in a litter based on where its cave is. He's out near Dog Lake."

"She means us," Sam says, punching George in the arm. "We're the volunteers."

"And me," Gareth says.

"I'm game," Ben says.

Mia glances at me. Do I feel guilty for not volunteering to litter out a four-hundred-pound bear? Not really.

"Sounds like we have our team," Jenny says. "We'll meet here at o-five-hundred tomorrow."

A collective groan goes up. Ben turns to me. "Lucky you."

"You did volunteer."

"Special pay, I reckon."

"Good point."

Jenny issues a few more instructions, and then the meeting breaks up as everyone's radios crackle. "Rescue on Tuolumne Peak," Jenny says. "All hands on deck."

Time to go to work.

The team assembles early the next morning. I can hear them groaning and shuffling around outside my tent and smell the sharp tang of camp coffee. I think, briefly, about getting up and going with them, but the rescue I'd gone on the day before had been difficult and I'm still worked. So I turn over and get a couple of hours extra sleep, then get up at seven and decide to make breakfast for the crew when they return. I mix up a large batch of pancake batter and rummage for some syrup in the bear box where we keep common supplies. I start a fire. When the coals are glowing red, I put the cast iron pan on and wait for it to get piping hot. I put the syrup in a pot off to the side so it warms, then make a large pot of coffee. Mia's hanging at one of the picnic tables, monitoring the radio. By the time I'm done, she tells me that they aren't far off.

"That smells amazing," a voice says behind me.

It's Petal, blinking at me slowly beneath that same hole-filled hat she was wearing when we talked before Jada and Jim's rescue, though it isn't hat weather. She's wearing a ripped backpack I've seen her use before, and her journal is under her arm, a pen sticking out of it. Jada's standing next to her, looking determined.

"Petal, Jada . . . What are you doing here?"

"I thought I'd take you up on that offer of a climbing lesson," Petal says.

I glance at Mia. She's on her phone, uninterested. "Oh, right. It's . . . not a good time."

Jada walks to the nearest tent and touches the canvas. "Because of Smokey?"

"How did . . . What?"

"Sandy has a ham radio," Petal says. "She likes to listen to the traffic. Depending on the day, we can hear all your traffic, too."

"You can?"

"It's pretty easy when you know how."

"You shouldn't do that."

She shrugs.

"You live here?" Jada asks.

"Yes."

"Kind of primitive."

"It is."

She turns to me slowly, assessing. "Thanks again for saving me."

"All part of the job."

"Jim thinks we should try Tenaya again. Get back on that horse, or whatever. His dad's always saying that."

"What do *you* think?"

"It was scary. Feels like a bad idea."

"You should trust your instincts."

She looks down at the ground. She's wearing a new pair of hiking shoes, barely muddied. "Jim can be pushy sometimes. It's hard to say no."

"Don't let him push you up something you're not comfortable on, okay? That's a way to end up killed."

"I wasn't going to *die*."

But she could've died. If Jim hadn't arrested her properly, she could've tumbled down enough vertical to break her. She doesn't seem in a mood to hear that, and I don't want an argument. "Maybe not, but you shouldn't have been on that pitch."

Petal's watching us like she's trying to memorize our dialogue.

"I don't like people telling me what I can't do," Jada says.

"I get it. I did a lot of stupid things when I was your age. I still do."

Petal clears her throat. "Your syrup is burning."

"Shit, thanks." I rush to the fire and pull the pot from it, burning my hand in the process. I nearly drop the pot, but save it just in time, then bring my hand to my mouth, blowing on the burn. It's mild, but it was dumb not to use a pot holder.

Mia walks up to me and holds out a wet towel. "Here, wrap it in this."

"Thanks."

"Those girls getting on your nerves?"

"No," I say, speaking low. "It's okay."

"Say the word and I'll shoo them off."

I smile at her and wrap the cloth around my hand, making a mental note to put some cream on it later. "Where are they?"

"About to—"

"Oh, look!" Jada says, pointing to the woods. "Oh no! Poor Smokey!" She rushes past me, her phone up as Ben, Gareth, Sam, and George come down the path, each holding a litter pole. Smokey is asleep on the platform. He looks peaceful. "What did you do to him?"

"Jada, step back," I say firmly. "He's sedated. He's fine."

She turns the phone on me. "Why's he sedated? What did he do? You're not going to kill him, are you?"

"Please put the phone down, Jada."

"Not until you tell me what's going on."

Jenny comes up behind Jada. She looks tired and stressed.

"I'll explain everything if you just put that down," I say. "It's all standard procedure."

Jada's face flushes with anger. "I know what you mean! I was reading about it online the other night on *Bear Aware*. You *say* you believe in bear preservation, but if the bear gets unruly, then you euthanize it. You murder the bear!"

"That's enough now," Jenny says, plucking the phone from Jada's hand.

"Give that back!"

"I'm going to turn it off and then we can talk about this calmly." Jenny turns to Ben and the others, who've stopped what they were doing. They're tired, ready to put the litter down. "Take him to the road. The truck is waiting there."

"You got it," Ben says.

"No! Where are you taking Smokey?"

"We're taking him into custody," I say. "He'll be fine."

Jada's near tears. "Custody! Like a criminal? What's his crime? I want to know the charges."

"Jada, please lower your voice."

"No, I won't! I won't. Everyone needs to know what you're doing here." Her eyes look wild, and for a moment, I'm worried that she'll try to grab her phone back from Jenny, a move Jenny won't tolerate.

"Jada," Petal says, her voice flat but commanding.

"What?"

"They aren't going to answer you if you keep yelling."

"Okay, yeah, okay." Jada takes a couple of slow, shallow breaths. "I understand. But you have to give me my phone back."

"I will, but you should delete that video and leave the SAR site immediately."

Jada holds out her hand. "Give me my phone."

Jenny puts the phone in it. Jada closes her hand around it tight, then turns and storms away.

"Do you know this girl, Cassie?" Jenny says, watching the rigid set of Jada's shoulders. "Can you talk sense into her?"

"I don't know . . ."

"I'll talk to her," Petal says. "We've been hanging out. Maybe she'll listen to me."

"She should delete that video," I say. "She doesn't want to call that kind of attention to herself and Smokey again."

Petal meets my gaze. Again, the slow blink. "I'll try."

Petal walks away without saying goodbye. I take a moment to calm down, then turn my attention back to making breakfast for the guys as Jenny leaves to supervise Smokey's removal.

When Ben and the others get back from bringing Smokey to the road so he can be transported to the animal lockup while he awaits his trial, they're tired and grateful for the meal. Ben tells me about the hike—where the cave is, behind Dog Lake and half a mile off the trail. His den is well hidden, and it's only because of the tracking beacon that they were able to find him. I fill him in on Petal and Jada, her reaction, the video.

"She'll calm down," he says.

"I'm not so sure."

"What's bothering you?"

I shake out my hands, trying to dispel the anxiety that's building between my shoulders. "I've been through her social media, and that video . . . We should've deleted it."

"Jenny didn't have cause to do that."

"I know, it's just . . . I feel like it's not the last we're going to hear about it."

PHOTOGRAPH—A bear staring at the camera with bars over it like a jail cell

Liked by **mamajada** and **23,017 others**

@JadaJohnsonInsta IT'S TIME TO SAVE SMOKEY!

Did you know that if the Park Service deems a bear as "problematic" they "euthanize" it? That's a fancy word for bear murder. All Smokey ever did was dare to walk into a campground in his OWN TERRITORY! It's not his fault he doesn't understand that he's supposed to stay away from humans! He's NEVER hurt anyone, and now he's in JAIL.

But we can #SAVESMOKEY. He can be retrained. There are programs to relocate bears after training so they don't have to be euthanized. I've set up a #GOFUNDME to pay for it—LINK IN BIO!

There's still time! His "trial" (ridic!) is in a couple of days. Let's show up and make our voices heard!

#BearsHaveRightsToo #PETA #SaveSmokey

mamajada Don't go courting trouble, Jada. What does Jim think about all this?

bellasgram You are my S-HERO!

KatieWicksWriter Signed the petition! Let's gooooo!!!!

jimislivingthedream @mamajada I support Jada and Smokey.

BearsAreMammalsToo This is YOUR FAULT!

LaurenBaileySays Love this!

theyfreedBritney @BearsAreMammalsToo Why don't you DO SOMETHING instead of just attacking people all the time?

Papajim The deep state reaches deep, Jada. Beware. Trust the plan.

Papajim @BearsAreMammalsToo I've researched you and you should be careful. The storm is coming.

JUNE 21

CHAPTER 13

PRELIMINARIES

Now

After I tell Jenny that I need to think about whether or not I want to speak to a lawyer, they decide to bring me to Eric rather than have him come to the Heli Base. He's busy dealing with the local police, Jenny explains, while I sit next to her in a van that bumps along the road to the Tuolumne Meadows Ranger Station.

A ranger I don't know is driving, and Gareth and Ben are in the back. Jenny and I are in the middle row, and I can't help feeling like I'm in custody. I want to turn around and look at Ben, to say something that will wash away the cold glint he had in his eyes when we got into the van. But what can I say? There's nothing.

There's nothing that can help me. That's what Jenny thinks. That's why she told me to get a lawyer. She thinks I'm in trouble. And maybe she's right.

Oh, she definitely is. So I hold my tongue while we drive through the night.

It takes us over an hour to get there, and when we arrive at the Ranger Station, I'm divided from the others. They leave for the SAR site, while I'm escorted by Jenny into the building, the bright porch light over the entrance almost blinding me. It's painted dark brown like many of the buildings in the park, and it almost disappears into the night.

Inside, Eric's waiting for me with a police officer I recognize. Her name is Captain Cole, though I don't remember anything else about her. She's in her forties, stocky, with green eyes behind cat-eye glasses. Eric doesn't say anything and neither does she. We're mute as Jenny leads me into Eric's office and sits me in a chair, her hands pressed firmly into my shoulders.

There's a map of the park on the wall behind Eric, his jurisdiction laid out in green tight peaks and light pink features. I have one like it pinned up in my tent, full of string and pushpins, marking locations, potential sightings of missing persons.

"Cassie," Eric says, "have you met Captain Cole?"

"Yes, once or twice."

"She'll be assisting me tonight."

"All right."

"I'm going to record this."

"Of course."

He reaches into his desk and takes out a silver mini recorder. He turns it on, its red light like a warning as he puts it in the middle of his desk. "Eric Moser, interview one with Cassie Peters, August fifth at nine thirty p.m. Captain Sarah Cole is accompanying me. Good evening, Cassie."

"Good evening."

"Can you please provide your date of birth for our records?"

I state it.

"And your full name."

"My legal name is Cassandra Adams, but everyone calls me Cassie Peters. That's my maiden name."

"You were married to Kevin Adams?"

I swallow slowly. "Yes. I *am* married to him. We're not yet divorced." *But he's dead*, my brain screams, and that's another way to dissolve a marriage.

"And the body you brought back with you tonight, that's Mr. Adams?"

"Yes."

"You were present when he died?"

BOOM!

"Yes, yes . . . I—I'm not sure I can talk about that yet."

Eric nods slowly. "All right, let's try something different. Let's start at the beginning. Why did you come to Yosemite this summer?"

I breathe in and out slowly. "I left my marriage and I needed a job."

"And you contacted Jenny Evans for that job?"

"Yes."

"When was that?"

"In the early winter. I don't remember the exact date."

"So you'd been planning to leave your husband for a while?"

"Yes."

"Did he know that?"

"No."

"Do you mind if I ask why you didn't tell him?"

"Yes, I do mind."

Eric tilts his head to the side. "I'm going to need you to answer just the same."

I look down at my hands. There's dirt caked under my fingernails, and maybe something else. Blood.

"I didn't think he'd take it well, my leaving."

"Why not?"

"Because he'd said so, once or twice." I meet Eric's gaze, focusing as hard as I can on keeping the tone of Kevin's voice when he'd said what he'd do if I left him out of my head. He had such an odd smile on his face, like he was discussing the weather, or what to order for dinner.

"How did you know there'd be a job on SAR?"

"I didn't."

"But you knew the winter was late for staffing? That the team would usually already have been assembled by then?"

"Yes, I . . . Sorry, I *did* know when I called Jenny. I saw in the Facebook group—you know, the SAR one?—that someone had pulled out and they were looking for a replacement. It felt like the perfect solution. I could slip away and go back to my old life while I tried to decide what to do next."

"When did you leave?"

"In May. A few days before I came here."

"Did you tell him then?"

"No, I left when he was out. I left a note, but that's it." I think back to the way my hand shook when I wrote it. How every noise in the hall sounded like Kevin's keys in the lock. It felt like I was having a heart attack, my pulse only returning to normal when I was hidden in the crappy motel in Jersey.

"Did you contact your husband after you left?"

"No."

"Did you tell him where you were going, in the note?"

"No."

"But he could guess that you'd come here?"

"I met him when I was living in Colorado. I never told him I was from Mammoth. I know it sounds weird, but Kevin wasn't a curious person. He didn't care about things like that."

"Did you keep it from him intentionally?"

"Maybe I always had a sense that the less he knew about me, the better. But I also wanted to leave this life behind after everything with Cameron Mack's disappearance. I moved across the country and didn't spend much time thinking about it."

"I see." Eric clicks his pen, then writes something in his notebook.

"Did he contact you after you left?"

"He sent me some messages. I have pictures of them on my phone. I changed phones after I got them."

"We'd like to see those."

"Okay."

"And after that, did you hear from him again?"

"No, I . . . Maybe."

Captain Cole leans forward and puts her hands on the desk. "What do you mean, maybe?"

"I threw my phone away, the one I used in New York, but I was getting messages on my new one. A few of them."

"What kind of messages? Threats?"

"Yes. But I don't know who they were from. Probably him, but the number was always blocked, and he didn't sign them."

"Did you tell anyone about these messages?" Eric asks.

"No."

"Why not?"

"I thought I could handle it. If it was Kevin—he was on the other side of the country. He didn't know where I was."

"But he found out?"

"Clearly."

"How?"

"I don't know. I guess I wasn't that hard to find."

"Why would he come here?"

You'd have to ask him, I almost say, but of course they can't. "He said . . . He said he wanted to work things out. That he wanted me back."

Captain Cole rocks back on her heels, her arms behind her

back. "How did he know where you'd be specifically? Out there, that far on the trail . . ."

"He followed me. He must've been tracking me."

"How?"

"I don't know. But he's the reason I went into the woods in the first place."

June 25—Lee Vining

Lots of drama around here!

 The other night, when I couldn't sleep, I was listening to the radio chat-ter on Sandy's ham radio. It's kind of soothing, the static, the truckers talking to each other, cutting in and out, or sometimes, the police. It's like messages from another planet, or a movie that you're watching in a drive-in, the speaker propped on the side of your car.

 That's when I heard them—two of those rescue people talking about how they were going to have to get Smokey and put him in jail before he hurt anyone. I texted Jada about it, and she was THAT ANGRY. Talking crazy about how she was going to put a stop to it.

 We ended up going to the SAR site early in the morning, and things got a little out of control. She took a video of the sleeping bear coming out of the woods being carried by four guys like he was a king. Only Jada said he was a prisoner. He looked pretty peaceful to me, but she was looking to disturb the peace. She posted her video and used all the right hashtags and it BLEW UP. Like, I think #SaveSmokey was trending for two days, and lots of stupid girls posted videos of themselves crying, thinking about what was going to happen to Smokey and shit like that.

 WEAK-ASS, that's what Daddy would call them, and for once, I kind of agree with him. Bears are dangerous, wild animals. Not pets. And it WAS kind of Jada's fault Smokey was in the trouble he was. She shouldn't have fed him. There are signs EVERYWHERE about that. Don't feed the bears! Duh. But maybe that's why she's so hell-bent on saving him. Because she knows that she's the reason he's behind bars in the first place.

Tonight was the hearing. "Bear Court," they call it, like the People's Court, only for bears.

I don't know what these meetings are usually like, but this one was PACKED. Standing room only. Jada and I got there early, and Sandy came along for the entertainment value, she said, but I think she wanted to get a better look at Jada. I've mentioned her one too many times, and now Sandy is jealous. I find it funny, but Sandy not so much.

There were people with signs, and Jada was sitting in the front row, holding her phone like it would save her. Jim was there too, his arm around her, holding her close.

I keep trying to describe Jim, but I feel like I can't quite get him. When I try to draw him, all I draw is a mask, like one of those ones from that movie Scream, all melting and scary. It's not rational. Maybe I do feel something romantic for Jada, only I don't think so.

I didn't follow all the legal stuff, but there was some back and forth about the bear—T923 apparently, not Smokey—and then Jada stood up and she asked if she could speak, and the judge person said she could. Everyone clapped even before she said anything, except for Cassie and that guy Ben, who were sitting off to the side with their arms crossed like grown-ups.

Then Jada started to speak and the room went silent, like totally STILL, and she talked about how she made a mistake and that Smokey shouldn't have to pay for her mistake. She'd done some research, and it was possible to do behavior modification so Smokey could unlearn about people. And then Jada announced that she'd started a GoFundMe and it already had $10,000 and she could raise whatever was needed to pay for the treatment. Then she held her hands out like she was begging and she said: "Part of justice is supposed to be about rehabilitation, and we can rehabilitate this bear. So that's what I'm asking you to do."

Then she sat down and a bunch of people clapped for her. Then the magistrate left for a minute and came back and said that they were going to try Jada's solution. Jada started crying and Jim was holding her phone, live streaming it, and for once he just looked like a normal guy, proud of his girlfriend. I was proud too, but when we left, Sandy was shaking her head like a mistake had been made.

"That girl is going to come to a bad end," Sandy said.

But when I asked her what she meant, she wouldn't say.

—Petal

CHAPTER 14

DEVILS POSTPILE

Then

July

It feels like I'm always waiting for something bad to happen.

For my rope to give when I'm out climbing. For my radio to crackle. For a text to arrive.

It's the nature of the job. I'm here *because* bad things are going to happen. I'd forgotten how that feeling edges into your life and takes up residence, seeping into everything. It's like the low-level anxiety that crept into my life in New York. I was always expecting something bad to happen there, too, and sometimes it did.

I do what I can to push those thoughts away through work and climbing and sleep, and the days slip by again, and now it's the July 4 weekend, the busiest weekend in the park. There seems to be an extra-large group of morons doing stupid things this year, and we all work ourselves to the bone doing rescue after rescue. A spiral fracture on a young kid who was jumping from rock to rock and went one rock too far. A twisted ankle. A guy who thought he was having a stroke, but it was just the heat. Someone who went off-trail and ended up getting hypothermia overnight because he didn't have the proper supplies. Rinse, repeat.

Each night I fall into bed exhausted, still hearing the crackle of the radio even though it's silent. My dreams are fractured, full of images from my past—Cameron's missing poster, the odd angle of her head when we found her, my first day on campus in Colorado, the flight to New York when Kevin got his seat switched so he was next to me, the motel room I stayed in after I left him, the texts.

When I wake up, I'm bathed in sweat and my hand is clutching the gun under my pillow.

My phone remains silent. I check it once a day, my heart in my throat, and each time there's nothing. I should throw this phone away but I can't afford another one and I need to be able to contact people. In the meantime, I save every penny I can, almost never turning down a job, even though I'm exhausted and need some time off. When this summer's over, I'm going to have to move on to something else that I haven't figured out yet. A few years running an art gallery isn't a marketable skill in most places. Maybe I'll go to LA and be swept up into that enormous city. Find some small place where I can see the ocean, or at least smell it.

I can't think about that right now. I just have to finish getting through these next two days and then I can go shake it off at the party at the Devils Postpile with the rest of the team.

The party was Gareth's idea. I think he mostly just likes saying "party at the Devils Postpile" as often as he can. He's been telling everyone about it—the SAR teams, everyone in the campground who's staying long-term. It's going to be *epic*, he says, but all I can think of are the high school parties I used to go to there, tailgates where whatever cheap liquor we could get our hands on got mixed into a terrible soup that got you immediately drunk. Those nights always ended with fights and police sirens, and it feels like this one won't be any different.

The last party I went to at the Postpile was right after my high school graduation. It felt like the whole school was there. I'd just broken up with my boyfriend because he was a jerk, and my girlfriends were refilling my red Solo cup repeatedly to make me feel better. It didn't, though. I just felt worse and worse, watching my ex dance around the fire, his hand locked with this girl from Bishop I didn't know.

Cameron was there that night, too. She and her boyfriend, Chris, were the golden couple of their grade, King and Queen of everything, including the party. Cameron was seventeen and glowing. No longer the annoying kid who'd follow me around the tennis club begging me for matches, she seemed to have lapped me in life. Taller, prettier, a better boyfriend. I remember staring at her—at them—as they laughed, while I bit the edge of my cup, full of envy. Unlike most of my classmates, I wasn't going away to college in the fall. I couldn't settle on what I wanted out of life. I only knew that I wanted to slip on her life and shed mine. But instead, all I did was throw up in some bushes while my friends rubbed my back.

I was wrong to envy her. She was two years away from dying. I'm still here.

So I get up and get through the day, and the one after that, and now I'm in Ben's truck heading to the Devils Postpile with a six-pack of beer on my lap and the radio on Ben's favorite station, which plays the Grateful Dead on a loop.

"We survived," he says. His hair is wet from his shower, and he's wearing a dark blue T-shirt with a hoodie that suits him. He smells good—clean, soapy, fresh. We've been working well together these last few weeks—more like friends, even though I can feel the edge of his want sometimes in a look, or a touch that lingers.

"I'm so tired," I say. "I feel like I could sleep for a week."

"We don't have to stay the night."

"Gareth will disown us if we don't *party 'til dawn, dude.*" I do a bad imitation of his way of speaking.

Ben laughs. "I bet there's so many people there, he never even notices."

"One can hope." I shake myself. "God, I sound a million years old. Fuck it, let's party."

"Feel free to change your mind."

"Thanks."

Ben takes the turnoff. The Devils Postpile is closed in winter, but the snow's all melted now, so the road is accessible. It starts off paved but ends up on dirt and gravel. The truck bumps along, rattling through the ruts until we reach the parking lot, which is full. Getting all of these cars out of here safely later is going to be a hassle, but that's not my concern. We've got sleeping bags, and sleeping under the stars doesn't sound like a bad idea. The night is warm and inviting.

"You know the history of this place?" I ask Ben as he parks the car between a camper van and an old dark green Subaru.

"No, actually."

"If I'm remembering right from school field trips, it's the best example of columnar basalt in the state. Maybe the country." I point to the rock face, which is made up of black columns of rock, like wavy cardboard. Below it is the Postpile—a jumble of rocks that have fallen off the cliff over more years than it's possible to fathom. "It goes up over sixty feet in the air and it was made from lava flow a hundred thousand years ago."

"Nice."

We climb out of the truck. "You think I'm a geek."

"Nope."

"I was in high school."

"I find that hard to believe."

"Believe it." I grip the beers as we walk toward the party.

There's already at least fifty people here, laughter and music echoing through the woods. The Postpile is in a separate park from Yosemite, one created just for it—a spectacular waterfall and the surrounding forest—and it has its own campground. The sites are on a first-come-first-served basis. Gareth and Mia came out here days ago with all the tents they could find to reserve as much of it as possible to reduce the possibility of complaints. I heard earlier that they'd secured fifteen spots, which was impressive.

A fire warning's been in effect for the last couple of weeks, so we can't have a bonfire, but everyone's brought lamps, which are scattered across various picnic tables, and Sam's hooked up his phone to a portable speaker, which is blasting some early 2000s playlist. I recognize about half the people—our SAR group, the one from the valley, Bri, some of the rangers, and, surprisingly, Jada, Jim, Petal, and Sandy.

"What are they doing here?" I ask Ben, nodding toward where they're huddled around one of the picnic tables, several bottles of wine atop it. Jim looks like he's holding court, telling some story with his arms waving wildly.

"Gareth invited the whole campground," he says. "Petal's always hanging around, isn't she, so I guess he invited her too?" He frowns at me. "You okay?"

"Yeah, I just . . . Did you see that video Jada posted of me?" Mia had shown it to me on her phone, the one where Jada confronted us about the bear. I looked like I didn't care about the bear, when all I was trying to do was calm Jada down.

"I did," Ben says.

"I look like a nut."

"You look like a responsible member of the SAR team."

"I guess."

"Forget her. Let's go see the others."

"Sure."

We walk toward Gareth's booming voice. He and Ben slap hands and hug even though they saw each other this morning. Mia embraces me, and I decide right there and then to try to have a good time.

I've been carrying my past around on my shoulders like a weight, and it's not helping. It's been so long since I let loose. My friends in New York were all older than me—Kevin's age, in their early forties—and they were more into expensive dinners and yoga classes than dancing on tables. I'd adapted my taste to theirs, changing almost everything about myself in order to fit in. The way I dressed, what I drank, even what made me laugh. Like the Dylan song, I was so much older then. I feel younger than that now.

But if I'm going to get into the spirit of things, I'm going to need some of these beers and maybe something more, too. Mia smells like wine and weed, so I ask her if she's holding. She pulls me aside and we share a joint under the canopy of a tree.

"I haven't done this in years," I say, inhaling deeply, letting the acrid taste spread through me. I can feel my limbs loosen, the tension being erased.

"How come?"

"My hu . . . It just wasn't a thing I did in New York."

"Your husband wasn't into it?"

I inhale again and release it slowly. This stuff is strong. I need to pace myself. "Ben tell you about that?"

Mia takes the joint. "I googled you."

"Oh."

"Sorry. Just, when you used my phone that time, I saw that you'd been googling someone and I was curious."

The edge of fear I'd just decided to release is back. "Okay."

"Cassandra Adams. That's you, right?"

I kick myself for not deleting my search history.

"I don't want to talk about it."

"I get it."

I stare into her dark eyes. They're hazy. "You do?"

"Who hasn't fantasized about walking away from their life and starting over?"

"I guess."

"Only, your life looked pretty great."

"Did it? I guess it was, in some lights."

"Why'd you leave, then?"

I take one more toke and hand it back to her. My head is spinning. "Not really party conversation. Thanks for this."

I walk away, weaving through the crowd. I'm not sure what my target is, but when I see Ben, I release the breath I'm holding. The music is pumping and everyone's having a good time. I can too. I'm thirty. I'm still young. I still have enough time to make a bunch of stupid mistakes and patch them up again.

"Hi," I say to Ben.

"I was wondering where you got to."

I motion to where Mia is returning from the trees.

"Ah," Ben says. "I didn't know you smoked."

"Sometimes," I say. "Sometimes I do." I tap him on the chest, a challenge in my voice. "You don't know everything about me."

"That's an understatement."

"Hey."

He laughs. "That's how you wanted it, right?"

"Honestly? I don't know what I want."

"Oh yeah?"

I take his beer from him and swallow some of it down, our eyes meeting. I hand it back to him. "Did Gareth assign us a camping spot?"

"He did."

"Want to check it out?"

"You sure?"

"I am." I can't think of the last time I made a move on a man, and my cheeks are already burning at the effort.

"I'll get the sleeping bags from the truck. It's site twelve."

He touches me briefly on the shoulder, then leaves. I go to where the coolers are gathered on the ground and grab two beers. I pass by the picnic table where Petal and co are sitting.

"—it'll be epic. You'll see, Jada."

"Sounds dangerous," Sandy says. Her hands are wrapped around one of those portable steel wineglasses and her teeth are stained red.

"What do you know about it?" Jim says.

Petal looks up at me. She shakes her head slightly, telling me to stay out of it, so I walk past them, clutching the cold beers against my chest. I grab a lamp off a table and use its light to guide me to site twelve. It's away from the party, in the far part of the half-moon of camp sites. There's a small tent in the middle, a picnic table, and a fire circle. I put the lamp down on the table and sit, looking up at the stars. The sky is full of them, the night empty of clouds.

"Hey," Ben says.

"Hey."

"I brought your bag, too."

"Thank you." I hand him a beer. He takes it, twisting the top off. The party is a distant sound—music, laughter. Closer to us is the sound of the trees, a bird rustling.

He takes a slow sip of his beer, his eyes on me.

"So," I say. "It's been a while."

"For me too."

"I doubt that."

"It has." He puts his beer down on the table. "What about your husband?"

"Kevin?"

"Is that his name?"

"It is."

"What would he think of all this?"

"It doesn't matter. I left him." I take a step closer to Ben, the beer and weed making me feel bold. He smells like a mix of soap and Tide, like he's been freshly laundered. "Does it bother you?"

"Not if you're single."

"In every sense but legally, yes."

"Good." He reaches up his hand to my face. His fingers are cold but gentle. "Can I kiss you?"

"No one's ever asked me that before. They've just done it."

"That makes me sad."

"It's okay. And yes, you can kiss me."

His hand moves up my face to my hair as he lowers his lips to mine. They're soft and taste like beer. He pulls away. "Good?"

"Yes. More." I tug on his waist, pulling him toward me. Our lips meet again, our mouths open, as our tongues mingle. His hands snake around my back and we're pressed against each other. It feels so good, his touch, his hands sliding up under my shirt to my back. I want it to last forever, but I also want more. I want—

Get the fuck off me!

We break apart.

"What was that?" I say as more shouts reach us. The unmistakable sounds of a fight.

"We should go see what's happening."

I agree. The shouts are louder now, a man and a woman, someone else yelling something about the police. We hurry back through the woods to the clearing.

When we get to the bottom of the Postpile, there's a large group of people standing in a circle, watching a fight. I can see the top of someone's head, and hear the scuffle of feet, but I can't tell who it is.

Ben and I push into the crowd, weaving through the bodies that smell like alcohol and weed. One more push and we pop through the circle. Jim and Sandy are tussling on the ground, while Gareth and Sam try to pull them apart.

"Stupid bitch!" Jim says.

"Get the fuck off me, asshole," Sandy grunts back.

Jada's next to me. "Make them stop." Her face is streaked with tears.

"Hey!" I say. "Hey! Stop it!"

Gareth and Sam finally succeed in pulling them apart, their arms wrapped around each of them as they hoist them up and to opposite sides of the circle. Sandy is dusty from the ground. Jim's eyes look like fire.

"What the fuck?" Sam says. "You hit a lady?"

"She hit me first!" Jim says, sounding like a petulant child.

I search the crowd for Petal. She's on the other side of it, clutching her sides, tears streaking her face.

Ben backs Sandy up, closer to her. "Are you okay?"

"Yeah, that kid doesn't know how to hit."

"Show's over," Gareth says. "Clear off, everyone."

I can sense the reluctance around me, the lure of an accident too strong. But when Gareth gives his command again, the crowd starts to pull away. Jim has stopped struggling in Gareth's arms, and Jada walks to him slowly, like she's approaching an animal that's behaved unexpectedly.

"Jim?"

He raises his head. "I'm sorry, baby."

She steps into his arms, and he buries his head in her neck.

We're all watching them, and it seems to wake Petal up. She walks to Sandy and mimics Jada's moves, but without the tears.

"What happened?" I ask.

"He was getting in my face," Sandy says over Petal's shoulder. "Talking shit."

"I didn't *say* anything," Jim says, his head rising from Jada's arms.

"I think you all should go home," Ben says in a firm tone. "Call it a night."

Jim agrees and yokes his arm around Jada's shoulder. They walk off, Jada casting a look back as she does. Petal looks away and takes Sandy's hand. "Let's go."

"Stupid asshole."

"I know, babe, but forget him, okay? Forget all of them."

Sandy hesitates, then gives in. "I've got work in the morning anyway."

"That's right. Better to get a good night's sleep before the richies at the alpine store start up with their unreasonable requests."

Sandy smiles at this, and Petal tugs on her hand, making a soothing noise. They walk in the opposite direction of Jim and Jada, and within minutes I hear the sound of a car door opening, then see lights cut across the other parked cars.

"What happened?" I ask Gareth.

"Fuck if I know."

"Jim said something homophobic, I think," Mia says. "But Sandy was kind of goading him. Like, acting jealous of Jada. Like she thought something was going on between her and Petal."

"They're friends, right?" Ben says. "I see them together in the park a lot."

"I've seen them hang out a bunch too," Mia says. "Mostly with Jim, though."

"Well, I know one thing," Gareth says. "They know how to end a party."

"I bet you know how to get it going again," Ben says with a wink to me.

"Hell yes. Come on, Mia, my services are required." They walk off together, Gareth's voice booming about *getting this party restarted!* When he gets back to the crowd, he cranks the music up and raises a bottle of wine over his head.

"That's going to bring the popo," I say.

"Probably." Ben turns to me. "Not how I imagined this night going."

"Which part?"

"All of it, to be honest."

I smile. "You regret it?"

"Hell no."

"Good."

"You?"

"No."

He frowns. "No, but . . ."

"It's complicated. Not just Kevin . . . my life."

"I don't mind complicated."

"You say that, but . . ." I expel a breath. It's visible in the night, a marker that I'm here. "I ran away from him. I didn't even tell him I was going, or where."

"Why?"

"I had to."

"Was he hurting you?"

I meet his eyes. "I can't talk about it."

"Okay." He pulls me to him.

I want to resist but I can't. It's too much to be treated this way. Gentle. I give in.

"I don't want to hurt you," I say into the front of his shirt.

"You won't."

"You don't know me."

He rests his chin on the top of my head. "I want to."

I pull away, shaking my head. I can't do this. It's too much. Now that the pot's been burned off by adrenaline, it's been replaced by regret. "I'm sorry."

"It's okay. You want to join the fray?"

The party's already rocking again. Gareth's leading a conga line around a collection of lamps, everyone all smiles, but I can feel the touch of the fight creeping in, the party about to take a darker turn despite Gareth's best intentions. "I think we should get out of here."

"Sure. Let me just go get our stuff."

"I'll meet you at the truck."

He leaves, and I walk slowly toward the parking lot. Cars are parked haphazardly, and I can spot Sandy and Petal in a car, the inside light on, kissing passionately. I turn away. Some couples get off on fights, the reunion part of the attraction. Maybe they're like that.

"Ready?" Ben says.

"Yep."

We maneuver between the other cars and trucks, over the bumpy track and out to the main road. As we turn toward Lee Vining, I can hear sirens and see lights whirring in the background. "Uh-oh."

"Maybe it's some other emergency and they're not going to the Postpile."

"Hope so. Eric will be pissed otherwise."

"And Jenny."

"Her too."

I lean my head against the glass, letting the road lull me to sleep. The next forty-five minutes pass in a haze. I'm aware of time passing, but I don't care. Then the truck stops and Ben says, "We're here."

I open my eyes. We're at the SAR site. "Thanks for bringing me back."

"No worries."

"I'll see you in the morning?"

"You will."

"Have a good rest," I say.

"You too."

I climb out and grab my bag, then walk to my tent. I should take advantage of the quiet to take a shower alone, but it's too cold and I'm too tired. I change into some different clothes for sleeping and crawl into bed, trying not to overanalyze what happened, to simply let myself give in. To let go of this night.

A flash of light catches me right before I fall asleep. My phone, which I left on my nightstand. I pick it up, knowing already that there's a text.

I don't want to read it but I can't help myself.

You should've done a better job of covering your tracks, it says, followed by an image. I click on it with trembling hands. It's a screenshot of a map—Reno when I look more closely. There's a pin with a bright red bulb set down in the middle of it. And even though it's not rational, it doesn't mean anything, it doesn't mean he's here, or that he ever will be, I can't help but feel like that pin is a bullseye that's been attached to my back.

Because X marks the spot.

That's what they say, isn't it?

PHOTOGRAPH—Map of Yosemite's Tuolumne trail system

Liked by **mamajada** and **250 others**

@JadaJohnsonInsta Time for a change of SCENE.

We've explored all there is to around here and now we're going out into the WILD!

Oh the places we will go!

We've been gathering supplies for days it feels like, packing everything up and then starting all over again when the pack was way too heavy for me to carry. We're going to #McCabeLakes, which is an almost THIRTY-MILE round trip!

It's going to take us at least three days, but I think we should do it in five to savor it! Beautiful lakes, vistas . . . this hike has it all! No cell service, though, so don't expect updates. I'll #photodump you on the flip side.

Wish us luck! If we don't make it, I love you all.

Maybe we'll see Smokey!

#JadaandJimForever #FeelingFree #IntoTheWild #SmokeyIsFree

mamajada Be careful, baby! You were joking about the no cell service, right?

bellasgram No showers for five days! How romantic.

TheWildOne Now she's going AFTER the bear? WTF!

BearsAreMammalsToo She never cared about the bear . . .

theyfreedBritney Don't listen to the haters @JadaJohnsonInsta!

Papajim Jim is right, Jada. Three days is more than sufficient for that hike.

YosemiteBot Promote it on www.xyntz.com

JULY 5

CHAPTER 15

IT'S HAPPENING AGAIN

Then

July

"**J**ada's missing!"

The words echo around the SAR site like a gunshot. The voice is high-pitched, panicked. Like someone who's been waiting for days to release the information and has finally found the courage to do it.

I open the door to my tent, letting in the outdoors. It's a little after seven, the sky lightening, clouds half blocking the rising sun. I scan the site until I find her. Ben's holding Petal by the arms near one of the picnic tables as she strains against him. One of her long braids has come loose; the other is hanging on by a thread.

"What's going on?" I ask them.

Petal locks eyes with me. "It's Jada. She's missing."

"What do you mean?"

"Her mom filed a report last night. I just heard it on the radio."

I left my radio in the tent. I always turn it off at night, even though I'm supposed to leave it on sometimes. If I'm wanted, they can page me—its soft purr on my makeshift nightstand is something that frightens me less than a staticky voice suddenly talking to me in my sleep.

"I just heard it myself," Ben says. "I haven't seen her and Jim around the park for a bit. Didn't think about it."

"I haven't seen them since the Fourth. Petal, when's the last time you saw her?"

"That night. They were going on a long hike the next day. They were supposed to be back by the ninth at the latest. She and Jim. But they didn't. They didn't come back."

I keep my voice calm and assured. "Come, sit here."

I walk to the picnic table and pat it, an invitation. Ben and Petal follow, Ben releasing his grip. Petal wraps her arms around herself, her thin T-shirt inadequate for the morning chill.

"Sit, Petal. Please?"

She sits down and I pull a notebook out of the pocket of my cargo pants. There's a pen threaded through the spiral top. I turn to a fresh page and note the date—July 11. I pause, clenching my hands together, then resume. I write Petal's full name in block letters across the top.

"Okay," I say, looking at Petal across from me. Ben's next to her, his hand on her shoulder, holding her steady. "Tell me everything you know."

"Why?"

"If they're missing, the more we know about where they might have gone and why, the better."

Petal takes a deep breath. "She and Jim left on July fifth to go to McCabe Lakes. Some long hike that they wanted to do, a point-to-point I think they called it?"

"That's a thirty-mile round trip," Ben says.

"Yeah, that's what she said. They wanted to push themselves, see the high country."

I note the information down. The McCabe Lakes Trail is not

difficult and it's well-marked. It's not where people usually go missing, but anything can happen in the high country.

"Did she tell you anything about the route they were going to take?"

"Just the usual one, I think. She didn't show me a map or anything. It's not really my thing."

"Do you know what gear they took?"

She shrugs. "I don't know. But the Airstream's still there in the campground. She asked me to check on it. I went every day, and two days ago, she was supposed to come back. That's what she said. They were going to do it in five days. Jim wanted to do it in three, but that was stupid."

"Maybe they decided to take a bit more time?" Ben says.

Petal turns to him. "That's what I thought at first. Like, when they didn't come back the first day it was no big deal. But then I remembered that she said she wanted to come back in time for her mom's birthday, which was yesterday. She wanted to make sure she'd be able to call her. That's what she said to Jim—*we need to get back in time so I can call my mom on her birthday.*" She mimics Jada's voice well. Petal meets my eyes. Hers are dark, clear, certain. "She's missing."

"Sounds like they both are," Ben says.

Petal scoffs. "I bet Jim shows up. That would be just like him."

"What's that supposed to mean?"

"He's not a good guy."

"What are you saying?" Ben asks. "That he did something to her?"

"It wouldn't surprise me."

My pen hovers over the page. The paper is thin, and I've perforated it more than once as I've written down the information Petal's given me. "Have you seen something, Petal?"

"We've all seen things, haven't we? Look at what he did to Sandy. A man who'd hit a woman is no good."

"Is Sandy okay?"

"She's fine, but that wasn't the first time Jim's put his hand on a woman, I can promise you that."

Ben and I share a glance, both remembering that pattern on Jada's skin when we rescued her on Tenaya. What looked like a thumbprint.

"We'll keep that in mind," Ben says.

"Do you know anything else?" I say. "Has she posted anything since she left? Have you heard from her at all?"

Petal pauses, then shakes her head. "No. I checked all her socials. Nothing since the morning they left. But they left their phones behind. They're in the Airstream."

"What?" Ben says. "Why would they do that?"

"Jada said it was the only way to truly explore nature. Like, if she was thinking about how to capture it all on camera the whole time, she wouldn't be really appreciating what was around her."

"Bad time to feel that way about it," Ben says, reaching for his radio. "Dispatch, this is SAR Cowell, I have some information on the two potential missing hikers you mentioned a few minutes ago. A couple, early twenties. Jada . . ."

"Johnson," Petal says. "And Jim Carlisle."

"Jada Johnson and Jim Carlisle. A Black female and a Caucasian male, both in their early twenties. Their intended path was the McCabe Lakes Trail. Expected back two days ago."

"SAR Cowell, this is Dispatch. Yes, we've had a report from Ms. Johnson's mother that she didn't check in when expected. Please assemble a blitz team to check that route."

"Yes, we'll go now. SAR Peters will assist."

A different voice cuts in. "SAR Cowell, this is Sierra 1," Jenny says. "SAR Peters should lead the investigation here. I'll alert the rangers and someone will be out to assist. SAR Peters?"

I take the radio from Ben and speak to Jenny. "Copy."

"Find out if there's any other possible location they've gone to while the blitz team operates. We'll rendezvous at o-seventeen-hundred."

"Roger."

"What does all that mean?" Petal says. "What's a blitz team?"

I close up my notebook. "Two rescue workers are going to run the trail looking for them. In the meantime, I'll investigate down here to make sure there's not some other explanation."

"Thanks for your help, Petal," Ben says. "We've got it from here. Cassie, I'll get Gareth."

"Okay, good. Stay in touch."

He strides away quickly. Time is always of the essence when someone's reported missing. If something went wrong on the first day, it's been nearly a week that they've been out there.

I tuck the notebook into my pocket. Nervous energy floods my chest.

"What are you going to do?" Petal asks.

"I'm going to go to the Airstream."

"It's locked."

"Can you come with me? Let me in?"

"Okay."

"Give me a minute." I duck into my tent to grab my radio and my phone. Then I change my camp shoes for a pair of hiking shoes, tying the laces tight.

When I get back out, Petal's standing where I left her, looking lost in thought.

"Ready?"

Petal nods and follows my lead down the path to the section of the campground where Jim and Jada parked their RV. It only takes a few minutes to get there, and I try not to let my thoughts get away from me. But that's easier said than done. It all feels like history repeating itself, but history doesn't do that. Something's always different. Something's always off.

We get to their camping spot, and it looks like it did the last time I was here. I walk around the Airstream slowly, checking to see if there's anything that's been left on the ground, but it's buttoned up tight. No trash, nothing out of place.

"You have the key?" I ask Petal.

"Jada gave me a spare." She fishes in her pocket and hands it to me.

"Stay out here."

I unlock the door. Inside, there's a light switch near it and I flick it on. My eyes adjust to the light, and I survey the cabin methodically. The Airstream is neat as a pin, everything tucked away, nothing out of place. The interior is blue and tan, and it's about twenty feet long and eight feet wide.

There's a bed at the back and a kitchen in front. Under the window, the table's pulled out and there are two phones and two empty water glasses on it. I touch the phone nearest to me—it has a pink case with stars on it—Jada's phone. I tap the screen. It fills with notifications—missed calls and social media tags. But when I try to check them, it asks me for a password. I try the same with the other phone—Jim's. It's dead, its battery run down. Their passwords probably aren't rocket science, but that will be someone else's problem. I grab a bag from under the sink and put them inside so they're easier to transport.

Past the kitchen, the bed is made with hospital precision. In the drawers beneath the bed, the clothes are folded, like they were just sitting on a table in a clothing store. One or both of them is a bit OCD.

The only personal touch is a small corkboard above the bed,

which is covered in photos of Jada and Jim together. It's odd to see printed pictures like that. The last time I saw photos arranged this way was in Cameron's room, when I explored it to look for clues to where she had disappeared to, ten years ago. There's even a shot of Jada and Jim similar to the one I took off the wall back then to help identify her and Chris. Both of them looking into the camera, Jim's arm around Jada's neck in a way that's more possessive than casual. But they're grinning, about to embark on some adventure, back before they thought of coming to this place.

I reach out to take the picture from the corkboard, the déjà vu almost disorienting. A couple missing. A search about to begin.

Ten years ago, it ended in death and sent my life spinning off its axis.

Is that what's happening again?

CHAPTER 16

CAMPFIRE DAYS

Then

July

For good or bad, there's nothing like the adrenaline of a search. Anticipation is a weird state to be in. That low thrum of epinephrine waiting to release. It can be draining, wearing away at you like a thought you can't quite grasp, a name you can't quite remember. And then, when the thing you're waiting for happens, there's an odd mix of release and panic. You're happy to be doing something, finally, but you're afraid too. That you might screw up. That you won't measure up. That you won't get there in time.

I feel all of this and more as I monitor the blitz team's progress up the McCabe Lakes Trail. It's their job to run up the most likely path where the missing person is, calling out their name and trying to locate them. They don't deviate from the trail. They don't go down side trails and follow hunches. They stick strictly to the marked-off parameters, and that usually produces a result. People hear their name ringing through the woods and come out of where they've stopped because the stream was pretty, or an ankle was twisted. Sometimes, others on the trail have seen them and can help to pinpoint their location. Often, they don't even know they're considered missing—that's a good day. Other times, the blitz team turns up a scared group of people who got into something they didn't anticipate and didn't bring the right equipment for. And then, rarely, but not rarely enough, the blitz team is unsuccessful and a bigger operation is necessary.

It's too early to tell where this search is going to end up. The trail to McCabe is long, and they're going to have to go all the way to the end before they can determine if Jada and Jim are on it or not. Even at speed, it's not something that can be completed in a couple of hours—they'll need to stop and rest unless they find them early.

In the meantime, I roam the campground, looking for leads. Even though they said they were going on the McCabe Lakes Trail, I need to make sure they didn't change their plans at the last minute or that others haven't seen them around. I come up with nothing but confirmations of their original plans. They were popular in the campground and told a lot of people about their trip.

Petal stays with me for a while, then drifts off, saying she has to get back to Lee Vining, that Sandy will be wondering where she is. She asks me to let her know if I find anything, and I watch her go without regret. It's easier to talk to people alone.

After an hour, I end up interviewing an older couple who's been in the park for a couple of weeks—the Watsons. They're in their seventies, living out of a big RV and seeing America, they tell me, while they still can, whatever that means. She's sitting in a camp chair, knitting, letting her husband do the talking. But she's the one who remembers the details, which she fills in when he pauses for breath.

"They were a nice a couple, always happy," Mr. Watson says, his hands on his hips, his beer belly thrust out.

"I wouldn't go that far, dear. No one's happy all the time,"

Mrs. Watson says, not missing a beat with the pink wool she's turning into a blanket for their next grandchild. She's small and delicate in appearance, but I bet she has hidden strengths.

"What's that?"

"All couples have their disagreements. They weren't any exception."

"Did you see something?" I ask her.

Mrs. Watson knits one and pearls two. "There was that time when she was crying."

Mr. Watson looks puzzled, then has a flash of memory. "Oh yes, yes, that one time. I guess they did have a disagreement. But that was the girl." He rocks forward and back on his heels. "She was making an awful racket. Her time of the month, I bet."

"You have no way of knowing that, dear."

He looks discomfited. "Why else would she be so upset? Though, come to think on it, he was talking to that other girl."

"What other girl?" I ask.

"You know the one," Mr. Watson says. "That girl with the white hair and the dark eyes. Named after a plant or a flower."

"Petal?"

"That's the one," Mrs. Watson says, looking up at me with her watery blue eyes. "She was making trouble."

"With Jim?"

"What else would she be doing around here all the time?" Mr. Watson says. "That's a good-looking young man. Stands to reason that she'd be interested in him."

I stifle a laugh. "You sure about that?"

"What's so funny?"

"She's gay, dear."

He rocks on his heels again, taking a step back. "Well, I don't have any problem with gay people, myself. Not everyone feels that way, though."

"Not her. The girl. Petal."

"That pretty young thing?"

"I don't know what that has to do with it."

"Oh, well . . ."

"What happened, exactly?" I ask. Talking to the Watsons is a bit dizzying. "Mrs. Watson, maybe you can tell me?"

She puts her knitting needles down into her lap. "I'm not too sure. They were all at the grocery mart, getting ice cream, that Petal girl and Jim and Jada. It was that hot day a couple of weeks ago. You know the one a few days before the Fourth? Right after we got here. Everyone was cranky. Anyway, you don't want to hear about that. But that Jim, I heard him say something about the other girl. About Petal."

"See, what did I say? Girls fighting with girls, making drama."

"No, dear. That's not what happened at all."

"Why was she crying, then?" Mr. Watson asks.

She gives a small shrug. "He was needling her all day. Trying to get her to do some climb she wasn't comfortable with. Saying she shouldn't be afraid. Then Petal showed up. He wasn't happy about that. He said something about her being around too much, wanting to know what she wanted with Petal, why they were hanging out. Jada laughed at that, and Petal wasn't happy. But it seemed to calm Jim down. Then they all went to get ice cream. When they came back, things seemed calmer, but then Jada's ice cream fell on the ground. That's when she got upset and started crying."

"Doesn't seem like much to go on."

"You asked if we'd ever seen anything. That's what we saw. But you never know what's going on behind closed doors, you know?" She gives her husband a look then, and I get what she means.

No one knew what was going on in my marriage. No one

wanted to know. All the women I hung around with—at yoga, and spin, and in wine bars—they wanted free and easy conversations without the guilt of real emotions hanging over us.

"Okay, thank you. Can you think of anything else?"

"No, that's all."

"If you do think of something, please come to the Ranger Station or the SAR site. My name's Cassie Peters."

"We'll do that. Gosh, I sure do hope you find them."

Next, instinct drives me to the small convenience store the Watsons mentioned. It's a tourist trap with a burger stand next to it, full of branded gear and five-dollar chocolate bars, but this is where they must've got the ice cream.

I walk through the front door, a bell tinkling above it. The guy behind the cash register, Gary, has been here almost as long as Bri, and I know him from way back. I explain what I want—security footage that shows Jim and Jada if he has it, and he nods under his trucker hat and takes me to the back room. He shows me how to use the machine that records the camera footage, how to scroll back and forward through the days. Only two weeks are kept at a time, though, so there might not be anything, depending on the day they were there.

I start with July 3 and start scrolling. The picture is surprisingly clear, though it's in black and white. At four times speed it's like watching a cartoon—people come and go quickly, holding their purchases in their arms, their movements jerky.

A few minutes later, there they are. Petal walks in first, looking around like she's casing the joint, though I'm sure it's just a trick of the camera. Jada comes in next, bouncy, excited. She puts her head on Petal's shoulder for an instant, then floats away toward the ice cream freezer. Jim is last, calm, casual. He smiles at Petal and then they follow Jada out of frame. There aren't cameras everywhere, so I wait until they come back into view. One minute, two . . . it feels like a long time.

Then, finally, there they are, each holding a frozen cone wrapped in paper, the kind with nuts on top. Jada has her arm linked with Petal and Jim is smiling at them, amused. They walk to the cash register and pay. An unremarkable transaction. Maybe Jada did get upset over nothing. Everyone's entitled to that once in a while.

I'm almost about to stop watching when they turn toward the door. They're walking directly toward the camera now—it must be positioned above the doorframe. Jim stops to let Jada and Petal leave before him, and then his smiling mask falls. His face is set in a mean expression, like he's about to do something bad, and though I don't think he intended to look directly at the camera, he does.

A chill goes down my spine as our eyes lock. It's like he's looking right at me, like he knows I'm watching him. And then he shakes himself and the smile is back. If I hadn't seen the transformation, I would never think anything about it.

But now that I've seen the true Jim, it's impossible to forget.

July 11—Tuolumne Meadows

Sandy doesn't care that Jada and Jim are missing.

She didn't say that exactly, but that's how she's acting. Just going to work like nothing's happening. Moving around the RV and HUMMING a tune to herself.

It was weird, the humming. Like, if you're upset at something, if you think something is going wrong, you're not humming a little tune, you know?

It was driving me nuts. When I couldn't stand it anymore, I asked Sandy why she was so happy Jada and Jim were gone that she was singing about it, and she gave me this weird look like she didn't know what I was talking about. So I started imitating her, adding in the words this time. It was an old song, one Mama used to sing along with on the radio like it was about her life. "When You're Gone" by that Bryan Adams guy, though I always used to call him Ryan Adams to drive Mama crazy. But he got canceled. Ryan, not Bryan.

Anyway, I always thought that song was some kind of love song, a song about pining, but the way Sandy was humming it, it was like a victory song.

Sandy says I'm nuts, that of course she's concerned—about Jada anyway, because Jim is a jerk. I don't blame her for thinking that. Jim did get in that scuffle with her at the party at the Devils Postpile, which was so weird because one minute we were all just sitting there, drinking, laughing, having fun, and then Jim said something, I don't even know WHAT, and the next thing I knew, they were on the ground and there was a ring of people around them.

That's what it feels like with Jada's disappearance. Jada and Jim, I mean.

Like they were here one minute and now they're just GONE.

Cassie says they'll find them, that they almost always do. They probably decided to take a side trail—Jim too confident like he always is, in his ability to get himself out of anything.

White Man Confidence.

Sandy apologized for the humming. But she ALSO said that it was nice that it was just the two of us again. I knew what she meant. I'd been spending a lot of time with Jada, and Sandy didn't like it. Not in the way that Sandy's scared of, but just because she's more my age and we have things in common. Or not THINGS, really. Jada grew up with shit— friends, a house, high school, then college—that I didn't. But she gets me in a way that Sandy doesn't.

Like sometimes, it feels like Sandy is my mama, not in a gross way, but in an age way. She'll use these expressions I only ever heard Mama use, like "panties" and "broken record" and I guess they're the same age or whatever. Maybe Sandy's older. I never really thought about it until I started hanging around with Jada and she asked me how old Sandy was.

After Sandy left for work, I was trying to think of why it was that I liked hanging with Jada so much, even with Jim around, and that's what it came down to, I think. I feel old around Sandy. Not as old as her, but older than I am. Like I've already lived a lifetime and this is the second time around. The SECOND HALF. But with Jada, I felt young. Like sometimes, one of us would say something and it would make the other giggle and we'd just laugh and laugh until our sides hurt.

Old people don't laugh that way. Sandy and I never laugh that way. Mama and Daddy never did either.

It's not a way to live, laughing your way through everything, but it's nice to have a break sometimes.

All of which is too hard to explain to Sandy.

But now it's just the two of us again. And that WOULD be good in a lotta ways if Jada wasn't missing. If she'd just gone home at the end of the summer like she was supposed to, promising to stay in touch, even though I knew she wouldn't. Jada isn't the type of girl who's going to remember someone like me when I'm not right in front of her. She didn't have to tell me that—I just KNEW.

But Jada hasn't gone home.

Maybe Jada isn't ever going to go home again.

And I can't get past the thought that a thing that makes me feel bad is something that makes Sandy sing.

—Petal

CHAPTER 17

FAMILY TIES

Then
July

In the afternoon, I take Jim's and Jada's phones to Eric.

Gareth and Ben are pretty far up the trail, with no sightings of Jada and Jim or anyone who's seen them, even. That's not too surprising—they left a week ago. Even if they took two to three days to hike to the end of the trail, it's unlikely anyone they passed on the way there would still be on it. It's an out-and-back, not a loop, so you cover the same ground on the way in as the way out. Maybe when they get to the campground itself and check in with the rangers that patrol that area regularly, they'll have something to report.

Eric's office is in the Ranger Station, an old building painted dark brown and made out of logs felled on the property in the 1920s. It's surrounded by tall pines, and the frames of its large windows are painted forest green. They let in enough natural light to push away the gloom inside.

When I walk into his office—neat, organized—he's sitting behind his battered old desk, talking on his phone. Forty, he's got dark brown hair and a matching beard that covers most of his face, except for his eyes and nose. He's wearing his ranger uniform—a khaki shirt, green tie and green pants, and his tan hat is resting on his pristine desk. He motions for me to take a seat while he finishes up.

"I can't discuss that at the moment," he says into the black, old-fashioned headset that goes with the ancient rotary phone. "But can I ask how you learned she might be missing?"

An indistinct voice comes through the phone, high-pitched and vigorous. Eric takes some information down on a yellow legal pad, then ends the call.

"Well, this is a clusterfuck," he says. His dark brown eyes are difficult to read, his voice deep and cautious.

"What's up?"

"That was a journalist from CNN wanting to know if it was true that Jada Johnson is missing."

My mouth goes dry. "What? How?"

"Apparently, it's on Instagram? Is she famous or something?"

I lay my sweating palms flat on my knees. "She's the one who got involved in Smo—in that bear court?"

Eric frowns. "That girl?"

"That's the one. Have you spoken to their parents?"

"Her mother is the one who called in the initial report. I haven't heard from his parents."

I take out Jim's and Jada's phones. "Maybe their number is in here?" I say, pointing to the phone I assume is Jim's. "But it's password protected. Do we have someone who can break passwords?"

"I don't think so."

"They shouldn't hear about this through the media. Are they going to report on it?"

He rubs at his beard. "CNN won't run the story without double source confirmation. But that doesn't mean some less reputable organization won't do it. I need to see what's on that social media thing."

"We could look on your computer."

"You don't have it on your phone?"

"No." I walk around his desk so that I'm standing in front of his computer. It's ten years out of date, but at least it connects to the internet. "Okay if I look?"

"Sure, go ahead."

I wake the screen up by banging the mouse against the desk, then google "Jada Johnson Instagram." A long list of women with that name comes up in the search results. I add in "Smokey the bear" and now the first hit is to an Instagram account with a photograph of Jada smiling saucily at the camera. The link takes me to her page, those squares of photos filling up the screen. I click on the latest one. It's a photograph of a map that was posted on July 5, talking about the trip they were about to take.

The photograph has hundreds of likes and the section below it is full of comments. Some from the hours after she posted it, and then newer ones from the last few days. I skip over the older *go you!* and *you got this!* posts and scroll to the end. The concern started two days ago.

@bellasgram Bitch, where are you? I've tried to call you a million times!

@mamajada Baby girl, you better call me.

@mamajada We're very worried now, baby. Please call.

@Papajim Jada, your mother has been calling me for two days. It is very irresponsible not to return phone calls or call her on her birthday.

After that, the comments are from strangers, with a user named @LifeisLife starting the speculation that maybe she'd gone missing, and then hundreds of others piling on, an odd mix of concern and misogyny. Someone told her it was karma for interfering with Smokey. That post had fifty likes.

The internet sucks.

I click through to @LifeisLife's page, but there's no photo or biographical information. The page looks like it belongs to a bot, but I don't know if bot accounts are sophisticated enough to post the sort of things this account has. Probably, which is scary. But if so, why would a bot seek out Jada's page to stir up trouble? That didn't make any sense.

"You see all this?" I say to Eric, pointing to the posts. "This is where the rumor comes from."

His eyes rove over the page, his mouth turned down. "Can we make them stop?"

"No. But look here, that's his dad. We can send him a direct message to let him know to get in touch with us."

"How do we do that?"

"You need an account."

"I can't make one on this computer. There's rules about that."

My shoulders creep up, tension building along my neck and radiating down. "I can do it."

"Great."

It's not great, but I navigate to the sign-in page anyway. I look at Eric over my shoulder. He's watching me expectantly. I move my body so I'm blocking as much of the screen as possible and sign in, wondering if it's going to work. It's only been a couple of months since I checked Instagram, but it feels longer. My mind fills with questions. How long does it take until it assumes you've abandoned the page and you can't log in anymore? Is that even a feature? If I do log in, is someone going to be alerted? I never shared my passwords with anyone, but passwords can be broken.

"Is there a problem?" Eric says.

"No. Sorry. I was blanking on my password."

I enter my username and password, and my page loads. My headshot is a picture Kevin took soon after we started dating. It's Central Park in fall, leaves swirling around me, my scarf trailing off to the left in the wind. My posts were infrequent. A meal at my favorite Italian place. A group shot with my friends, all a decade older than me, but sweet and undemanding. No shots of Kevin, who isn't a fan of social media.

As my eyes scan over the photographs, the top of the page lights up. I have hundreds of notifications and tags. I don't want to know what that means, so instead I navigate to Jim's father's page and press the button to send him a message. Thankfully his DMs are open.

Hello, this is Cassie Peters from the Forest Service in Yosemite. We need to speak to you urgently about your son, Jim. Please contact me or Eric Moser as soon as you can. I put my number in and then Eric's. I wait a minute to see if he'll respond. While I'm waiting, I want to check my notifications and see what the fuss is all about, but I can't do that here. Instead, I sign out and close the browser.

"I sent a message to him and gave him our numbers."

"What if they respond through the app?"

"I'll check it frequently. I can use Mia's phone."

"Do that."

I go back to the chair in front of his desk. "What now?"

Eric writes something down on his legal pad, then checks it off. "The blitz team should be at the end of the trail soon. Did you find anything else on your canvass?"

"No. If they went somewhere else, they didn't tell anyone."

"Did you check their permit?" Everyone who stays overnight in the park needs a permit for the specific destination where they plan on staying.

"Not yet. I'll do that next."

"Any idea how much food they took? Or what equipment?"

"They were supposed to be gone for five days according to Petal Fernandez and Jada's Instagram post. I'd assume they have enough to last that long, maybe a bit to spare. Based on my own observations, I'd say they have some wilderness training, but not much."

He drums his fingers against the desk. His nails are clean and well kept. "They've been gone a long time. Not good."

"Agreed. Do you want me to start checking side trails off the McCabe Lakes Trail?"

"No, hang tight for a couple of hours. I want you to be here if the parents get in touch."

"Okay. I'll wait at the SAR site. And check those permits."

"You should call her mother, also, and give her an update." He consults the file and writes something down on a yellow sticky note. "This is the number she left."

My mouth goes dry. I've never liked making these kinds of calls, talking to the stressed and bereaved. But I have no reason to say no. "Will do."

"Do we know anything else about them?" Eric asks.

"It's probably not relevant, but Jim has a temper. He got into a fight at a party on July Fourth with a woman." I tell Eric about the fight at the Devils Postpile, which he's heard about but did not know the details of.

"Who's this Sandy person?"

"Sandy Cramer. She's Petal Fernandez's partner. Older, working in Mammoth at one of the sports stores, from what I've heard."

"What's the connection between the four of them?"

"They met at an RV park in Lee Vining a month ago. Petal and Jada became friends. They'd hike together sometimes. I gather this has caused a bit of friction between Jada and Jim, but I still don't know what the fight at the party was about. Jim mouthing off, maybe. Being a frat bro about them being gay . . . Jim seems like that kind of guy."

"Charming."

"He can be."

Eric bites the edge of his lip. "But they're both missing."

"Yes."

"So it's unlikely to have anything to do with this."

"I agree."

"Let me know if you learn anything more."

"I will."

"Thanks for your quick work on this."

"No problem." I stand to leave but I can sense that Eric wants to say something more. Something's holding him back, though. Politeness, maybe. "Is there something else you need?"

"How are you handling all this?"

"How do you mean?"

"Being back here . . . Another couple missing . . ."

I clench my hands into fists. "They're not Cameron and Chris."

"No."

"Couples go missing sometimes. We usually find them."

"True."

"I'm fine."

"All right, but if you need to not be on this case, that's fine too."

"Thanks, I—"

The phone on Eric's desk rings. He holds up a hand to stop me and picks it up. He listens for a minute, then points to the phone and makes a gesture like it's going to be a long call, holding his hands out from each other while he cradles the phone under his chin. *We'll talk later*, he mouths.

I escape gratefully out into the bright day. I don't need other people treating me like glass that might shatter. I'm good enough at doing that to myself.

Back at the SAR site I go to the picnic table to monitor the radio for updates from Ben and Gareth. Mia's there, cleaning up after a meal.

"How was your rescue?" I ask.

"Minor sprain. No big deal."

"That's good."

"Gareth and Ben are almost at the end of the trail. No sign of them."

"That's *not* good."

"Nope."

"Maybe some of the people camping there will have seen them?"

"Here's hoping. I do not want to do a full-scale search." Those searches were exhausting and can feel endless. Every trail has to be checked. And the longer it goes on, the more you know you're never going to find them alive.

I sit at the table. "I hear you." I take out my phone. "I've got to call Jada's mother."

Mia grimaces. "Those calls are no fun."

I put in the number Eric gave me.

"Hello! Hello!"

"Mrs. Johnson?"

"Yes, who's this?"

"This is Cassie Peters. I'm from the Park Service in Yosemite. I've been asked to call you with an update."

"You found them?"

A lump forms in my throat. "No, ma'am, I'm so sorry. Jada and Jim do seem to be missing. We have a team looking for them now."

"Oh my God, oh my God, I knew it. I knew it when she didn't call me on my birthday. My baby girl, my baby girl."

I swallow down my guilt. "Ma'am, I want you to know that most people are recovered without any significant injury. She hasn't been missing for long. We're doing everything we can to find her. And Jim."

"Oh my God. Oh my God."

"Are you in contact with Jim's family?"

"Yes, yes, I have their number somewhere."

"Can you give that to me?"

"I . . . I'd have to look for it. I . . . I can't . . ."

"Mrs. Johnson is there someone there with you?"

"No, it's just me."

"Mr. Johnson?"

There's a bitter sound on the line, followed by a sob. "He's gone too. Long gone."

"Is there someone you can call? A friend, a relative? Someone to be with you?"

"Yes, yes, okay."

"I will let you know as soon as I have an update. You can call this number anytime, or the other number I gave you."

"Where is she? Where's Jada?"

My heart squeezes. "We don't know, ma'am. Hopefully we'll know soon."

"I . . . I have to go."

"I'll let you know as soon as we know something. And if you can ask Jim's father to call me . . ." But the line is dead.

"That sucked," Mia says, her eyes full of sympathy.

"Yeah." My hands are shaking as I look down at the screen. I should've taken Eric up on his offer to leave this case, but I can't do that. "Can I use your phone for a minute?"

"Why?"

"I want to check Instagram. I wrote to Jim's dad there. It doesn't work on this." I shake the phone in my hand.

"Sure, okay." She hands me her phone, putting in the password first.

I sign into my Instagram account. I look at the red heart, the number of messages in my inbox. All those notifications I noticed earlier. Am I strong enough?

I hold my hands steady as I check the message I sent to Jim's father first. There's no way to know on Instagram if he's read it. Hopefully, Jada's mother will let him know and he'll call me. In the meantime, I can't help but dip into the other messages. It's a mix of confused notes from months ago from my New York friends, my hasty group email saying I was leaving and thanking them for their friendship not sufficient to allay their concerns.

Where are you?

What the hell, Cassandra? Not funny.

Everyone's worried about you. Can you please answer?

I tried calling your phone, but it's been disconnected. What's going on?

I want to answer them, especially the last one from Tawny, who's the nicest of the bunch, but the messages are months old. I faded from their view as quickly as I joined their group after Kevin and I got engaged. Better to leave well enough alone, but I can't pretend it doesn't hurt. A few messages of concern and that's it. Somehow, I knew no one would go to the police, that I could slip away without anyone searching for me.

There are several messages from Kevin, too, which surprise me because I didn't know he had an account. Did he have it all along or only after I left? The messages are also older and similar to the texts I'd received at the airport in Reno. Profanity-filled and angry, but not worried. Not asking *why*. Then again, he knows, better than anyone, why I left.

I toggle back to my notifications, because the messages haven't answered the puzzle of why there are so many. Those are more recent, and once I realize that, I know in my bones what caused them.

Jada's post about Smokey. That stupid video she shot when Smokey was taken out of the woods. She didn't tag me—she didn't know my Instagram name, but the video went viral. Someone from the climbing gym in New York recognized me. She'd tagged me in a comment, and a few others from the gym, telling them to come look.

Fuck.

My heart is pounding as I check each comment—the original post and three other people who were wondering where I'd gotten to. *Question answered*, one of them said. *Crazy*, someone else said. I'm not sure if they mean me or the situation, but I don't care. These women aren't connected to anyone else I know in New York. No one knew I was going to that gym. I paid for my membership in cash and hid my climbing gear at the back of my closet.

But then there's a final comment on the thread that stops me cold.

Should we tell the husband?

CHAPTER 18

IT'S THE HOPE THAT KILLS

Then

July

It takes till eight at night for Ben and Gareth to reach the campground at McCabe Lake. They've also spoken to the rangers who patrol that section of the park. No one's seen Jim or Jada. If they'd actually gone up the McCabe Lakes Trail, there'd be some sign of them.

When I check the permit office, they had a five-day permit. Day hikers don't need one, but anyone planning to stay overnight has to. Jada and Jim's permit was issued on July 4, the day before they left—Jada was the one who obtained it. The permits don't get checked religiously, but there's a heavy fine for being in an area that isn't covered by the permit, all of which would've been explained to Jada when she got it.

Either they decided to take a different route anyway, or they wandered far off the trail early on their journey. Either way, the procedure now is to start a wider search. Ben and Gareth will stay the night at McCabe Lake and then do a slower hike back tomorrow. This time, they'll search the most likely places where they might've gone off-trail. There aren't any campgrounds along the way—hikers can set up camp where they want. In the meantime, new teams will be assembled to start searching the other trails. If they're not found in the next couple of days, then teams might be pulled in from other areas in the park and from outside too.

I call Jada's mother. She's not alone this time. Jim's parents are there, and Mrs. Johnson's sister. Mrs. Johnson is just as emotional as she was when we spoke earlier, and Jim Senior quickly grabs the phone and takes over.

"We're coming there," he says in a gruff voice.

"Sir, I'm not sure that's a good idea."

"I don't care what you think. We've booked a flight for the morning. Text me the details of where we should go."

"Where are you flying into?"

He tells me that they've chartered a small plane to fly into Mammoth, then they'll rent a car in town. They should be at the park by midday. I'll tell the entrance station they're coming so they can enter without a permit. I give him the coordinates for Eric's office, then I tell him I'll let him know if there's anything that develops overnight. It's only then that he shows any sign of breaking.

"Is it cold?" he asks, his voice full of emotion. "Is it cold at night? Jim never did like the cold."

My own breath catches. "It does get colder at night, sir, but it's full summer. They have a tent, sleeping bags . . . They'll be fine." I say this even though it's easily untrue. Yosemite is massive, and even searching this section of the park is a huge undertaking. The only thing we can be fairly sure of is that they're probably within walking distance of the campground. There are shuttles in the park, but a canvass of the drivers has turned up nothing. They should be on one of the trails out of Tuolumne Meadows, which narrows things down, but not by much.

"Thank you for saying that."

"We're doing everything we can to recover them."

"Whatever resources you need, I'll make sure you get them."

We hang up, and then I call Eric to fill him in on the fact that they're coming tomorrow. I also tell him about Jim Senior's offer.

He sighs. "All right, thanks for the heads-up."

"You want me to take one of the trails tomorrow?"

"We'll decide in the morning. Meeting at o-six-hundred."

"Got it."

I hang up and let Mia know about the meeting in the morning.

"You sure there was nothing in the trailer?" she asks, hugging herself in her puffy. "No other routes?"

"She posted a map on Insta. It looked like they considered other routes."

Mia takes out her phone and opens the app. She navigates to Jada's page and finds the photo. She widens it on her screen so we can see the detail. There are ten routes they thought about, all long out-and-backs that will take multiple days to search.

Mia looks up at me, worry clouding her face. "This is going to be a shit show."

"Looks like it."

"Better get a good night's sleep. Won't be much of that in the coming days."

We say goodnight and I go to my tent. I change quickly into the clothes I sleep in and climb into bed, deciding to forgo brushing my teeth. The moon is bright outside, and it's casting shadows on my tent through the branches. They look like tentacles crawling over the walls, and it gives me the shivers. I wrap my hand around my medallion, the metal warm in my hand from being pressed against my chest all day, and close my eyes, trying to block out the images, but they come anyway.

Cameron's distended, bloated face.

Her blue eyes clouded over with a million-mile stare.

I'd rearranged my life to avoid ever having to see anything like that again.

But what's that expression? Man makes plans and God laughs? God is laughing.

Jada's mother, Gayle, arrives with Jim Senior and his wife, Sue, the next day in the late afternoon. Even under stress because their children are still missing, I can tell that they're an incompatible group of traveling companions.

Gayle is an older version of Jada—petite, pretty, with close-cropped dark hair, and large gold hoop earrings. From a distance, she looks like she's off to an office job, a silk scarf around her neck, her shoes sensible. But up close, I can see that she only put mascara on one eye and one of her earrings is in backwards. Her hands are twisted in front of her, her eyes bloodshot. She looks alone, isolated, and my stomach hurts just looking at her.

In life we do a lot of things without thinking about the consequences. If you thought too much about how your actions might impact others, you'd be paralyzed. This is true in alpinist pursuits and many other things—you forge ahead anyway because *you* want to do the risky thing, *you* want to change your life, *you, you, you*. It's selfish, but people are. I thought I'd accepted that about life, about myself. But here's the evidence of the consequences of Jada's choices. A broken woman who might never recover. Not if Jada never comes back.

In contrast, Jim Senior is a force of nature, and by that I mean a hurricane. He's six feet and barrel-chested, his hair gray and military cut. His voice is bombastic and commanding. He's wearing hiking boots and combat pants, and he comes off like a drill sergeant about to lead his troop on a multiday campaign to toughen them up.

Sue shrinks next to him, her hair dyed dark orange with two inches of gray roots, and she's wearing a bright red lipstick that doesn't match her skin tone. She's dressed in athleisure wear, and her body is soft and yielding. She looks almost as broken as Gayle, but they don't seem to be comforting each other, each an island alone in their pain.

Jim Senior tears into the SAR site demanding answers, the force of his anger exhausting and unhelpful. I'm happy it isn't my job to placate him. That task falls to Eric and Jenny, who listen for a few minutes, letting Jim Senior wind down like a toy whose battery is failing. Then Eric leads them off to find accommodations since they can't all stay in the Airstream. Gayle will sleep there while Jim Senior and Sue will be put up in a motel right outside the park. During the day, they can stay in the Ranger Station, listening to the radio chatter, getting minute-by-minute updates.

I watch them go with relief. I don't have the bandwidth to deal with their energy, and being around them makes me feel guilty. Instead, I volunteer to spend the afternoon searching the short Lembert Dome Trail, knowing there's no chance of their being on it.

Ben and Gareth arrive back at camp after dinner, dirty and exhausted. They take showers, then wolf down the stew Mia made like they haven't eaten in a week. Searches have a way of depleting your energy.

It's like politics—it's the hope that kills.

After they fill us in on what they found on the trail—nothing—we all retire for the night. I can tell in moments that I'm not going to be able to sleep. Those spooky tree fingers are moving over my tent again, the same images behind my eyes. I start to slowly count to a thousand and eventually it works.

The next morning, I can see the stress around Eric's eyes at our morning meeting. There have been no new developments in the night. Searching at night is hard—flying is dangerous, hiking too, and we want the team to be safe. Losing people to find others is not a calculus we want to engage in. Eric does his best to explain this to Jim Senior, while Gayle and Sue shrink on either side of him.

When he's settled them down and explained the day's plan, he hands out assignments. There are eight of us on the search now—a team has come up from the valley floor to help us. It already feels more serious having the others here, and my memory fills in what it's going to get like in the coming days. The people hovering around, the lookie-loos. By now it's common knowledge in Tuolumne that a couple is missing. Their faces have started appearing on posters, and a few of the regulars have volunteered to help. The media won't be far behind.

Like last time.

I push those thoughts away and volunteer with Ben to search the Ragged Peak Trail, one of the other, longer trails out of this part of the park. It starts on the Lembert Dome Trail, then continues on for miles. It's going to be a long, slow hike, and we'll probably have to camp out overnight, so my pack is heavier than usual with the supplies we'll need.

We drive to the trailhead and park our vehicle. The radios across our chests are constantly cutting in with updates, as other teams set out and check in. It's a strange sort of music, the static, the hollow voices. It feels dark and ominous though the sky is high and clear, the sun beating down on my neck. I slather on some sunscreen and add a layer of bug spray while Ben does the same, then we start down the trail.

We walk quickly, stopping every few minutes to call for them in the woods, the words *Jim* and *Jada* echoing around us. No one answers. Once we get past Lembert Dome, the trail isn't nearly as well traveled.

"This is where we came to get Smokey," Ben says. "His cave is about a mile from here."

"Is he back there now?" Smokey had been to "bear rehab" and then was released last week.

"No idea. Hopefully he'll stay out of this part of the park."

I shiver and cup my hand around my mouth. I yell out *Jada! Jim!* and wait. Nothing. We resume walking, doing the same, never getting a response.

After a couple of miles we come to the trail that leads to Dog Lake. My heart speeds up as we hike down it and stop at the lake. I'm sweating in the heat of the day, but I feel chilled at the same time. I bend down and splash cold water on my face to try to snap myself out of it.

Ben opens his canteen and takes a drink, then holds it out to me. He looks around at the water surrounded by quiet woods. "Is this where you found her?"

My hand freezes on the container. "You mean Cameron?"

"Yes."

"No." I release the canteen and walk past him up the trail. We don't need to search around Dog Lake, as another team did that the day before.

He follows after me. "I guess you don't want to talk about it?"

"No, it's fine." Maybe it will help. Maybe putting the images that haunt me into the sunlight will wash them out, give them less potency.

"It was on this trail?" Ben pushes, and I wonder what it is that prompted him to ask about this now. Is it as simple as we're on another search for another couple? Or has he been digging into me, googling me like Mia did?

"Not exactly. They'd decided to hike Ragged Peak, and they got turned around at the top. Instead of coming back down to the trail, they went down the backside and ended up near Young Lake."

"How did you find her?"

"Her boyfriend, Chris, told us where she was."

"What?"

I pull the straps away from my shoulders. My shirt is soaked through with sweat. "Yeah . . . It's not . . . She'd twisted her ankle, and eventually he went to get help. He fashioned a compass out of a bottle cap and a needle—you know, like they teach you in Scouts? Anyway . . ." I look down at my feet, choosing my steps carefully on the rocky trail. "He eventually found his way back to the Meadows, but he only had a vague idea of where she was. He'd left everything with her, though—the tent, the food, some water. He was in bad shape."

I think back to the conversation we'd had with him after he'd stumbled into the Ranger Station, his legs cut, his mouth parched. He was crying, almost incoherent, and once he'd had some water and food, he'd drawn a map explaining where he thought she was. Not quite at the lake, which would've been easier to find, but stuck in the woods about five hundred yards from it, under dense cover. Jenny and I had volunteered to search for her. I'd volunteered because I knew her, Jenny because she was always volunteering for everything.

We both came to regret it.

"Anyway, Jenny and I . . . it took two days for us to find her because Chris's map wasn't that helpful. By the time we got to her, she'd been out there alone for five days." But dead for much less than that, the coroner eventually determined. Not long enough to implicate Chris, though the suspicion continued to swirl around him. Had he left her there on purpose, knowing she couldn't survive? Was he a monster, or just someone who'd gotten in over his head?

"She died of exposure?" Ben asks, his voice behind me.

"She had a head injury. She'd run out of water, and they think she was trying to get to the lake. She slipped, hit her head, and knocked herself out. Maybe never regained consciousness."

"That's terrible."

"It was."

"You knew her, right?"

I turn around slowly. Ben's face is red, his hair mussed. "It's hard to talk about. Especially here."

"I understand. You don't have to."

I start walking again, thinking about Cameron—how happy she was, how light on her feet. She was one of those people who seemed to float through life. "Cameron and I grew up together. She was a year younger than me, but we were in tennis together and she used to follow me around a bit when she was a kid."

"Kind of like a younger sister?"

"I guess. I mean, we weren't close. She was kind of wrapped up in Chris, if I'm being honest."

"People thought he left her there on purpose?"

"Yeah."

"And?"

I hear a sound, like a branch snapping. I scan the woods. We've passed a few other hikers on the trail on the way here, or it could be an animal. I don't see anything. "He didn't."

"But he did leave her out there."

"He did."

"A mistake, clearly."

I glance back at him. "Not necessarily. We only found her because he came out. The search teams hadn't made it all the way back to where they were because they were so far off course. They could've both died if he hadn't taken the chance."

Ben runs a hand through his hair. "I don't know how I'd live with myself."

"He was a mess for a long time. Last I heard he was living in a shack in Bali, trying to center his heart or whatever."

Ben laughs gently. "There are worse places to be."

I hear a snap again, and my head turns to the side. Petal is standing there, watching us. "Petal! What are you doing here?"

She steps out of the woods holding a walking stick. She's wearing busted running shoes and three-quarter hiking pants that have a stain on the thigh. "I'm looking for Jada."

"You should leave that to the professionals," Ben says. "Or volunteer for the search party formally."

Petal shrugs. "That was taking too long."

"Did you find anything?"

She meets my eyes. "No."

"Where have you been?" Ben asks.

"I walked all the way to Ragged Peak and back."

"What made you come on this trail?"

"It's one of the ones they were talking about doing before they left."

Ben puts his hands on his hips. "Any idea why they might've changed their plans?"

Petal makes a face. "Jim probably has something to do with it."

"How so?"

"He's a child. A spoiled baby brat." She twirls the stick in her hand. "You meet his daddy?"

"I have."

"Then you know. I saw his parents last night and . . . It's obvious that neither Jim has ever been told *no* in his whole life. They don't know what struggle is. Just like a little kid."

"Okay," Ben says, "but what does that have to do with Jada and Jim being missing?"

"I'm just saying that whatever happened out there, it's probably Jim's fault." Petal steps past us. "Good luck with your search."

She turns her back and starts to walk down the trail, her blond braids bouncing against her back.

"What do you make of that?" Ben asks.

"I have no idea."

"What should we do?"

"What we were told. Walk the trail. Look for them."

"Okay." He starts to walk again, then stops and calls for Jim and Jada. The only thing that greets his call is the symphony of the woods, but he calls again anyway, because there's always the possibility that the next time will work.

Like I said, it's the hope that kills.

CHAPTER 19
A FACE IN THE CROWD

What does that mean?" Eric says across the desk from me in his office. "That you went into the woods because of Kevin?"

I try to focus on Eric's face, but it's hard. I'm so tired and my eyes don't seem to be working properly and I feel cold all over. "It's going to sound crazy."

"Try me."

I look away. The room spins less when I don't try to focus on anything. "I saw him. At least I think I did."

"You were seeing things?" Jenny says.

"I don't know."

"How can you not know if it was him?"

"It's hard to explain. We were all under a lot of stress. All that media. Searching day and night. We were exhausted. And there were so many people in the park and in Mammoth . . . All those reporters and their crew."

"Did you talk to the person you thought was Kevin?"

"I couldn't. He was there and then he wasn't."

It was like seeing a ghost. No, not a ghost. A specter. Someone taunting me. Like I was awake in a dream. And then that dream became a nightmare because he was there, he was right there.

BOOM!

"None of this makes sense, Cassie," Jenny says.

"I know. I'm sorry."

"Where did this happen?" Eric asks.

I shiver, though it's not cold. My teeth start to clack together, *rat-tat-tat*, like gunfire in my mouth. "The first time was in Mammoth. I was in town to see my mother." It's hard to get the words out, and they're slurred, like I'm drunk.

I wish I was drunk.

"When was this, Cassie?"

"Right after I got the text."

"What text?" Eric says. "Cassie. Cassie, you need to focus."

I list to the side, my vision blurred, my hearing like I'm underwater. I feel like I'm drowning, here in the open air. Like the air is wet and taking it in is filling my lungs with fluid, pushing out the oxygen, sucking me down.

"Cassie! She's going into shock . . ."

Someone's got their arms around me now, but I can't tell who. I'm slumping toward the floor, into darkness, and the only thing I see is the face I thought was Kevin's, haunting me.

July 18—Lee Vining

As Mama used to say: it's been a WEEK.

A week since Jada and Jim went missing.

A week since I stopped being able to see my life like a straight road going out in front of me forever.

A week since it feels like everything changed, since I've slept well, since I've been able to collect my thoughts.

Jada and Jim—they're still missing.

And I feel guilty, guilty, GUILTY. Because I was LOOKING for stories. That's why I became friends with Jada, why I listened in on their conversations, why I watched them climbing, why I spent so much time in the park. Ever since I met them . . . it feels like all of it has been about them. As I tried to "shape a narrative," as that writing teacher lady would say. As I tried to figure out who they were and what they were about. How they fit.

And now they ARE a story, oh boy, a much bigger one than I ever could've imagined.

It's all anyone talks about around here. Around anywhere, it seems.

A day after they were reported missing, the media arrived like a flock of geese hightailing it for warmer air in the fall. All honking cars and blocked roads and big white vans with aerials on their roofs. I've never seen so many people look out of place in my life. Women in blue suits and white blouses. Men with ties. Like they were attending a funeral before they'd even found a body.

It's weird because some of these journalists are celebrities—not celebrities, exactly, but those people you grow up watching on the TV telling you about all the bad things that have happened that day.

It's strange being around them. Their voices are so familiar, and their heads are larger than they appear on television.

And they might be famous, these Jakes and Katies and Toms, but they'll talk to anybody. You just tell them you have information about the missing person and BAM! a microphone is shoved in your face and they're looking at you with these earnest expressions, their heads tilted to the side and nodding. I never knew TV makeup was so god-awful up close, like clown makeup, a thick pancake that ends in a sharp line under the chin. Even the men wear it. I guess it's so they won't look green on television. Or whatever. It's freaky.

I didn't talk to the journalists, but Sandy did. They were roaming around Mammoth, and she was on her lunch break, she said, eating the sandwich I make for her every morning, out on a picnic bench, and she was approached by some young journos looking for a story. And instead of telling them to FUCK OFF, which would've been my best guess about how she'd react, she said she DID know Jada and Jim and she talked to them.

Only, she didn't tell the truth. She didn't say that she hated Jim and was jealous of Jada and that she thought it was GOOD RIDDANCE that they were both gone.

She didn't tell them about the humming.

Instead, she said nice things, like how sweet Jada was, how devoted they seemed to each other, how SAD it was when two people who wanted to have an adventure have something like that happen to them.

Not that she knew what happened to them.

I couldn't believe it when I watched it on my phone. Sandy had TEARS in her eyes. TEARS. I've never seen Sandy cry, not one time. Not when we fought. Not even after that fight with Jim when I know he hurt her because I saw the bruises the next day.

When I asked Sandy about it, she said she got caught up in the moment, and she believed that you don't say anything bad about the dead. And then I asked her what THAT meant, and she said I needed to grow *up. More than a week gone in the wilderness—that wasn't a search and rescue anymore, that was a "recovery operation." And then she explained to me what that meant, because I didn't say anything, like I was a child who didn't understand that people died sometimes.*

Like I didn't know that people can just DISAPPEAR.

I hate it when she talks to me like that.

Later, I found her counting the money in the mattress. Checking its weight, holding it up, checking the number of piles. I got real nervous because I've been taking some when I need it, not a lot, but it's added up. But she didn't seem to notice. She just patted it reassuringly and put it back where it came from.

"Never tell anyone about this," she said when she caught me watching.

I turned away. Who was I going to tell? My only friend is gone and never coming back, according to Sandy.

But where did the money come from, I want to know.

And why is Sandy so sure that Jada and Jim are gone forever?

—Petal

Jada Johnson: Another Missing Black Girl in America

Transcript of YouTube Video by CriminalMind

CriminalMind:

Y'all, I am OB-SESSED with this Jada Johnson case. No way she just disappeared into the wilderness. People don't just go "poof," like a magic trick.

If they were just going for a hike, someone would've seen them when they set off, or on the trail. Someone would know *something*.

Maybe somebody *does*.

What *I* want to know is, why aren't they investigating who else was in the park at the time of their disappearance? Like, what criminal elements are hanging out there?

I heard Jim got in a fight with someone the *day* before they disappeared. That's quite the coincidence. And you know I don't believe in coincidences.

I have so. Many. Questions.

Seriously, y'all. What are the police up to?

Are they pulling the video in the park? Aren't there cameras everywhere now?

The police or rangers or whatever they're called need to get on that.

Make a list of prime suspects. And like Michelle McNamara said: *Work that list to dust.*

Find out everyone they talked to and interrogate them until they get a confession.

People don't just disappear.

But in America, our Black and Brown sisters do. Time and time again.

It's an epidemic, but there's no vaccine for racism. Only boosters brought to you by the algorithms.

The only reason anyone ever heard about Jada Johnson is because her boyfriend is white and his daddy is connected. That's the truth.

Because I can tell you one thing—if this was a white girl who was missing, we'd already know what happened.

CHAPTER 20

WELCOME TO THE CIRCUS

Then
July

When are they going to call it?" I say to Ben more than a week after Jada and Jim were reported missing.

It's deep into July now, the days hot and sticky, sunset after eight. Ben and I are sitting at the picnic table early in the morning, trying to shove down enough calories to get us through another exhausting day. Jenny and Eric are conferring off to the side, their heads bent toward each other. It all feels like theater. The helicopters flying overhead. The media vans. The establishing shots they take of Eric and Jenny, looking serious. How Gayle seems to shrink into herself day by day. Even some of Jim Senior's bluster is gone. When he arrived, he acted like if he just yelled loud enough, then something would happen. But our yelling in the woods didn't bring them home, and yelling at the SAR team didn't produce any results either.

All of the trails have been checked thoroughly already, and so now, the only option left is to drop people deeper into the wilderness and have them fan out through the woods. It's not an option that's normally pursued because it creates dangers for the searchers, but it's under discussion.

The tension seems to be getting to others too. Yesterday, I saw Petal and Sandy having an argument outside of Eric's office. Petal had her arms crossed, and Sandy seemed to be pleading with her not to do something. Petal looked determined, but as Sandy continued to talk in a steady, low voice I couldn't make out, Petal softened. Eventually, Sandy reached out and drew her close, holding her, rocking her back and forth. Petal buried her face in Sandy's shoulder and hugged her back. They stood like that for a minute, then Sandy led Petal away and into their car. I watched them drive off, then went back to what I was supposed to be doing, wondering who else was going to unravel from the stress.

"We all know it's a recovery mission." Ben stretches his arms above his head, revealing a quick flash of his flat belly.

"If all this media wasn't here, then it would've been called days ago." Typically, a search lasts for between seven and fourteen days. If they got lost on the first day, it's been more than two weeks. Their chance of survival is statistically zero.

"For sure."

"It's not that I don't want them found."

"I get it. We all need to move on, unfortunately. Yesterday, it took too long to get to some idiot on Half Dome because half the team is up here."

"That's dangerous," I say.

"I'm just glad it's not my decision to make." He stands to take his dishes to the washstand.

He's gotten skinnier over the summer—we all have. Hiking all day, missing meals, surviving on protein bars. My pants are loose and my arms haven't been this thin since I was sixteen. None of us has had time to climb, and if this continues through the rest of the summer, we'll miss out on most of the season. But that's a stupid thought. Who cares if I can go climbing? It's just me trying to distract myself from what my brain wants to obsess over.

I have so many questions swirling in my head, it's hard to concentrate. No one could've predicted that this would get so out of control. It's worse, even, than when Cameron and Chris went missing. But ten years ago was before the peak of social media. Before everyone with a phone was an investigative reporter, and anyone with an opinion could get a million views on a conspiracy video.

I should've seen this coming, but I didn't, because I didn't think it through.

"What are they going to have us do today, you think?" Ben asks a minute later when he returns with his rinsed-out dish.

Jenny and Eric separate. Eric looks grim as Jenny checks something on her phone, pales, then slips it into her pocket. She searches the crowd until her eyes land on me. She motions for me to join her near my tent.

"What's up, Jenny?"

"New story breaking."

"What now?"

Jenny looks around her, making sure no one can overhear. We're as alone as we can be. "All that Cameron and Chris stuff— you know how they found out he'd been cheating on her when they went missing? That they'd had a big fight about it?"

"I remember." The community had been shocked. They'd always seemed like the perfect couple. No one ever knows what's going on behind closed doors. "Was Jim cheating on Jada?"

"Not that I know of. But you know these internet sleuths. When they get ahold of something, all kinds of speculation starts up. And then sometimes they find things that are helpful . . . Anyway, some video has turned up."

The back of my neck feels prickly. Something wicked this way comes. "Video of what?"

"A stop they made when they were driving here. In Idaho or Iowa . . . Anyway, it's from a gas station. Jada was crying and someone says that they saw Jim hit her."

"Is that on camera?"

"No, and the gas station attendant didn't do anything about it at the time. But now that her face is plastered all over the news, he came forward. The owner of the gas station pulled the camera footage, and presto, the news cycle is fed for another forty-eight hours."

"Christ. That's the last thing we need."

"You don't seem that surprised," Jenny says.

I pause, considering my words carefully. "Honestly? I'm not. He always seemed like a jerk, and he had that fight with Sandy. Ben and I saw a bruise on Jada, too, that time that we rescued them."

Jenny frowns. "You did?"

"It was the size of a thumbprint, but it could've been caused while she was climbing that time they needed to be rescued."

"Why didn't you report this?"

"Report what? That a climber had a bruise?"

"You should've told us this before."

"Why? They're *both* missing."

"But Cameron . . ."

I tighten my jaw. "Jada isn't Cameron, and Chris didn't do anything to Cameron but try to save her."

"Are you sure about that?"

"What are you saying?"

Jenny runs her hand over her face. "I don't know. This just all feels so weird and similar, you know?"

"I do. But people go missing. Couples go missing. And Jim hasn't suddenly reappeared."

"I know. I just feel haunted."

I take her hand. "I felt like that for so long, I ran away for ten years."

She smiles. "I'm glad you came back."

"I'm not sure I can agree with that."

"I get it." She pulls her hand away. "Anyway, I wanted to let you know. About the story, and that a reporter's already asked me about Cameron."

"What about Cameron?"

"About me—us—finding her. Someone dug out the old report."

"Christ."

"They asked about you too."

My heart speeds up. "What did you say?"

"That it was a long time ago."

"Who was it?"

"That Charlie McMaster guy. Have you read his stuff? Over-the-top sensational."

"Does he know I'm here?"

"I don't know. You know reporters—they ask questions, they don't answer them. But it's not like there's an online registry of SAR."

"Right. But you—"

"Are one of the public faces. Lucky me."

I kick my toe at the dirt. "Fucking vultures. Why don't they just help with finding Jada and Jim instead of making things worse for everyone? Why don't they just go home?"

"It'll all be over soon."

"How?"

"We made a decision. Today is the last day of active search."

My stomach clenches.

"Are you okay?" Jenny says.

"I'm just tired."

"Why don't you take today off? We're pulling back the teams. I don't want you to burn out before the end of summer."

A day off. I hadn't even considered it. You don't take a day off when someone's missing. "Okay, thanks."

"Why don't you get out of the park? Avoid the vultures."

"Yeah, good idea. I should see my mother, anyway. It's been a while."

"You can borrow my car if you like."

"Thanks. You don't have to . . ."

"Stop it."

I hug her. I know what this is, but I'll take it anyway. Jenny's worried, worried I'll talk to the press and tell the real version of what happened to Cameron all those years ago. The one that didn't make it into the report.

"I'll just go get changed."

"Sure. Find me when you need the keys."

"Will do."

I walk to my tent. I never did get breakfast, but I don't have an appetite. I'll eat something in Mammoth. Or drink something. Maybe the latter. I'll need the reinforcements to handle my mother, who's been calling me frequently ever since the news about Jada and Jim broke.

I enter my tent and turn on the light. My phone is resting near the bed. I pick it up to text my mother to let her know I'm coming into town, but there's a text waiting for me from a blocked number. It's a link to an article.

Cases of Missing Couples Linked? the headline asks, and my hands start to shake.

CASES OF MISSING COUPLES LINKED?

Recent Disappearance in Yosemite Baffles Rangers

BY Charlie McMaster

July 20 · 9:20 a.m. PST

The disappearance of Jada Johnson and her boyfriend, Jim Carlisle, in Yosemite has baffled search and rescue teams since it was reported on July 11. Ms. Johnson, who rose to Instagram fame after she championed the rescue of a black bear known as "Smokey" from being euthanized, and Mr. Carlisle drove to Yosemite from Ohio with plans to spend the summer. Ms. Johnson posted about their trip on Instagram frequently, documenting their stops along the way in photos, captions, and hashtags, as well as their various adventures in the park.

But since they disappeared, the search and rescue efforts have turned up nothing. Their Airstream sits abandoned in the Tuolumne campground, and no one has seen or heard from them since July 5. Their families are understandably frantic, holding press conferences to draw attention to the plight of their children. Multiple teams of searchers have been mobilized, both from within and outside the park, but to date, they have no leads on where they might be or what might have happened to them.

It is common knowledge that the chance of being found alive goes down drastically after the first twenty-four hours. One person familiar with the search and rescue effort who wants to remain anonymous put the chance of them being found alive at this stage at less than 1%.

The head law enforcement officer for Yosemite, Eric Moser, says that "everything is being done to find them," and has assured the families as late as yesterday that this is still "very much a search and rescue operation." But sources have revealed that unless something changes, today will be the last full day of searching, as the rescue teams will shift the focus of their investigation to recovering the bodies if—and when— they are found.

The couple was planning on hiking to McCabe Lake, a remote site in the backcountry, fifteen miles from their starting point in Tuolumne. The current theory is that Ms. Johnson and Mr. Carlisle decided to diverge from their intended path and that one or both of them were injured along the way. "They have a tent, food, and there's lots of access to water. Even if they are deep in the wilderness, they have the skills to survive," Moser assured us. "We are confident that we will find them soon."

As two anxious families wait for answers, an eerie parallel has emerged. Ten years ago, Cameron Mack and Chris Stevens went missing from the Tuolumne Meadows area. They were also missing for more than ten days and believed to be lost forever. Then Mr. Stevens emerged from the woods, hungry and severely dehydrated. Ms. Mack had been injured, he explained, and he had eventually decided to walk out to get help. Two days later, Ms. Mack's body was recovered from the wilderness by search and rescue workers. Mr. Stevens survived, and while no charges were ever brought, many believed that he was—at the very least—highly irresponsible to leave Ms. Mack alone.

It was also revealed that Mr. Stevens had been cheating on Ms. Mack, something that she apparently discovered not long before they left for their trip. People who were close to the couple at the time said that the trip was supposed to be a chance at reconciling.

Trouble might have been brewing between Mr. Carlisle and Ms. Johnson as well. Video has emerged of Mr. Carlisle in a potential altercation with Ms. Johnson while they were traveling to Yosemite from Ohio. As has been reported elsewhere, an eyewitness saw Mr. Carlisle strike Ms. Johnson at a gas station in Oklahoma. The incident was not captured on video and is being investigated by the police there.

In another eerie coincidence, the current head of the search and rescue division, Jenny Evans, was one of the members of the search and rescue team that located Cameron Mack ten years ago. She and another member of the team, Cassie Peters—who recently rejoined SAR and also goes by the name Cassandra Adams—have been active in the search and rescue efforts to find Ms. Johnson and Mr. Carlisle.

Ten years, two couples, the same two search and rescue workers. Is it all just a coincidence, or is something more sinister at play?

CHAPTER 21
PASTS COLLIDE

Then
July

Mammoth looks like it always does—childhood memories, close together pine trees, the mountains in the background.

My mother's house is in a new development away from the main strip on Old Mammoth Road. She bought it when I was in high school, her real estate career taking off, the bank doing her a favor on the mortgage rate because of all the business she'd thrown their way. It's a Pacific West Coast design, with dark green shingles and cedar trim, with soaring ceilings in the great room and a wall of windows that lets in the sunlight in the long winter months.

I didn't live here long enough to feel at home, but as my mother fusses in the kitchen, opening a bottle of wine even though it isn't noon yet, I wander down the hall to my old bedroom. I push open the door, wondering what I'll find. My bed is there, my dresser and desk, but the paint is new, the bedspread different. Like me; I'm enough like the girl who used to live here, who dreamt of being elsewhere, of traveling the world and going on adventures. But I've also been changed, rendered blander, with less personality. Dreams cast aside, wandering a bust.

The wandering had brought me to Kevin, and now he knows where I am.

What's he going to do about it? He'd texted me the link to the article without anything more. He'd also blocked his number—why? That wasn't like Kevin. When Kevin made threats, he didn't couch who they came from. But who else would want to threaten me? Because that's what that text was, whether it said so or not.

"Cassie!"

"Coming!"

I walk back to the kitchen. It's got light gray cabinets and a lot of white marble. There are two glasses of white wine sitting on the counter in oversized glasses, the light yellow liquid glowing in the downlighting.

She hands one to me. "Such a terrible business."

"You mean Jada and Jim?"

"Of course. Bringing all of this up again. Julie Mack is a mess."

"I didn't know she was still in town."

"She never left." My mom takes a large swig of her wine. She'd promised to make me breakfast, too, but that doesn't appear to be happening.

I walk to the fridge. It's filled with containers from some weight-loss system, each meal portioned out and sealed away in a semi-translucent plastic container. "Is there anything else in here?"

"There are some eggs at the back."

I push the containers aside until I find the eggs. I take them out along with some low-fat cheese and non-fat milk. I know better than to ask if there's bread. I put them on the counter and pull out a bowl, a pan, and a fork. I whip up a quick omelet and then pour the mixture into a pan with some oil.

"You don't seem that concerned," my mother says.

"About what?"

"Julie Mack."

"I'm sorry for her, but there are bigger things on my mind right now."

"She never got closure."

I close my eyes for a moment as I push my eggs around. "She did, though. We found Cameron."

"You think that's closure? With that man still walking around?"

"Chris?"

"Of course, Chris."

"He almost died too."

She's holding her wineglass by the stem, gripping it tight. "Why do you always defend him?"

"I don't."

"You do. Back then. Now. I know you had a crush on him, but he's not a good person."

I can feel the heat rise up my neck. "I didn't have a crush on him."

I had a crush on *them*. They looked so perfect together, so happy. I wanted that. I still do.

I turn the heat off and put my eggs on a plate, then bring it to the counter with a fork. "But even if I did, it doesn't change the facts. Cameron died of natural causes. There's nothing unexplained. They went the wrong way on a trail and one of them is lucky to be alive. It's a fucking tragedy, but it wasn't a crime."

"Don't raise your voice at me."

I take a deep breath and shove some eggs into my mouth. Coming here was a mistake, as it always is. "I'm sorry."

"Everyone is on edge."

"I understand. I am too. It's been a long couple of weeks."

"It doesn't help that I see him everywhere."

"Who?"

My mother blows out her cheeks. "Chris."

I put my fork down slowly. "What?"

"He's working at that outfitter on Old Mammoth Road. You know the one on the corner near the Vons?"

"Since when?"

"He came back last year, but no one knew he was back for a while. His parents died and he came to deal with their estate. But then he stayed. And he just walks around like he has a right to."

"Mom, honestly. You'd think *you* were Cameron's mom."

"Julie's a close friend."

"I get it, but he can live where he wants to. What's he supposed to do? Kill himself? Would that make you happy?"

She reaches for the bottle and pours herself another glass. "That's a terrible thing to say."

"It's how you act."

"You don't know. You don't live here."

"You're right, I don't." I push back from the counter. "Thanks for breakfast."

"Where are you going?"

"I've got to get back."

"You said you'd spend the day."

"Did I?"

I give her a quick hug. She smells the same as she did when I was a kid, like some expensive perfume I never remember the name of. Sometimes I'd catch a whiff of it in New York, walking behind some older woman in a suit, and I'd think it was her for a second, my body stiffening in anticipation. But then she'd turn her head and it was just some middle-aged woman with the same perfume. That's what it's like when you leave one life behind and slip into another—the old one haunts you.

"I've got to go."

"When are you coming back?"

"I don't know."

"Soon?"

"I'll try."

I pull away and walk to the door. I turn back to look at her, feeling terrible, but unable to do anything about it. I can't stay here or I'll scream bloody murder.

I don't mean to go to the outfitters where Chris works, but it's like the car drives me there itself while I mull over what my mother said.

But no, that's not what happens. I want to see him. I don't even know if he'll be working there today, but I take a chance.

The store is like many in town, and it's full of hiking and skiing equipment. I used to get my racing skis here when I was a teenager. Skiing is like walking in this town—kids get let out of school early to ski the afternoon away. I specialized in giant slalom but did all the disciplines, including downhill. Insane crashes, knee braces, concussions . . . it was all a normal part of growing up in an outdoor town.

I walk through the store slowly, unrolling more memories, looking for Chris. I don't spot him on the first floor, so I walk up the winding wooden stairs to the upstairs level full of on-sale items and things that are out of season. All of these stores have the same layout, like Irish bars, and smell the same, too. A mix of wool and ski wax, like winter bundled into a candle.

At the back of the second level is a wall of skis and snowboards, and that's where Chris is. He's helping a customer, his arms folded across his chest, but not unfriendly. I have no trouble recognizing him. His hair is still the light blond of a surfer, his arms tanned and strong in his dark blue polo work shirt. The man he's helping is in his mid-thirties with a streak of sunburn across his nose.

I hover near a rack of ski jackets, flipping through them slowly as I steal glances at Chris. My heart's beating quickly, like it used to when I was eighteen. I can't decide if I want to talk to him or run.

"Cassie?"

My shoulders stiffen as I turn around to face Sandy. She's wearing the same shirt as Chris and a name tag. "Hi, Sandy."

"Can I help you?"

"Just browsing." I flip my hand through the rack.

"Shouldn't you be looking for Jim and Jada?" Her tone is sharp, and a nearby customer's head snaps up. Those names are famous around here. Around everywhere.

"It's my day off."

"They don't get a day off from being missing, do they?"

I step away from the rack, suddenly sweating. "I'm sorry?"

"I just don't . . . Why can't you find them?"

"We're doing everything we can."

"Clearly not."

"No offense, but what's it to you? You didn't even like them."

Sandy's eyes narrow. "Petal's upset."

"I know."

"No, you don't. You don't know her at all."

I put my hands up in front of me. "Okay, Sandy, I'm going to go."

"What's going on?" Chris says from behind me. "Cassie?"

I spin slowly. He's standing five feet away, like he's social distancing from me, like I'm contagious. His face is tanned and there are crinkles forming around the edges of his eyes.

"Hi, Chris."

"What are you doing here?"

I try to smile. "Would you believe shopping?"

He shakes his head. Sandy didn't buy my excuse and neither does he. "Here?"

"It was a mistake."

"A mistake."

I'd forgotten that he does this, repeats the last thing he's heard like he's testing it out. Not a question, or an affirmation. *I like you. You like me. No one will know. No one will know.*

"Yes."

He blinks at me slowly and I can feel Sandy hovering behind me. I don't know what I was thinking when I came in here, but whatever it was has gone with the wind. I need to get out of this store, but I feel trapped. By the past, by the present. Between Sandy and Chris.

"I'm going to go."

"Wait," Chris says. "Wait."

I hesitate, but I don't want to have this conversation with half the store listening. "I'm at the T-SAR site if you want to reach me."

He blinks again and I take that second to leave. I hustle through the floor to the stairs and start down them, my heart speeding, my breath cut short.

And that's when I see him.

Kevin.

He's leaving the store too, down a level, his hand on the door. I'd know the back of that head anywhere, the way it's shaped, the set of his shoulders. I've followed it down a street enough times—he was always walking three steps ahead of me, never slowing down to let me catch up.

I almost call out his name from habit, but it catches in my throat, strangling me. And then, because I'm not paying attention to where I'm going, my shoe catches on the uneven stair and I pitch forward, reaching for the railing too late. I tumble down the rest of the stairs, landing in a heap, half against the bottom step, bruised and winded.

"Cassie, Cassie are you okay?" Chris says, his gentle hands

touching me, helping me up. His touch feels like a memory, one that burns.

"I . . . I'm okay."

"What happened?"

"I tripped," I say, but my brain is screaming that it's Kevin's fault.

That even when he couldn't touch me, he was still able to hurt.

CHAPTER 22

THE LONG AND WINDING ROAD

Then

July

When I get out of the store, Kevin isn't anywhere to be seen. I search up and down the streets, driving around, looking for that familiar shape, but he's nowhere.

After a while I begin to think I was imagining the whole thing. That I'm so caught up in my past and paranoia, I'm seeing things. What other explanation could there be? If Kevin's in town and saw me, he wouldn't just cut and run. That's not his style.

When I give up hope of finding him or an explanation, I drive to the ski hill and take the chairlift to the top. I haven't been up here in ten years, and there's a bunch of new chairs I don't recognize, but the mountain—its large spread, its multiple peaks—is so familiar, like the rocks I've climbed over and over again in Yosemite. I know every nook and cranny, the trail map laid out in my head. I've always felt centered up here, the view calming. I breathe in the thinner air and take in the full 360. I center myself and try to reconcile what's happened today.

I made several stupid decisions. I went to see my mother—never a good idea. I went to see Chris—ditto. I thought I saw Kevin, but that must've been a mistake. In fact, I can check on that.

I take out my phone. I go through the steps to block my number and call Kevin's office. It rings once, twice, three times. An odd, stuttered ring like I'm making an international call.

"Kevin Adams's office." This voice is not familiar either, but his assistants came and went over the years because working for him was difficult, so I'm not surprised.

I try to mask my voice, adding a bad British accent. "Is Mr. Adams in?"

"Who may I say is calling?"

I grasp for a name. "Sophie Turner."

"And what is this regarding?"

"I'm looking for a new investment advisor."

"I'm sorry, Ms. Turner, but Mr. Adams is out."

"Do you know when he'll be back?"

"He's out of town right now. But I can take your details and have him call you?"

I end the call, my hands shaking. Kevin's out of town. Double shit.

I want to call back and ask where he's gone, but his assistant isn't going to tell me that.

Kevin is away. Kevin's out of town. It's hard for me to breathe, knowing that.

But wait. Just because he's out of town doesn't mean he's here. He traveled often for work. That's the most likely explanation.

If he knew where I was, he wouldn't be hanging out in Mammoth.

He'd be in Yosemite.

I never thought he'd come after me, not really. Threatening me from afar by text—that I can believe. But traveling all this way to find me? That seems like too much effort for Kevin. It's why I risked coming here. For someone who knows what they're doing, that journalist has proven I'm not that hard to find.

I look at the phone in my hand. I could call him and ask, but that's a terrible idea. I don't want to hear his voice again, feel that anger vibrating through the phone. I don't want to hear his pleas for my return, or the threats he'll make if I don't comply. Would he even tell me where he is right now?

No.

So I'm screwed. I'll never get the answer. I have no way to track him—

Wait. I do. I *do* have a way to track him.

Only I can't do it from my phone.

I arrive back at the T-SAR site in the midafternoon. I return Jenny's car to the Ranger Station, stopping inside to bring her keys back.

"Hey, Cassie?" Ben asks behind me.

I turn to him and smile. "How are you?"

"I'm okay. You?"

"I . . . Can I talk to you about something?" I ask.

"Sure."

"Not here. Can we go to your tent?"

"Sure. Lead the way."

We walk the short distance to our part of the campground. Gareth and Mia are at the picnic table, and he lets out a loud whoop as we go into Ben's tent without stopping to talk to them.

"He's so mature," I say.

"He's harmless." Ben sits on his bed. "What's up?"

"I was wondering if I could check something on your phone."

"What?"

I bite my lip. "I think I might've seen Kevin in Mammoth today, and I need to check his location."

Ben rests his hands on his thighs. "Kevin?"

"My husband."

"Okay."

"I know it sounds crazy."

"Why would he be in town?"

"We didn't end things well. He's not a nice man."

"Not a nice man how?"

I rock my body back and forth slowly. It is so hard to talk about this, and I've never done it face-to-face. Saying the words, letting them out, it's an act of will. "He has some anger issues."

"Did he hit you?"

I nod slowly, even that hurting. I don't talk about this. I've almost never talked about this. Because the first time Kevin hit me was such a shock. The blow, what caused it, all of it. Afterwards, I spent weeks looking for signs. Should I have seen it coming?

"I'm sorry, Cassie."

"Thank you."

"But why would he be here?"

"He's not happy I left him. And I've been . . . I've had a few texts . . ."

"From him?"

"Maybe."

"How do you not know?"

"The number's blocked, and the messages aren't signed."

"How can you track him?"

"Through our iPhone account. That Find My iPhone feature. I needed to know when he was coming home sometimes. So I could prepare."

Ben looks like he might be sick to his stomach. That's how I felt too. Seasick, like the ground underneath me was pitching and rolling all the time. Like the boat might tip at any moment and throw me overboard.

"Are you only telling me this because you need my phone?"

"Mia asks a lot of questions."

"Okay."

"I'm sorry."

"It's fine." He reaches into his pocket and takes out his phone. "Here."

"Thank you."

I take it and go through the process of signing in to the account online, nervous that he'll get alerted when I do. I click on his phone's icon. It shows that it's in our apartment in New York. I let out a sigh of relief.

But wait. His assistant said he was out of town. He wouldn't travel without his phone. So, what does that mean? That he turned the tracking feature off? That he got a new phone?

"Cassie?"

"Yeah?"

"What is it?"

"He's not here." I look up and hand him back the phone.

"You sure?"

"Yeah, I'm sure."

Ben takes my hand and I close my eyes at the sensation. I'm acting on instinct now, even though my instincts have gotten me into more trouble than I like to think about.

I open my eyes and take a step toward him so I'm standing between his legs. I don't want to talk about this anymore or think about what it might mean that Kevin is out there in the world, maybe close by, without his phone on him. Or not his old phone anyway.

"We should get back to work," Ben says as I put my hands on his shoulders.

"I have the day off."

I bring my face close to his, breathing in his scent. My body feels alive and hungry, hungry for something. Hungry for Ben.

"What are you . . ."

"Do you want me to stop?"

"No, I just want you to be sure."

"I am," I say as I bring my mouth to his.

His lips are soft but firm, and our kiss escalates quickly. His hands move to my waist, pulling up my shirt. When his hands touch my skin, I shiver.

"This okay?"

"Yes. Very okay."

He starts to unbutton my shirt, tracing his hand along my skin, over my clavicle and down my chest. It rests on my medallion.

He touches it with his forefinger. "I've never seen this. What is it?"

I tilt it toward him. "It's meant to symbolize hope."

"Does it work?"

I let it drop and lean toward his lips. "Not so far, but I still have hope."

He smiles as he pulls me down to the bed on top of him, our legs tangled together over the side. I hold his face and kiss him, exploring his mouth, his tongue, while his hands rove over my back. I can feel the excitement build, the heat between us. It's been so long since I felt this way, it's a bit overwhelming, but I try to push everything else aside, anyone, until there is just me and Ben.

He rolls us onto our sides and brings his hands to my breasts. I suck in my breath at the contact as I feel him harden against me. It feels extra illicit to do this in daylight, the sounds of the camp around us.

"I want you," Ben says.

"I want you too."

Things move quickly now, our clothes discarded on the floor, a condom removed from his wallet, his hands and lips everywhere, and then he's inside me and it's all I can do not to cry out because I feel good and scared and happy and sad and this man, this man is trying to heal me, but I'm broken beyond repair.

Early the next morning, I turn over in bed and reach for Ben's phone on the nightstand. I roll my body so I hide the light as best I can, cupping my hands around the screen. I check the account again. Kevin's phone is still where it was earlier. Somehow, the small dot reassures me, even though I know it's unlikely to be Kevin.

I was overreacting before. I'm not even sure I saw Kevin in Mammoth. What did I see? A man with dark hair from behind. He could've been anyone. I've made the mistake before—there have been other men I thought were him, especially when I was scared to run into him in an area of Manhattan where I wasn't supposed to be. It was how I'd learned about the iPhone tracking. The first time I went to the climbing gym, Kevin had said something about it, wondering what I was doing there. He'd let me know that he was tracking my phone, smirking, like I was stupid not to have realized it before. But he'd made a mistake, telling me. I changed gyms and learned to leave my phone behind. After I thought I saw him outside my new gym, I started checking where *his* iPhone was before I went anywhere.

It was a sick game, but that's what we were—a couple who was dying a slow death. And we stayed that way until I finally had the courage to leave.

I put the phone down and turn back to Ben. He looks peaceful, sleeping. He must be as exhausted as I am, as we all are. Despite my misgivings, it's good we took this moment to rest.

"Cassie! Cassie! Where's Cassie?" The voice outside the tent is panicked, loud. Ben stirs next to me.

"What's going on?" he says, his voice hoarse.

"Stay here, I'll check." I get up quickly and throw on my clothes. I open the door to Ben's tent. Sandy's standing by the picnic tables looking wild-eyed.

"Sandy, what is it?"

She turns to me. Her face is streaked with tears. "It's Petal. She's missing."

July 21—Lee Vining

I found it—I found OUT.

I know where the money came from. Sandy's been lying to me this whole time.

Daddy used to say: if someone accuses you of something it's because they done that thing themself.

Daddy isn't a nice man, but he knows people, and he used to do that, call so and so a liar when it was him that was one. Say he was dangerous when it was him that was the menace. Say Mama was a whore when it was him that was screwing around the trailer park.

Daddy never liked Sandy. He made that plain. At first, I thought it was just because of who she was—who we were together. But I guess it was more than that. He saw what she was beneath the surface.

That money—it comes from drugs.

I got on one of those public computers at the library in town and I googled her. I've never done that before. Who cares what a computer tells you about a person? It's what they show you that counts. That's what I always thought.

But I was wrong. What Sandy's been showing me, it's only part of the picture. I should've listened to Daddy and done my due diligence.

She was with some bad people. She's got arrest warrants waiting for her in Florida. Drugs. Violence. In her mug shot, she looks like a different person, her teeth bared like a dog who's been cornered. It's been three years since she skipped some muggy town in the swamps as the DEA was closing in on her.

She got tipped off, stuffed her car full of cash, and skedaddled.

A year later she showed up in my life with her sweet words and her big plans and her saying I could escape all of this. And I bought it. I fell into her life and let her take me away because what I had was worse than whatever it was she was promising.

I thought we were taking a leap of faith into our new life. I didn't know I was on the run.

And now I'm wondering—did Jada know about her past? Did Jim?

That fight at the bonfire—Jim was needling her. Saying he knew she was keeping something from everyone, that she was some kind of weird sex cult leader like R. Kelly because why else would she have a hot woman by her side? That her and me together was CRIMINAL. That's when Sandy hit him.

She wanted to shut him up. That's what I thought at the time. But now I see it was more than that. He was going to say something else. He was going to tell me about her. Maybe he was going to turn her in.

The next day, he went missing.

That sent chills down my spine.

Is Sandy controlling me? Is that why I'm with her? When I look at my life now, that's the only explanation I can think of. One minute I was taking a class in junior college, working toward something, and now I walk trails all day looking for someone I don't even know.

Sandy did this to me. But she's not going to get away with it.

—Petal

CHAPTER 23

BE HERE NOW

Now

My eyes flutter open.

"There you are," Ben says.

I try to sit up, but he puts a gentle hand on my shoulder and pushes me back down. "You need to rest."

"Where am I?"

"Medical station."

"What happened?"

"You passed out. Shock."

I tilt my head back and focus. I'm lying in a hospital cot, blankets pulled up around me. It's warm in here, and I feel sleepy. It's late, maybe the middle of the night, but it's hard to know. This whole day has been too long, like the day I left New York, like there was a time change involved, and maybe an international date line.

"I'm in trouble," I say. I turn my head to look at him. He's leaning forward in his seat, his hands on his thighs. He looks tired, worn-out. But the kindness is there in his eyes, what drew me to him in the first place.

"Is it really Kevin?" he asks.

"Yes. He found me."

"How?"

I close my eyes. "The video, I think. The one Jada posted when you took Smokey out. Some friends of mine in New York saw it. Or maybe it was that article. The one where the journalist mentioned my married name. Or maybe I just wasn't that hard to find."

"So it *was* him you saw in town the day we . . . ?"

"I don't know. I don't know when he got here."

"Why did he come here?"

"What do you think?"

"Did you hurt him?"

I turn away. Kevin's dead. Someone hurt him and that has to be me, right?

"I was defending myself. He was . . . He had a gun."

Ben sucks in his breath. "Where is it?"

"What?"

"The gun. Where's the gun, Cassie?"

I turn back toward him slowly. "I don't have it?"

"I went through your pack. It wasn't there."

"Why did you do that?"

"Jenny asked me to."

The implication is clear. Jenny asked him to make sure there wasn't anything incriminating in my pack. To let her know if there was. They think I'm guilty of something. But if Ben's asking me about it, that means Jenny's trying to protect me. She's been doing it ever since I got off the Huey.

"I . . . It fell, after . . . I dropped it."

"It's too late to look for it now. Someone will have to go back in the morning."

Back to the clearing, he means. What will they find if they go there? It's a crime scene now. Will it be taped off with yellow ribbon? Will crews descend in hazmat suits to collect samples and evidence? What, besides my gun, is there to find?

"I had to, Ben. Do you understand?"

He shakes his head, and I'm not sure what that means. That he doesn't understand? That he can't?

"There's something else you should know," Ben says.

My heart starts to pound. I don't know how much more of this I can take. "What?"

"Gareth just radioed it in. They found another body, and they're pretty sure it's Jim."

CHAPTER 24

THE PATTERN

Then
July

The media's going to go crazy. One couple missing is already a big story—bigger than usual. Jada's photogenic and already had an online following because of Smokey. And Jim's dad has connections and he used them to get as much attention for the case as possible. We were just about to wrap this up. The search had been called off, that information about to trickle through the online ecosphere.

But then another person goes missing—a friend of the couple's?—and now it's not just a tragedy, it's a pattern.

On that warm morning outside Ben's tent, Sandy knows it too. In those moments when I find myself holding her as she falls to the ground, taking in her scent of bergamot and fear, she shudders and says "no." *No, no, no, no, no.* She says it when I say I'll call the disappearance in. In the moment, I think it's because that makes it real. An official report. But later, I'm not so sure.

I lead her inside and Ben, Jenny, and I sit down to talk to her. We make an odd quartet. Ben and I in our hastily unshed clothes rearranged with equal haste. Sandy with a sweater that she's put on backwards over her work polo. Only Jenny is calm and composed, her tone capable and firm.

"Am I in trouble?" Sandy asks.

"No, of course not," Jenny says. "We just need to understand what's going on so we can help find Petal."

"Okay."

We're sitting around a dark brown picnic table in one of the Forest Service buildings. The morning sunlight is filtering through the windows, touching the map behind Sandy on the wall. Ben is next to her, his face unshaven. His eyes keep darting to mine, like I might have the answers to the questions Jenny's about to start asking Sandy.

"Can you tell me your full name, Sandy?"

"Sandy Cramer."

"How old are you?"

"Fifty-four."

"Where do you live?"

"At the trailer park in Lee Vining." Sandy gives her the address.

"Petal's your girlfriend?"

"Yeah."

"What's her full name?"

"Petal Fernandez."

"How old is Petal?"

"Twenty-three."

"When is the last time you saw her?"

"Two nights ago when we went to bed. In the morning she was gone. I thought maybe . . . but she didn't come back all day, or all night, either . . ." Sandy gulps back a sob and Ben puts a hand on her back. She looks at him gratefully.

"How long have you been together?" Ben asks.

Sandy takes in and releases a slow breath. "About two years now. We met when I was passing through her hometown."

"Where was that?"

"Cape Cod. A town called Wellfleet."

I'd been there once, with Kevin. We drove past it on our way to Provincetown, where we were staying in a Victorian bed-and-breakfast painted sky blue. All I remember of the town are the dunes, the long pale grass waving in the breeze, and the sense that it was a place that time had abandoned. It still had a drive-in movie theater, and we went there one night when we'd run out of things to do, watching a silly action movie in our car, Kevin complaining about the sound quality.

That whole trip was out of character for him. He preferred fancy hotels and five-star experiences, but I'd never been to the Atlantic Ocean, and he decided to take me there as a surprise for our first anniversary. I would've loved it, too—I *did* love it—right up to the moment when he yelled at me because he thought I was looking at a man at dinner. That the man was clearly gay and there with his husband didn't matter to Kevin.

It was the first time he'd talked to me like that, and I was scared. I should've walked right out the door and away from him forever. Instead, I accepted his tearful apology and we saw a Marvel movie. And I never told anyone in New York about it. I didn't keep a diary or take photos. I didn't collect the evidence. I didn't want to turn myself into a crime scene. If I did that, I'd have to admit what was happening. And I couldn't. I didn't. Not for years and years.

"What have you been doing for the last two years?" Jenny asks.

Sandy gives her a dead-eyed stare. "Traveling around, mostly. Never stay in one place for long. But here, we were going to stay here."

"Why did you come to Lee Vining?"

"Petal wanted to. Her mom . . . she told me her mom sent her a postcard from here once. Mammoth, anyway. She left Petal a long time ago, but Petal was always looking for her."

"Did she find her?"

"That woman doesn't want to be found. And it was years ago that she sent that postcard. Can you imagine, just abandoning your kid like that? As a mother?" Sandy wipes a tear away. "It wasn't right."

"So why did you agree?"

"Because we were sick of being on the road. It was time to settle down. This seemed as good a place as any."

Jenny leans back, assessing Sandy. Does it matter why they came here? They're here. At least one of them is.

"Is it possible she's out searching? For Jim and Jada?" I ask.

Sandy turns her eyes to me. They're drooping at the edges. "No."

"We found her doing that, once." I nod to Ben.

Sandy leans back in her chair. "She's been doing that since they went missing. Spending her days out here, hiking all the trails. She's obsessed."

"Why?"

"I don't know. I mean, she and Jada hung out a bit before. They were working on that bear thing together. I guess the whole thing just . . . It's a lot, you know, when someone disappears without an explanation."

"So maybe that's where she is?"

"No, she's missing, I told you."

"Why did she come here the other day?" I ask.

Sandy brings her eyes to mine slowly. "What's that?"

"Two days ago. I saw you both here. Petal seemed upset."

"We'd had an . . . argument."

"That doesn't explain why she came to this office."

Jenny puts her hand on my arm. "What was it about, Sandy? The argument?"

"She . . . She found out something about me. Something I didn't tell her."

"What?"

Sandy shakes her head. "It doesn't have anything to do with this."

"You don't know that. If you want to find her . . ."

Sandy looks at her hands. They're callused, the nails short. Climber's hands, though I've never seen her climb. "I did some stupid things a few years ago. Something . . . It wasn't right."

"Something illegal?" Jenny guesses.

"Yes."

"What?" I say.

"I don't want to say. I don't have to, right?"

"No, you don't," Jenny says. "Why don't you tell us what you can."

Sandy's shoulders droop. "She was upset. She'd been upset at me ever since Jada and Jim went missing."

"Why?"

"Because I didn't think it was that big a deal. Not enough to keep going out there every day."

"Did you argue about it?"

"Yes."

"But what does that have to do with what she found out about you?" Ben asks, his face crinkled in thought.

"It made her think . . . Because of that fight I had with Jim . . . She said maybe *I* was the reason they were missing."

"Is it?" I ask.

"No, of course not. But before I could convince her, she bolted and came here." She looks at Jenny. "I guess she wanted to tell on me. To turn me in."

"And then?"

"She left the trailer and drove here. I followed her. I talked to her outside this building, I guess that's what you saw. I apologized, told her that whatever she was thinking was crazy, that it didn't make sense. She hadn't been sleeping. She wasn't thinking straight. I didn't have anything to do with Jim and Jada going missing, but if she told you that I did, then it was going to be trouble for both of us. She agreed to come back to the trailer. To talk to me."

"And did she?"

"Yes. We drove back separately. We had dinner, we talked, she calmed down. She said she understood . . . what I did. That she knew I didn't have anything to do with Jada and Jim. That she wouldn't say anything. And then we went to bed—" Sandy's voice cuts off with a sob. She takes a minute to compose herself. "The next morning, when I woke up to go to work, she was gone."

"Was there a note?"

"No."

"Did she take anything?"

"I'm not sure. I . . . Her backpack, I think."

"What about her car?"

"It's here. That's how I . . ."

Jenny leans forward. "How you what?"

"How she knew that Petal was here, right?" I say. "You tracked her car?"

Sandy looks at me then nods.

"How?"

"One of those things you can put in your luggage. In case it gets lost." She takes out her phone. "There's an app . . ."

"Does it store data?" I ask.

"I don't know. Maybe?"

"Can we see it?" Jenny asks.

Sandy opens the app and hands her phone to me. I haven't used this app before, but it's easy enough to navigate. Technology has made stalking easier than ever.

There's a log of where the chip's been. A quick perusal shows a predictable pattern—to the park, the trailer, to Mammoth. I show it to Jenny.

"Can we keep this?" Jenny asks.

"I need my phone."

"Let's figure out a way to download the information when we're done here."

"Okay," Sandy says. "But what about Petal? Her car, it's in the lot, and she's just . . . Gone."

"Couldn't she be hiking?" Ben says. "Looking for them like you said before?"

"She's not searching. She's *gone*. If she was searching, she would've come back last night. Something happened out there. Something happened to her." Sandy's eyes pool with tears. "Please. Can you please find her?"

"We'll alert the teams to be on the lookout for her, certainly," Jenny says.

Sandy angrily wipes her tears away with her fist. "You're not going to search for her?"

"If she doesn't return tomorrow, then yes. We'll start a search."

"Only tomorrow?"

"Let's give it another twenty-four hours, just to make sure, okay?" Jenny says gently.

"She's missing. What's there to make sure of?"

Jenny stands. "We'll be in touch with you. Please let us know if you hear from Petal."

Sandy stands up. "This isn't right." She turns and leaves the building, slamming the door behind her so it shakes.

"What do you think?" Jenny asks.

"She's not telling us everything," Ben says.

"And the girl?"

He shrugs. "Maybe just a lovers' quarrel."

"Maybe," Jenny says. "We'll see."

CHAPTER 25

SEARCH PARTY

Then

July

Petal doesn't come back that day.

While she hasn't yet opened an official missing person's case, Jenny makes a copy of the log of Petal's movements, telling me privately that it makes her *that angry* that someone would do that to someone they love. Jenny's life has been relatively innocent. She doesn't know the half of what someone might do to someone they love, so I bite my tongue, then go out on a rescue that involves a gruesome cut to the leg. When I return to camp with the scent of blood caught in my nostrils, everyone's buzzing about Sandy's visit and the fact that Petal hasn't reappeared.

No one knows what to make of it. Did she simply leave after her and Sandy's fight? Is she out there in the woods?

Jenny finds me at the washstand, cleaning the blood off my hands. "What do you make of all this?"

"Petal missing?"

"If she's even missing."

"Why so skeptical?" I scrub under my fingernails, waiting for the water to turn clear. The hiker I saved is going to be okay, but they're going to have a nasty scar for the rest of their life.

"What's your assessment of Petal?"

"She seemed a bit lost. Latching on to Jada like that . . . She was kind of following them around, right? That day that Jada and Jim got into trouble on Tenaya . . ."

"What is it?"

"I just remembered something. She had a journal. She carried it around with her a lot."

"That could be helpful," Jenny says. "To give us a window into her thinking."

"Assuming she left it behind."

"Right. Maybe Sandy would know."

"You think she'd give us that?"

Jenny's shoulders rise. "Don't ask, don't get."

"True."

"She does genuinely seem to want to find Petal."

"Yeah."

"But there's something she's not telling us."

"Also true."

Jenny folds her arms over her chest. "Can you ask her?"

"Sure. You want me to go now?"

"Better to have all the information. If she doesn't turn up tomorrow, we might have a head start."

"Okay."

"Take Ben with you."

"Will do. He's better with people than me, anyway."

Jenny smiles at this. "You're fine with people."

I finish cleaning my hands, and though I've scrubbed for several minutes, it feels like it's going to take more than that to get them truly clean. My mind is a skipping track that doesn't stay on one idea for long. It feels like I might unravel soon.

I wipe my hands dry, then go to find Ben. He's at the picnic table talking to Mia, Sam, and George. I explain the errand, and he agrees to go with me.

We get changed and climb into Ben's truck and drive out of the park.

"You okay?" Ben asks after a half hour of silence.

"Yeah, just in my head a little."

"About last night?"

In the turmoil, I'd forgotten all about our night together. But I know that's not the right thing to say. "All of it, honestly. It's a lot to process."

"I don't regret it." He smiles. "It was great."

"It was." I point out the window. "I think it's just up here."

Ben slows down to turn into the drive. It's the trailer park Ben and I passed in May on our way to the park. A new addition since I left the area, nestled into the space between the highway and a high embankment. It looks small from the road, but once we pull into the parking lot, I realize that's an illusion. There are two rows of trailers, and behind them is a large, wooded area, dark and shady because of the embankment. It looks like somewhere someone might hide a body.

"What are you thinking?" Ben asks from behind me.

"It's creepy as fuck back there."

"You don't think . . . ? I mean, Petal's car is in the park."

"Yeah, I know. My brain is full of maudlin thoughts."

He puts a hand on my shoulder and squeezes. "Let's get this over with, shall we?"

I follow him to Petal and Sandy's trailer. It's older, beige, much less fancy than the Airstream, though a bit larger—the trailer I saw them buying in Bishop back in May.

We knock on the door and after a moment, Sandy appears. She's wearing the same clothes she was this morning, though her sweater is on the right way around now. Her hair's still a mess, though, and the dark circles under her eyes have expanded.

"Have you found Petal?"

"No, I'm sorry. Not yet."

"What do you want, then?"

I smile gently, like I would to a startled animal, my hands in front of me, my tone soft. "We were wondering if we could see Petal's journal?"

"Her journal?"

"The notebook she carried around with her? I think she drew in it too?"

Sandy looks confused. "I don't . . . She was writing?"

"I think so."

"I didn't know that."

I clear my nervous throat. "Maybe I misunderstood, but I thought, if it was here, then maybe it might have some clues . . . some indication, of what she was thinking. Where she might have gone."

"Oh," Sandy says. "I . . . I don't know."

"Have you seen it around? It had a black cover."

"I . . . No."

"Could you look for it?"

She glances over her shoulder at the RV. "I can't."

"Maybe later?"

"No, I . . . You look, okay? I can't go through her things. I can't handle it."

"You don't mind us doing it?"

Her eyes track to mine. They're filled with tears. "Please. If it will help find her."

"Okay."

She steps out of the RV and pushes the door open wider, leaving space for us to go in.

Ben enters first and I follow, letting my eyes adjust to the light. The first thing I notice is a moldy, musty odor mixed in with some kind of cleaner. Bleach, maybe. Something strong for sure. Someone's cleaned this place fairly recently, but not necessarily today.

The walls are paneled dark wood, that fake plastic kind that you see in seventies basements, and the countertops are yellowed, chipped Formica. The place is messy, but not dirty, clothes and papers strewn about.

"What are we looking for?" Ben asks.

"Not sure. Petal's stuff, I guess. Wherever she might hide a diary."

"It feels weird going through someone else's things."

"I know."

We walk through the trailer slowly. Past the kitchen, dishes in the sink, the remains of a meal on the stove. Then the "living room," papers strewn over the table, the couches' cushions in disarray, and back to the bedroom. Here, there's more order. The bed is made with a pretty, light bedspread and there's a shelf of books along one wall.

"She hasn't washed the dishes," Ben says. "But she makes the bed."

"Habit?"

"Maybe. You smell that cleaner?"

"I do." I smile at him. "You're CSI now?"

"Just observing."

"You see anything else?"

He points to the wall. "This looks like Petal's closet."

I pull back the sliding door. Most of the hangers are empty. "You think that was full before?"

"No idea. Seems like she always wore the same thing to me."

I picture Petal in my mind. Long cutoff shorts. That sweater full of holes. I never paid much attention to what she was wearing. The pull of Petal was the contrast between her white-blond hair, her warm, brown skin, and her dark eyes. "Sandy said she didn't know if she took anything, right?"

"Seems like something she should be able to be more precise about."

"I don't know," I say. "If you're upset, then maybe you didn't pay that much attention to the details."

"I guess. Odd couple either way."

"Now that, I can agree with." I flick my hand through her clothes. Cheap things, old. They tell a story of Petal's life—where she came from, what was important to her. Clothes are a costume we put on every day to project a story about ourselves. Right now, I'm playing outdoorsy rescue-worker Cassie. Everyone buys it. But everyone bought put-together art gallery Cassandra, too.

"What about up here?" Ben says, standing next to me. He points to the shelf above. There's a battered box on it, the kind you carry documents around in. He reaches up and pulls it down. It's light in his hands. He puts it on the bed and opens the lid. There are some loose documents inside and the book we've been looking for—a black Moleskine journal. It has a daisy decal on the cover, with a petal trailing away. "That's like her tattoo."

"This is what you saw her with?"

"Yes, I think so."

He takes it out and opens it to the last entry. I read it over his shoulder, the hairs on the back of my neck rising high as I absorb the words.

Is Sandy controlling me? Is that why I'm with her? When I look at my life now, that's the only explanation I can think of. One minute I was taking a class in junior college, working toward something, and now I walk trails all day looking for someone I don't even know.

Sandy did this to me. But she's not going to get away with it.

"Shit," Ben says.

"Understatement."

Ben points to the words. "This looks bad." He takes out his phone. "I'm going to scan it so I can send it to Jenny right away."

"Just this page?"

"Let's do the whole thing. It won't take long."

"Okay, good idea."

I flip to the first page and he takes a photo, then another as I turn the pages slowly. The first entry is May 20, the same day I arrived in the park—that night when we saw each other in the Mobil. My eyes race over the words, some jumping out. *Cassie, money, hiding place, Smokey.*

"You're in here," Ben says.

"I see that. And you." I point to the entry that says: *I recognized the one couple from the Mobil the other night, only I'm not sure they're a couple. The girl is Cassie, and the cute guy is Ben.* "She thinks you're cute."

He smiles. "And you?"

"Definitely. Come on, let's get this finished." I flip the page and he photographs it, and then again, and again. It doesn't take long. When we're done, I close the diary and hold it in my hand. I'll show it to Sandy, make sure she's still okay with us taking it. "We should get back to the park."

"Yeah, okay." He turns and I follow him out of the trailer. When we step outside, Sandy's standing there, looking lost. But she's right here.

"Did you find anything?" she says.

I hold up the diary. "This. You okay with us taking it?"

For the first time, she looks wary. "What does it say in there?"

"We didn't have time to read it."

"Uh-huh."

"We can leave it, if you like."

"No, you take it. You find Petal." Her voice wavers, and the tears are back.

"If Petal isn't back by tomorrow morning, then we'll start the search officially."

"She won't be," Sandy says, then steps into the trailer and closes the door behind her.

"What is she not telling us?" Ben says.

"I don't know." I hold the diary up. "Maybe the explanation's in here?"

CHAPTER 26
EVERYWHERE YOU GO

Then

July

When we get back to the SAR site, it's after the usual group dinner. Mia's cleaning up, and Sam, George, and Gareth are seated around the fire ring without a bonfire lit, drinking beers. They're halfway through a case, which isn't unusual, and understandable in the current circumstances. It's the end of a long search, maybe right before another one is set to begin. If I didn't know I'd regret it, I'd chase down my own pain with as many beers as I could hold, too.

As it is, I grab a cup of stew that Mia was nice enough to save for me and Ben, and the night passes like many have this summer around the fire ring, beers clutched in fists, stars above. There's an odd sense of relief, like we've been through a war that's over. Even though the news about Petal is swirling around the park like a Santa Ana wind, it doesn't have the same intensity as Jada's disappearance did. The sad truth is no one will care as much about Petal missing as they did about Jim and Jada.

Maybe she isn't missing at all, Gareth theorizes. She drove to the park and left her car because she knew Sandy was tracking her. It's easy enough to hitchhike out. People do it all the time. They were fighting, Petal was upset about Jada. She'd just found out about Sandy's past. It stands to reason that she might choose this moment to leave.

Ben and I exchange glances across the fire ring. Those words in her diary about Sandy controlling her, how she wasn't going to let her get away with it . . . It's hard to forget them. It's just as likely Sandy did something to Petal before she could tell on her. And telling us that Petal's missing is the alibi she needs to get away with it.

Around eleven, the chat dies down and we trickle off to bed. Ben joins me in my tent and before long our clothes are off. We make love quietly, but I shouldn't call it that. I'm not in love with Ben. I'm attracted to him and I like and respect him, but this isn't love.

I don't know what he's feeling. We don't talk about it, just like we don't talk about Kevin, my past, any of it. This bed is a refuge that we enjoy, exploring each other, hands and tongues and skin. That release, the moment where all you can think of is the person touching you, inside of you. The one moment where I feel free.

When we're done, we snuggle down and fall asleep. Half the night passes away quietly, but then the scratching branches penetrate my dreams and turn them dark. I'm in bed with someone and it feels illicit. I can't see their face at first, but their hands are familiar. I've been with this person before, maybe long ago. Unease builds within me as I start to think it's Kevin. A man I *was* in love with who turned sour and angry. For so long I thought it was my fault, that I'd done something to flip him from the charming, solicitous gentleman into the snarling, abusive husband.

But it wasn't my fault. And these hands on me in the dream, they're not Kevin's.

They're Chris's.

"Cassie?"

There's another hand on me, but this one's alive, pulling me out of my dream, shaking me awake. Ben.

I open my eyes slowly.

"Cassie?"

"Yes?"

"Were you having a nightmare?"

"I . . ." I sit up slowly. It's dawn, the morning light trickling in through the tent walls. My medallion hangs between my breasts, and I clutch it, centering myself. "Yes, I think so."

"You okay?"

"Sure." I look at him. He's cradling his phone. "Sorry if I disturbed you."

"It's fine. I couldn't sleep and . . . I've been reading Petal's diary."

I run my hands through my hair, trying to shake away the images, the memories. "Should you be doing that?"

"I don't know, but look, see what I found." He hands me the phone. It's opened to an entry from June, a few days after Smokey was put in custody. I read it, my eyes scanning her handwriting easily.

"They went to the cave?" I say, my mouth dry.

"Yeah, and I was thinking . . . Smokey. His cave. We never looked for Jada and Jim there."

"Smokey's cave?"

"Yeah," Ben says. "It would be a good hiding place. It's off the trail, dry . . ."

My throat is parched. I reach for my water bottle on the nightstand and take a drink. "But why would Jada and Jim want to hide?"

"Maybe that's the wrong word. I don't know. Remember in Jada's last Instagram post? Didn't she say something about seeing Smokey?"

"I . . . Yeah, I think she did."

"She did. Look here, see?" He taps at his phone, then shows me Jada's Instagram page. The post with the map. I reread the entry.

Maybe we'll see Smokey!

#JadaandJimForever #FeelingFree #IntoTheWild #SmokeyIsFree

"What are you thinking?" I ask Ben.

"Maybe that's where they went instead of where they were supposed to go? And Smokey was there. He was re-released, right? Maybe he went back there, or another bear was in the cave and things went badly."

I feel sick to my stomach. This has literally never occurred to me before. "You don't think he could be dangerous, do you?"

"He's a wild animal. If he feels threatened, he could do something. Even after the retraining."

"We could ask the wildlife services. He's being tracked. They'd know if he went there."

"Good point." He takes the phone back from me and sends a text. "We should go."

"To the cave?"

"We've looked everywhere else," Ben says. His hair is mussed, stubble on his chin. "Sometimes you have to follow your instincts."

"You want to go now?"

"You got something better to do?"

"I . . . No, I guess I don't." I start to get up, but Ben doesn't follow me. "What is it?"

"I found something else in the diary." He rubs at his face. "Sandy had money hidden in the trailer. Like, a lot of money."

"Where?"

"In their mattress, if you can believe it."

"I wonder if it's still there?"

"I'm guessing not. But that could be why Sandy was so upset. If Petal took it."

"Why not tell us about it?"

"It must be from something criminal."

"But why tell us that Petal was missing if she just ran off with the money?"

He shakes his head. "Several possibilities. Maybe, when she saw the car left in the park, she felt like she had to. Or maybe she was trying to cover her tracks. I mean, if she did something to Petal, then she's not acting rationally, right?"

I think about what he's saying as I get dressed. I grab a pair of shorts, because it's going to be hot, and my yellow SAR T-shirt. I run a brush through my hair and catch Ben watching me. "What is it?"

"You said another man's name."

"What?"

He tucks his head down. "When you were sleeping. That nightmare. You said 'Chris.' "

"I did?"

"Yeah."

"That's weird."

"What were you dreaming about?"

I pull a hair tie through my hair and double it over. "I never remember my dreams."

"That's lucky."

"Is it?"

His phone beeps. He checks it. "Smokey's not in the area."

"That's something, at least."

"So, will you go with me to the cave?"

I don't feel like I have any choice but to agree. "Yes."

He smiles. "Great. Give me ten and let's meet at the firepit."

"Sounds good. Can you forward me the diary in the meantime?"

"Why?"

"Four eyes are better than one. Maybe I'll notice something you didn't."

"Sure." He taps at his phone as he gets out of bed. "Wait. I don't have your number."

"Oh, right." I take his phone from him and put it in. "Now you do."

He looks at his phone. "And sent."

My phone beeps on the nightstand as he leaves. I pick it up. Ben's text is the only new message.

In all the chaos, I haven't thought about Kevin and the texts, what it all might mean. I need some time to stop and sit and think things through, but I'm not going to have that. Instead, I push him away and flip through the photographs of Petal's diary on my rudimentary phone until I get to the entry that made Ben think he knew where Jim and Jada were. I read it slowly, trying to absorb the details, but I can't help thinking the whole time that this is a mistake. That I'll regret it as I have so many things.

Oh, Petal. What have you done?

CHAPTER 27

INTO THE LION'S DEN

Then

July

It's a four-mile hike to Smokey's cave, nothing strenuous, as we often hike ten or more miles in a day. It's still early, just after eight, and my stomach is rumbling because I didn't eat anything before we started out. I should've, but I couldn't get anything down. Even though Smokey's signal shows him far from here and no other bears in the area, this whole thing is a terrible idea.

Ben is walking ahead of me, and I watch his back as he hikes. There are so many emotions swirling through me. Dread, sadness, fear, doubt. I've done my best to compartmentalize all of it, but the walls I've built are fraying. I could so easily turn around and run back down the trail and out of this park. But I already tried running, and this is where I ran to. So instead, I force myself to move along the trail until I catch up to Ben.

"Can I ask you a favor?" I say.

He glances back at me. "Sure."

"Talk to me. I need the distraction."

"Okay." He motions for me to come up next to him. The trail

is wide enough for us to walk two abreast. "Where do you think her money came from?"

"Sandy's money?"

"Yeah."

"A robbery?"

"Drugs, more likely," Ben says.

"Why do you say that?"

"What else has an illegal cash component to it?"

"She doesn't seem like the type, though."

"What type is that?"

"Are there that many drug-dealing women in their fifties?" I ask.

"Not on TV, anyway. Except for Smurf."

"Who?"

"From *Animal Kingdom*. She's the matriarch of a crime family."

"Is she blue?"

"What? No. She's played by Ellen Barkin."

I sigh. "Why are we talking about this?"

"You said you wanted me to talk."

"I did." I check the trail ahead. It looks like every other trail in the park. Dirt and rocks, trees and grass. "Do you remember where the turn is?"

"Yeah, I remember." He stops and takes his canteen off his hip. He holds it out. "Have some water."

"I'm okay."

"You look pale."

I want to argue, but it's easier to take the water and drink it down. My hand rattles on the container and I concentrate on steadying it. I take a long, cool drink, then hand it back to him as my radio crackles.

"SAR Peters, go ahead."

"SAR Peters, this is Sierra 1," Jenny says. "Petal Fernandez has not returned this morning and we're now treating her as missing."

"Understood, over."

"We're sending a quick team up the Polly Dome Lakes Trail. Her car was parked at the bottom of it."

"Copy that."

"All hands meeting at nineteen hundred if she doesn't turn up."

"Roger. SAR Peters out."

I look at Ben. "Fuck."

"Yeah."

"We don't have to do this," he says. "We can go back."

"No, we've come this far. Let's keep going."

The trail is narrower now, and he motions for me to go ahead, giving my arm a squeeze as I pass. We walk a few more minutes and then Ben points to the cutoff—a scar in the trees that must've been widened when they brought Smokey out. I take the turn and pick my way through the woods. We haven't seen anyone this morning. Some days are like that, life taking a respite.

"Keep to the left," Ben says, pointing to a small fork in the path. "We went the wrong way the first time."

I follow his directions, pushing tree branches out of my way, holding them so they won't snap in Ben's face. Each footfall feels heavier, harder to take.

"Should we call out for them?" I ask.

"Not a bad idea." He cups his hand around his mouth. "Jada! Jim!" His voice echoes away and then is muffled by the trees. He tries a few more times, but nothing comes back to him except the wind. "It's just up here." He walks ahead of me, pushing a particularly thick bush out of the way. We enter a small clearing, the mouth of the cave half-obscured by hanging moss in front of us, backing onto a higher cliff promontory. We stop, listening. It's deadly quiet. I can hear Ben breathing next to me and the sound of my heart pumping in my ears.

"Should we go in?"

"Okay."

We walk abreast. Ben pulls a flashlight out and turns it on, shining it into the opening. He reaches up and pulls the moss aside. The smell of something hits me then, something rotten, fetid.

"Ben . . . Be careful."

"I know."

I reach for his free hand, holding it tight as I take my own flashlight out of my pocket. We take a step inside together, our lights bouncing off the closed-in walls. I suck in my breath, expecting to find a form on the ground. The source of the smell.

But there's nothing. The cave is empty.

Well, almost.

Huddled back against the far end are three dry bags, rolled up tight, a bright red rain slicker, and a sweater I'd recognize anywhere. I walk toward it slowly and hold it up. It's loose and full of holes, the same sweater I've seen Petal wearing all summer.

"What have you got there?"

I turn around, holding it away from my body. "This is Petal's."

"She was here."

"She was here."

"When, though?"

"I can't remember the last time I saw her in it." I pick up the rain slicker. It's a larger size, one that could fit a woman or a man. I search the pockets. In the lefthand side there's something hard and sharp. "Ouch."

"You okay?"

"Something stuck me." I take out the object. It's a name tag with a pin holder on the back. I suck my finger as I turn it over.

Oh shit.

"Sandy," Ben says, taking it from me.

"She works in a store," I say. "In town. I saw her there a couple of days ago, wearing a name tag like this."

"This one exactly?"

"I . . . it could just be similar. If she lost this one . . ."

Ben nods, then shines his flashlight on the dry bags. "Wonder what's in there?"

Ben steps closer and shines his flashlight around. It catches a stain on the wall. Something brown, rusty.

"Is that . . . blood?" I ask, my voice shaking.

"I . . . Maybe?"

I feel queasy, and walk out of the cave and into the sunlight.

Sandy's name tag, Petal's sweater. *Blood.* I'm having trouble breathing.

"There's this, too," Ben says. I turn slowly. He's holding one of the dry bags, a waterproof cylinder made of thick canvas that climbers use to keep things dry. And even though it's sealed up tight, I can smell the odor from here.

"What's in there?"

"Not sure."

"Maybe we shouldn't open it?"

But he doesn't listen to me. Instead, he puts it on the ground and starts to undo the top clip, then the drawstrings. He works it open then turns his head away suddenly. "God, that's awful." The smell is so strong I think I might retch. He holds the bag away from him and turns it upside down. Nothing comes out so he shakes it. Rotting food slides out. Part of a sandwich. Two putrefied apples. And what looks like feces. "What the hell?"

The smell hits me again and I rush to some bushes, hunching over as my body heaves but nothing comes out. Then Ben is behind me, his hand on my back, rubbing.

"Are you okay?"

"No."

"Just breathe. The smell will dissipate."

I breathe in through my nose while Ben rubs my back. Eventually the feeling passes, my stomach unclenches, the smell seeps out of my nostrils, though it hasn't retreated far. I stand up slowly. "I'm not built for this."

"It's okay. No one is."

"I don't think that's true." I turn to face him. His face is pale, but he's more composed than me. "We need to report this."

"Yes."

"What . . . what do you think it means?"

"I don't know. Someone was staying here, and it must've been recently because Smokey would've torn those bags up."

"Sandy and Petal?"

"I don't think so. The rotting food . . . that's been here longer than a couple of days."

"So, someone else."

"Right, but who?"

Ben rubs his hand over his face. "Jada and Jim?"

"But why?" I clench my hands together. "And where did they go?"

"It could've been someone else. Someone on the run, maybe. Or a vagrant. People do strange things all the time."

"Yeah. But Petal was here—" I stop myself. "And this was Smokey's cave," I remind him. "Jada and Petal came here before."

"Maybe that's when Petal left the sweater?"

"I'm almost certain I've seen her in it since then. And if those bags had been there—wouldn't they have looked in them? She'd have written about it in her diary—in that entry about them finding the cave. I read it this morning. There's nothing about that."

"Right. And Sandy's name tag. I guess Petal could've brought it? Maybe that's her rain jacket?"

"It doesn't make any sense."

"Yeah." Ben sighs and runs his hands through his hair. "We should head back and talk to Jenny. They're going to want to send a team out here. And the police might want to . . . if that *is* blood on the wall . . ."

"What a mess."

"Not our problem now, I don't think," Ben says.

But yes, it is our problem. *Mine.*

"Ready?" Ben asks.

I nod, and we walk back down the path, each step pulling us farther away from the reality we just uncovered. Something bad happened in that cave, and now Petal is missing, adding to the total of lost people in the park. The search will start up again, maybe more intense than before.

And how many other rotten things will it uncover?

And Now a White Girl

Transcript of YouTube Video by CriminalMind

CriminalMind:

Y'all, I told you so. I feel bad bragging about being right about this, but I *knew* that Jada wasn't just "missing."

She and Jim did NOT walk off some trail and get hurt and lost and just die out there, no matter what the official line is. No.

If they were missing, why weren't they found? All those people looking for them? All those searchers?

I don't buy it.

And now we come to find out that Jim hit her? In public? Nah.

Jim did something to her and he's hiding her out there in the woods, I'm certain.

At least I was until this white girl went missing. Petal. And before you start slamming me in the comments, yeah, I know she's half Latina. Bitch, please. Her name is *Petal* and her hair is *blond*. You think the media's going to be parsing out her genetics?

She's white for all intents and purposes. For my intents and purposes.

Because hell yeah, I have an agenda. I'm here to expose how we get treated versus how *they* get treated. It shouldn't matter what someone looks like if they're missing. It should all be the same. The same amount of effort no matter how much melanin they have in their skin. And the fact that it isn't needs to be called out. So many missing Black and Brown girls that have *never* been found and *never* will be, either, because no one cares.

And don't go telling me Jada got plenty of attention. I already spoke on that. It's because of Jim and his Trump-loving daddy that we even knew she was gone.

So yeah, I'm good as hell, as Queen Lizzo says.

Okay, so, now that I got my rant out of the way, what the hell is going on in Yosemite, y'all? This Petal girl, this *flower*, she was Jada's friend. Did she know something? Did she *see* something? Is Jim following all this out there in his hiding place? Did he come and get her?

Wait, wait, wait. Hold on. I see you in the comments talking about someone named Sandy. Who's that? Oh, the girlfriend. That older lady who got in a fight with Jim?

You think she had something to do with this?

So what that she has a criminal record? Give me a break. 93% of violence against women comes from men, okay? Sandy isn't a perp, she's a *victim*. Jim hit *her*.

I'm not buying this. Not one bit.

It's just a matter of time before they find Jim. *Alive.*

You'll see.

ANOTHER WOMAN GOES MISSING IN YOSEMITE

The Young Woman Was Friends with Jada Johnson

BY Charlie McMaster

July 25 · 8:58 a.m. PST

Cape Cod—Just days after the formal search for Jada Johnson and Jim Carlisle was called off, a third individual, Petal Fernandez, 23, has gone missing from the Tuolumne Meadows area of Yosemite. Some have assumed that these two events are connected, but that might not be what's at play here. Our in-depth investigation has revealed numerous startling and previously unreported facts about Ms. Fernandez and her domestic partner, Sandy Cramer, 54, which may shed light on her disappearance.

According to Ms. Fernandez's father, Alonzo, 50, Petal was a troubled teen who was "always getting into problems over one thing or another." Her mother, Josephine, abandoned her at ten and she "got real angry and mean afterwards," a former classmate claims. After a few brushes with the juvenile authorities, she dropped out of high school, though she later obtained her GED. She worked for a few years as a waitress and at other odd jobs, but eventually decided to return to school. She was turning her life around, Mr. Fernandez says, before she met Ms. Cramer. "She was taking a course at the community college, about writing and things like that. She was real creative. But then she met that woman."

Ms. Cramer, who also goes by the name Alexandra Curry, has a sordid past. She was known to authorities in Florida and was believed to have been a mid-level drug mule in one of Miami's illegal drug importation businesses. She was facing numerous criminal charges for trafficking and wire fraud—charges that are still pending—when she made a deal to cooperate with the authorities.

"She was scheduled to testify before a grand jury," Detective Theodopolous told us. The grand jury had been impaneled to indict the Munoz crime family. "But she disappeared a few days before her court date."

The reason she left before she could testify can only be speculated at. "She was in business with some hardened criminals who didn't take kindly to their employees turning witness," Detective Theodopolous told us. "Frankly, I assumed she was dead, left in a swamp somewhere," he said in an unguarded moment. "Wouldn't be the first time."

But Ms. Cramer was not in a swamp. Instead, she packed her things and drove north, eventually getting to Cape Cod, where she met Ms. Fernandez in a gay bar in Provincetown.

"Things happened real quick after that," Mr. Fernandez said. "I didn't like her, and I made that plain to Petal. But that girl would never listen to me. She was going to find her mama, she thought, taking to the road like that."

Ms. Fernandez and Ms. Cramer left Cape Cod almost two years ago, when Petal was 21. For the next two years, they led a nomadic life, driving across the country and not stopping anywhere for long. Petal called her father sporadically and didn't seem to have left many friends behind.

Ms. Kathryn Newton, 23, went to high school with Petal and had an on-again, off-again friendship with her over the years, said that "she stayed in touch some from the road. We'd exchange DMs on Insta sometimes." Ms. Newton showed me these messages, short exchanges with a user who went by the handle LifeisLife. "That was Petal's favorite expression. Don't know why."

The last time Ms. Newton heard from Ms. Fernandez was six months ago, long before she reached Yosemite. She didn't speak much about her relationship with Ms. Cramer, but Ms. Fernandez gave her the impression that things were not always rosy.

"She had a temper, I think. Petal never said anything directly, that wasn't her way. But she told me a couple of stories that made me think that. No, I don't remember the details, sorry."

Beyond the pending drug charges, Ms. Cramer has two prior arrests for domestic incidents. We tried to track down her former domestic partner without success.

But a search for the handle "LifeisLife" on the internet turned up several posts on SHELTER ME, a domestic violence survivor's website where users can post anonymously and receive support from other victims. While the site claims to provide complete anonymity, its infrastructure is not what it should be. Upon investigation, several of LifeisLife's posts were geolocated to the same locations where that Instagram user had posted pictures in the same time frames.

LifeisLife did not post any details of abuse herself, but she did comment on several posts.

LifeisLife did also appear to be "shitposting" on several of Ms. Johnson's Instagram posts, particularly the ones about her crusade to save the bear known as Smokey. "Shitposting" is the increasingly common practice of trolling people's posts online, often without a purpose. It is unclear why Ms. Fernandez was making such posts on Ms. Johnson's Instagram when, by all accounts, they were friends.

During the course of our investigation, we were able to obtain a copy of Ms. Fernandez's diary, which had been turned over to the police by Ms. Cramer. An analysis was performed comparing the speech style of Ms. Fernandez's Instagram posts, the posts in the domestic abuse forum, and the diary, confirming they were likely written by the same person.

The diary itself gives few clues as to where Ms. Fernandez might be. It doesn't speak of abuse directly—though she and Ms. Cramer appear to have had a volatile and controlling relationship. It does, however, indicate that Ms. Cramer had a large stash of money in their home. Ms. Fernandez and Ms. Cramer had also been arguing about Ms. Cramer's apparent indifference to Ms. Johnson's disappearance, who Ms. Fernandez had befriended over the summer.

Sources also tell us that evidence found in a cave about three miles from Tuolumne Meadows indicates that Ms. Fernandez might've spent at least one night there. But in the days since that information was found, there haven't been any other signs of her despite a renewed search of the area.

Did Ms. Fernandez decide to leave Ms. Cramer of her own volition? It would be a relief to all if this turned out to be true. But many also fear that something darker is at work. As previously reported, Ms. Cramer had a physical altercation with Jim Carlisle the night before his disappearance, which is being seen in a new light given Ms. Fernandez's subsequent disappearance.

"I don't know what Ms. Cramer might do if she felt she was cornered," Detective Theodopolous said. "Anyone in danger has the potential to be dangerous themselves."

Anyone with information on the matter is asked to contact the police immediately.

CHAPTER 28

THE LOVELY BONES

Now

W here did they find him?" I ask Ben. "Jim?"

"It was near Smokey's cave."

"How near?"

"About a mile away. Deeper into the woods. Someone was camping off-trail and their dog got away from them. He came back with a bone."

"Oh."

"Yeah. It was pretty stripped, but there was some clothing attached."

"When did this happen?"

"It was called in yesterday."

I breathe out slowly. I'd left two days ago, or was it three now? I don't even know what time it is anymore.

"The bones are being transported to the medical examiner now."

"What about Jada? Or Petal?"

"No sign of them."

I close my eyes for a moment, feeling relieved. "Do they have an idea of how he died?"

"Unclear, but they said his hyoid bone was snapped."

"What's that?"

Ben points to his neck. "It's a bone in here. Apparently, when someone's strangled, it often breaks."

"Strangled?"

"Yes, though that's not the only explanation for a broken hyoid bone, from what I read online."

I grimace. "That's a gruesome search."

"I had time to kill."

"Bad choice of words."

"Sorry."

I swallow down my fear. "So, he was strangled?"

"Not necessarily. It can happen from other kinds of injuries. Usually in sports if someone gets hit in the neck in a certain way. It could be a fall. Or an animal could have broken it during . . . well, you know."

"How terrible."

Ben's face is grim. "Yeah. The medical examiner will figure it out, I guess."

"Can they tell when he died?"

"Must've been weeks ago from what I understand. But they'll be able to date that better in the postmortem."

I try to imagine it. His bones spread out on a table. Clothes and flesh still clinging to it. Combing over it to gather evidence. Was the same thing happening to Kevin?

"What happens now?" I ask.

"The area's going to be searched again for Jada. Cadaver dogs, the whole nine."

"If Jim's been dead for weeks . . ."

Ben rubs at his chin. "Yeah."

"Maybe there's someone out there in the park . . . Like a killer. A serial killer?" I say.

"It's possible. It's happened before."

"A long time ago."

"Evil doesn't expire."

"Believe me, I know." I hug myself. Is Jim's death the result of evil? Is Kevin's?

"Are you feeling better?"

"In the circumstances."

"It's been a rough couple of days."

I nod slowly. "How did you find me? In the woods. You and Gareth and the helicopter?"

"We were able to ping your phone."

"My phone?"

"Yeah. You gave me the number, remember?"

I didn't remember giving him my number. I thought I'd only given that number to my mom and . . . "Oh, my mom."

"She's been very worried."

"Where is she?"

"She's at home. Bri's with her."

"I should call her. Did you call her?"

"Yes, I let her know you were okay."

"Thank you."

Ben takes a beat, then asks, "Cassie, what was Kevin doing here?"

My throat closes up, the *BOOM!* of the gun echoing in my ears again. "I can't, Ben. I . . . That's how I ended up here. I couldn't get through it, even with Eric and that policewoman."

"Maybe it would be easier to tell me?"

I turn my head away and look at the wall. "Jenny thinks I should have a lawyer."

"She does?"

"I should have one, probably. I . . . I killed him."

"Because he was going to hurt you?"

"I can't . . . Please don't ask again."

"Okay, I won't."

I shift my body so I can see his face. I try to smile, but I don't quite make it. "Thank you. This is all such a mess."

"Yeah." He sighs. "Do you think . . . Could it have been him? Kevin?"

"Who hurt Jim you mean?"

"Yes."

"I . . . Why would he do that?"

"He hurt you, didn't he?"

"He was mean, he had a temper . . . He'd explode sometimes, and a couple of times he hit me, but . . . I, I don't think he could do something like that. Just kill someone he didn't even know."

"People can do all kinds of things when they feel threatened."

"I know, Ben."

"What if he was jealous? Did he get that way?"

"Yes. He was always thinking I was with someone I wasn't. If I looked at a man, or a man looked at me . . . It was all in his head, but that's when he'd get violent. Wait, why are you asking that?"

"Is it possible that he was here before Jim and Jada went missing? That he was stalking you?"

"I don't know."

"What if he was here? What if he found you a while back and he came here? What if his jealousy got the better of him?"

I think over what he's saying, and though my mind's confused, I know this isn't the answer. "No, Ben. He didn't hurt Jim."

"Why are you so sure?"

"Because if he was here, if he was watching me, it wouldn't be Jim dead. It would be you."

CHAPTER 29

AUGUST IS THE CRUELEST MONTH

Then

August

More than a week into the search for Petal, everyone and everything feels broken.

The team is tired and down. Even Gareth, usually so bright and sunny, is downcast, falling asleep during meetings and drinking silently by the firepit at night. Mia looks worried, Ben has dark circles under his eyes, and I haven't looked in the mirror for days.

We were already burned out from the search for Jada and Jim, our resources and energies exhausted. People only have so much attention span for tragedies.

I'd thought about that every once in a while, the ten years I was away. When someone would go missing or a war would start and the world would be behind it, watching, the twenty-four-hour news cycle churning out slogans and images and hashtags. Everyone changing their Twitter handles to words of encouragement and flags—I'd be waiting. Waiting for that moment when interest would start to wane and the world would turn away. When the bios would be changed for some new cause. Because it's not sustainable. Only the families can keep their hope in place until the lost are returned, and even then, only some of them do. Some families just give up and move on. Not from the hurt, but from the daily grind of it, and who can blame them? You can't live if you don't let go of the past. And if you don't let go, then one death causes others, causes too many.

And so it proves this time, too. The media is here, but there are fewer of them. Second stringers. Not those famous, large faces with too much makeup and out-of-place suits, but those on the come up, wearing puffy vests and doing their own hair and lighting. It's grittier, more raw. A once-a-day report rather than hourly, breaking news.

Resources are pulled back. The valley teams don't come and help this time. The only new thing is a search and rescue dog, who's given a scent of Petal's sweater and starts off along the trail near the cave with great enthusiasm. But then it gets to a river crossing and the trail stops. Like she disappeared or floated downstream. Like she was never there at all.

Sandy tells the police that the red rain jacket is Petal's, that she never went to that cave, that she wouldn't have had any idea how to find it and that she doesn't know how her work name tag got in the pocket, but she was always leaving them around.

But then I remember about the ham radio, how Petal said she'd listen to it, and when the police come to question Sandy in her trailer, it's still tuned to our channel—and they find a map of Yosemite, with Smokey's cave marked on it like it was a treasure map. She stopped talking after that, Jenny tells us, telling the police and Eric to leave her alone until they find Petal.

The forensic team examines the dry bags we found; they inventory food, some other supplies, and then some items of clothing that also appear to belong to Sandy—a pair of jeans, a hat. The potential blood on the wall and the other contents of the dry bags are sent away for DNA analysis, but that will take weeks and weeks. Maybe months. It won't become a priority unless someone finds a body, maybe not even then.

The headlines are lurid, but they don't solve anything. It's becoming more and more likely that it's Sandy's fault Petal is gone. Whether that's because she did something to her, or because Petal finally had enough, is anyone's guess at this point.

Or maybe not. Maybe Jenny and Eric know something they aren't telling me. I'm not part of that arm of the investigation, where they discuss theories with the police.

Sandy was arrested two days ago, held for extradition back to Florida. The papers carry a picture of her as she's being loaded into the sheriff's car, her hands cuffed behind her back, her head hanging low. She looks broken and lost.

At night, while Ben sleeps, I read Petal's diary, trying to make sense of the entries. She's different on paper, but so many of us are. Most people don't go around revealing their inner thoughts to everyone they meet. It occurs to me that I don't know Petal. I only know what she wanted me to, just like everyone only knows what I want them to know about me.

Even an open book has pages that can't be read.

The days trickle by, searching for someone who might not be lost, waiting for something to change, for something to break.

Nothing does, and now it's August. The days are hot, the air dry, and there's a forest fire fifty miles from here that brings smoke into the park, hanging low in the valley, tingeing the air, irritating the eye.

It's contained for now, but it's hard to fence in a fire. It can spread quickly, without warning.

All it will take is one misplaced spark.

When I wake up on the second day of August, I'm wearier than when I went to bed. When I couldn't sleep, I spent the night rereading online articles about Petal's disappearance on Ben's phone. Yosemite is a good place to disappear, more than one of them notes, and then they ask themselves the same questions, ones that have become almost rhetorical at this point.

What was Petal doing on the website for abused women? Was she abused by Sandy? Did she ever talk about that with Jada? Is that what they bonded over? Why was she posting on Jada's page anonymously? What was the point of any of it?

I pull back the covers and rise, leaving Ben asleep. They're probably going to call off the search today. With Sandy arrested and the scent grown cold, there isn't anything to go on. Life will move on, the scrutiny will diminish, and that's a good thing.

I take a shower and get dressed, then head to the small grocery store to get some supplies.

And that's when I see him, waiting in the parking lot next to a nondescript car like he was looking for me.

Chris.

"What are you doing here?" I ask, feeling nervous and off-kilter. He's wearing khaki pants and a short-sleeved shirt. His arms are tanned and strong, his hands roughened. His eyes are shaded by a pair of sunglasses, but when he sees me, he pushes them up onto the top of his head. He's tired, not sleeping. Like me.

"I was looking for you."

"Why?"

"Because I wanted to know why you came back. Why you were looking for me in town last week?"

I try to push past him, but he grabs my arm. "Let me go."

"No. Cassie, talk to me."

I look him in the eye. I don't think Chris would hurt me, but what do I know? I've proven myself a terrible judge of character time and again. "Please let go. You're hurting me."

Chris's eyes widen in shock, and he releases my arm. "I'm so sorry."

"It's all right."

"No, no it isn't. I'm not . . . I'm not a violent man."

"I know."

"No, you don't. Everyone thinks . . . Everything thinks I left her there on purpose. That I could do that to someone I loved."

I can't lie. That word hurts. "Love."

"Cassie."

"You didn't love her."

"I did."

"Then what were you doing with *me?*"

His eyes widen, like I'm telling him something he didn't know, when of course he did. He was there. A participant. The initiator, even.

It started on a climb on Cathedral Peak when I was nineteen. I hadn't gone to college like most of my classmates because I couldn't settle on what I wanted to do. Instead, I'd spent a year bumming around my mother's house and hanging with climbers. That day, I was trying to solo, and so was Chris. We hadn't planned to be there together, but that sort of thing happened all the time. I'd done plenty of unplanned climbs with Chris and Cameron, and sometimes her friend, Natalie, who wasn't as good as them.

That day it was just Chris. We decided to climb together, and we'd made good time. But then, near the peak, a storm came in suddenly, and we got stuck. It was too dangerous to go down, so we sheltered together for the night, waiting for the storm to pass as the wind whipped against our tent.

We huddled together for warmth, and talked to distract ourselves, and then our hormones took over. We were teenagers—that's my defense. Stupid teenagers who didn't think about hurting other people. So when Chris touched his hand to my face and the world quieted down, I responded. I clung to him. I let him peel off my clothes and explore my body and I loved every second of it.

In the morning, when the storm cleared, I was happy and he was guilty. It had been a mistake, he'd said. We never should've done it.

His guilt was contagious and leeched away everything good I was feeling. We couldn't tell anyone what had happened. He loved Cameron and he wanted to be with her. She'd never forgive him if anyone knew about this.

"Promise me, Cassie," he said, sounding desperate. "Promise me you won't tell."

I promised, and we broke camp and made our way down the mountain.

Bri was there when I got down. He was happy to see me and tut-tutted that we hadn't checked the weather properly, that we'd left it so late. And Bri could sense that something had happened between us. He was the only one paying attention. He asked me later if I had something to tell him, but I kept my promise.

That was early July. I thought that would be it. That Chris would go back to Cameron, and I'd go back to dreaming about getting out of Mammoth. The end.

But it wasn't. Two nights later, Chris scratched at my first-floor window. His hair was wet from a run, his clothes clinging to him, soaking in sweat, and he didn't even have to say anything. I didn't even *let* him say anything, just hauled him inside and into my bed.

It happened every night after that. Late, after midnight, he'd go for a run to purge his thoughts and he'd end up at my house, in my bed, then leave before dawn. It started to consume me. All day long, all I did was think about him. All night long, all we did was explore each other for hours on end until a rising day dragged him away from me.

We never talked about why he came back. Or Cameron. Or what was going on between us. I could tell he didn't want to discuss it, and I was too scared to break the spell.

And then it was fall. Cameron and Chris were going away to college. I kept waiting for Chris to say something—that he wasn't leaving, that I meant something to him—but he didn't. He just circled the date on the calendar that hung on my bedroom wall, so I knew that was the day we'd be over.

That last night together was so intense that even now, if I think about it, my cheeks blush. I've never been like that with another man. Not the boys I fumbled around with in college, not Kevin, even at the height of our passion. Not Ben. He unlocked something in me that I couldn't ever recapture.

I don't know if it was the same for him.

I just know that he got up as the sky turned pink and didn't even say goodbye.

"That was a long time ago," I say, blinking away the memory.

"You think that matters?"

He looks around, suddenly worried that someone might hear us. "Is there somewhere we can go to talk?"

I don't want to have this conversation, but I motion for him to follow me to a picnic table that's farther away than the others. We sit across from each other and it's strange. He's just a man, the boy I loved grown up. His face is wan and his hair is browner, and there's something in his eyes I don't like. Something dark.

"What do you want to talk to me about Chris?"

"I said, why are you here?"

"I needed a job."

"Here?"

"I . . . It was what I could do."

"You couldn't apply to another park? You had to come here?"

"*You're* here."

"Is that why you came?"

"No!" I lower my voice. "I didn't even know that you were in Mammoth. I wasn't thinking about you when I made the decision."

His mouth twists. "Why don't I believe you?"

"Nothing in my life now has anything to do with you."

"But you came to see me."

Something in me twists. I don't remember Chris like this. Selfish. Thinking that my whole world still revolved around him after everything? Or maybe he was always like this. Maybe he was always exactly like this. "I was . . . I don't know. Curious."

"We promised to stay away from each other."

We'd sworn it like some vow, like it was sacred. But what was between us wasn't sacred, it was terrible. The two of us together did a terrible thing.

"A lot has happened since then."

"I know."

"What do you mean?"

"I . . . I followed you," he says.

"You followed me?"

His hands flutter. "Not like that. I kept tabs on you. I wanted to make sure you were keeping up your end of the bargain."

"My end of the bargain?"

"That you wouldn't tell."

"I've never told anyone."

"Someone told those newspapers."

I stare at him. He looks tortured, not that different than the last time we saw each other, furtively, hiding in the woods outside of town. "It was Natalie," I say.

"What?"

"Cameron told Natalie. She bragged about it to me once, early in the search. Like she was competing with me, telling me she knew Cameron better. That's how everyone knew. That's how it ended up in the papers."

"If it was Natalie, she'd own it. She'd want the credit."

I pull in a deep breath. "No. She was afraid of me. I made sure she wouldn't tell."

"What are you talking about?" He pulls back from me in horror. "What did you do?"

"I protected us."

"You threatened her?"

"I told her to keep her mouth shut."

He shakes his head and I look away from him. There's a crowd now in the parking lot, people pulling up for their day hikes. Everyone's dressed much the same and that's why he stands out—a man out of place. A man searching for something.

And this time, I don't need to worry whether it's him or some trick of my imagination.

I know.

CHAPTER 30
RUN

Then

August

I duck and turn away.

"What are you doing?" Chris asks. He's looking at me like I've lost my mind.

"Keep your voice down." I move off the bench, keeping low, heading toward the side of the building near us.

Chris follows behind me. "Where are you going?"

"Shh!"

"Cassie, tell me what's happening right now."

I get to the side of the building and press myself against it. I pull Chris next to me so he's hidden from the parking lot. "I don't want that person to see me."

"Who?"

"Kevin." I glance at him. "My . . . My ex."

"What the fuck?"

"He's looking for me, okay?" I edge toward the corner of the building, pulling my ball cap low. I can see a small part of the parking lot. Two families at a picnic table eating lunch. An older couple consulting a map, each of them pointing a different way.

And Kevin, looking casual in a pair of dark jeans and a short-sleeved shirt, but watchful, scanning the lot, looking for something. Looking for me.

"Let's go," I say, taking Chris by the hand and rushing to the back of the building.

"Where are we going?"

"To the SAR site."

"But my car's back there."

"You can come get it later."

"Cassie, stop."

"Shh! Please don't use my name." I push a tree branch out of the way, then pause to get my bearings. Maybe the SAR site isn't the best idea. If Kevin's in the park, that might be his next port of call. But what's he doing here? What does he want?

"What's going on?"

I turn to face Chris. He looks enough like the boy I used to love that it tugs at my heart. But that girl is gone, and she needs to stay that way. "He's been looking for me. He's . . . abusive. I left him. I ran away."

His face creases with concern. "He wants to hurt you?"

"I don't know. But I don't . . ."

"Cassie, if you don't want to see him, just tell him that."

"It's not that simple."

"Why not?"

I shake my head. "You don't understand. You don't know what he does."

"So tell me."

"I can't, okay? Not here. Not now." I look around me again, trying to decide where I can go that Kevin won't find me immediately. It's not a rational reaction, this fear that if I see him, then I won't be able to control the consequences—but it's not irrational, either.

"Cassie."

"What?"

"I want to help you."

I close my eyes, my body feels limp. If only I'd made a million different decisions, then maybe that would be possible. Maybe I could reach out to this man and he could help me find a path out of here. But that ship sailed a long time ago, and I'm the one who put it out to sea. "Thank you, but . . . No. I'll be okay. Just go back to your car."

"I'm not going to leave you here."

"I won't be here for long."

"What does *that* mean?"

"Nothing. I . . ." I stop and look him in the eyes. They search my face, trying to find an explanation that I'm not going to give him. "Thank you, Chris, but I've got it from here." I kiss him on the cheek, then turn and run through the forest.

And I don't look back. I don't look back.

I don't look back.

I take a circuitous route to the SAR site, avoiding the road. When I get there, it's empty, everyone out on their assignments for the day. I should be somewhere too, but the plan has shifted. I dip into my tent and put my backpack on the bed. I change out of my SAR shirt and put on something less conspicuous, a black T-shirt and a fresh pair of hiking pants. I tuck my hair up inside my ball cap and check myself in the mirror. I look like a million other girls now, and I'm happy to be nondescript.

I'll leave, I think. I'll leave the park and go find a motel a hundred miles from here to sit tight in while I make a new plan. I'll ditch my phone and get a new one, and this time I won't give anyone the number. I'll leave a note saying that I quit, and I'll tell my mother I'm going out of town. No one will look for me, and Kevin will give up when he finds I've left.

I retrieve my phone off the nightstand and that's when I see it. Another message from a blocked number. *It's time*, it says, and I shudder.

Goddamn it, no. Not now.

But wait. Maybe this will work better. Kevin won't be able to follow me there. I'll be just as safe in the woods as in some anonymous motel that I don't even know how I'll get to.

My heart is thrumming, and I know I don't have much time to decide what to do. Stick with the plan or go?

Fuck it.

I start to stuff what I'll need inside my pack—a couple changes of clothes, a sleeping bag, all the food I have. A flashlight, my headlamp, my maps of the park, my GPS tracker. A sweater, a hat and gloves, my phone.

My gun.

I take it out of its hiding place and stare at it, lifting it slowly up and down, testing its weight. Ever since I've started spending the night with Ben, I've tucked it away where he can't find it. If you'd asked me yesterday, I would've said I almost forgot I had it, but that's not true. I knew where it was the whole time, and why I had it in the first place.

I've been marking time here until I'd need it.

And now I do.

I wrap it back up in its cloth and put it in the top compartment of the pack. Then I close it up and strap it all down and think for a minute about whether I need to leave a note. No. I need enough space between my departure and my return. I need to be able to control the timing to the extent I can. If I leave a note, someone could easily catch up with me.

Besides, I said enough to Chris. Once I'm gone for more than a day, once they start looking for me, he'll hear about it and tell them about Kevin. Ben knows enough to understand, and with any luck, they'll think I simply left.

Time to go. Kevin could be here any minute.

A shiver runs down my spine as I adjust my pack, thinking about that day months ago when I got off the plane in Reno. I'm so much stronger than I was then, in too many ways. But I'm weaker, too. Then, fear and anger were driving me, and that's still there, in my DNA, but other things have crept in too. Comfort, a purpose, a sense of my past, and maybe my future. If only . . . If only . . .

I stop myself. I've come too far to turn back now. There is no path backwards, only forward until it's done.

I check that my boots are double knotted, then peek outside the tent to make sure the coast is still clear. It's as quiet as it was before. Abandoned almost, like a sign.

I step out into the daylight and walk swiftly toward the woods. I'll take the back way to the Lembert Dome path, avoiding the busiest sections of the path. Avoiding the people, and anyone who might know me enough to ask questions.

And then I'll return to the scene of the crime.

CHAPTER 31

FINALLY, SOME NEWS

Chris went away, ten years ago, after he was done with me.

He left town with Cameron to go to college back east, and I didn't hear from him for a *year*. Not once. Not at Thanksgiving or Christmas or Easter or my birthday. Not when he came to town and left again, his movements being brought to me in small doses by carrier pigeons.

I spent that year adrift in a sea of guilt. I was working odd jobs, still trying to figure out what to do with my life. Eventually, Bri suggested I join SAR. I had all the skills, and it would look good on a résumé and give me options. A way out, maybe. It was okay to go somewhere new and make mistakes, he told me, his watery blue eyes wise with age. I didn't have to be yoked to this place. My mother, my fears. I could go somewhere else and start all over.

I could be someone new.

Maybe that's what planted the first seed.

Who knows how ideas take shape?

I applied for SAR and I got in. We had a celebration—a family dinner of sorts with my mother, who was always on her best behavior when Bri was around.

It was a tough summer. At twenty, I was the youngest member of the SAR team, me, then Jenny, who was twenty-one. She'd grown up in Jackson, a different mountain town, and we had a lot in common. We bonded over it, got close, went on rescues together, helped each other. In time, I fell into a routine, got my bearings and my confidence and I realized I was having a good summer. That I was happy for the first time in a long time, looking forward to a future.

Then Chris came back—he and Cameron. They came to the park in July, to the very climb we'd been stuck on. I felt rooted to the spot seeing them in the parking lot. Cameron was her usual happy and bubbly self, but Chris was cool, standoffish. She kept asking him what was wrong, wasn't he happy to see me? Didn't he want to tell me about all the cool climbs they'd been on in the last year? Chris mumbled something and went to check his fixed line and Cameron looked after him with a shaking head, like *what's wrong with this guy?*

I tried to smile but I didn't quite make it, and that's when I think she knew.

Something.

Soon, everyone was talking about it, that they were in trouble. Chris had done something—*someone*, maybe—and Cameron was devastated. I never got the details of what she knew. I tried texting him once and he told me to leave him alone, and then he blocked me.

He blocked me! I didn't make him come to me all those nights. I didn't make him cheat on his girlfriend. Even in the tent that night when we were trapped, with the storm raging outside, he made the first move. I was never a move-maker, always the passive recipient of someone else's desires. That was true for Chris and

Kevin, everyone except Ben. He's the first man I've ever come close to initiating things with, and even then, I did it at a safe distance.

Not safe enough for Chris. The way he treated me—it made me hate him. It made me mean. When I was told the rumors that he'd been unfaithful, I said I could believe it. That he was a flirty guy and Cameron could do better. Partly, I wanted to deflect suspicion away from me, but there was more to it. He made me into someone I didn't like, cruel and suspicious, caring too much what others thought of me and not enough about myself.

Eventually, the rumors died down, but the damage was done. Whether she knew it was me or not, Cameron didn't come around the SAR site anymore. When we passed each other in the park, she was distant and polite. It was agonizing not knowing whether she knew, but I couldn't make myself act like nothing had ever happened, even if my behavior made it all the more likely that she'd figure it out. I'd fantasize sometimes that she'd confront me. Would I deny it? Would I confess? If they broke up, could I have him for myself? Did I even want that?

I didn't. I just wanted to live my life in peace, the fragile state I'd returned to after a year of silence. I wanted to forget, to move on, to get in a time machine and erase what I'd done, the memories of his lips, his scent, his touch. That wasn't possible, so I worked instead. All the hours I could get, every rescue that was called in. I paid off my bad deeds by saving others, one by one by one.

Then Cameron and Chris went missing, and you know what? You know what I thought when I first heard the news?

I was *glad*.

It's ten years later now; hot, not a hint of rain in the forecast, the air is acrid from the not-so-distance fires, reminding me that danger is near even though I'm walking away from it. The insects buzz in the trees and the ground doesn't spring under my feet the way it used to. Everything is dry as bone, one match away from going up in smoke.

That's how I feel. Like my body is ready to be lit. Every inch of me is a live wire. I need to pull myself together or I'll never get to the end of this.

I keep my eyes down as I hike past others, not making eye contact, not stopping to say the friendly "hello" and "have a good day" that's the usual way of hikers. I don't want anyone to remember me on this hike. I don't want anyone to know I was here. Especially not Kevin.

Kevin.

Kevin is here. Kevin is *here*.

Why?

I hit my toe on a rock and stumble, putting my hands out to steady myself, my breathing thick in my ears. I right myself with a curse, then start to hike again, forcing out my breath, forcing out my thoughts.

This wasn't the plan, not the plan at all. I didn't come here to see him, to have to face whatever judgment he wanted to give me. I came here to get away from that, from him. To help others, and to purge myself, the way I tried to do ten years ago. The way I should've done back then.

Instead, everything has spiraled out of control.

This has all gone much further than it ever should have, no matter what the provocation. But someone has the answers, someone can explain, so I hike. I put one foot in front of the other and the miles tick away. Two miles, three, four. My shirt is soaked with sweat, and I don't even stop to drink, just take sips from my canteen, conserving water. I feel hunted on this trail, even though the people peel away, and soon, I barely pass anyone coming toward me. By mile five, I'm almost running, but I need to conserve my energy. I need to have my wits about me when I get to the end.

Mile six, mile seven, mile eight. Up ahead is the turn.

And it's then that I realize. It's my past that's following me, ten years not long enough to leave it all behind. That day with Jenny. The map. It was here. Right here where we made the decision that altered everything.

The small burst of happiness I felt at Chris and Cameron missing was quickly replaced by guilt and then by exhaustion. It was all hands on deck. This wasn't just some tourist who'd done something stupid, it was the local golden couple. We went all out searching for them. Hours and hours and hours on the trails, beating back trees, calling their names. We had more volunteers than we knew what to do with, almost tripping over each other. Her mother in agony, my mother hysterical, his parents cold and stoic—everyone I knew with a pinched expression on their faces.

And then the rumors started again, but they weren't just whispers now, they were a drumbeat. About Cameron and Chris. That he'd cheated on her. That she'd found out about it when they got back from college. How they'd been fighting. How they'd almost broken up. No one knew if it was true or where this had occurred. At college? In town? It felt like every woman who'd had anything to do with Chris came under scrutiny. But not me.

Not me.

I was almost insulted. Why wasn't I good enough to be someone's dirty little secret? I wasn't as pretty as Cameron, but I was pretty enough. It was only in Mammoth that I was seen as so undesirable that I didn't even make the suspect list.

It seems stupid now. But then, it was devastating. It made me want to tell. To confess that I was the person everyone was talking about. But what good would that do? Did I really want to put my-self in the middle of it? To be more involved than I already was?

I kept my mouth shut. I walked the trails I was told to, and I thought about how much of your life gets exposed when you're missing. All the little details that come to light. The garbage you leave behind. The things you never wanted anyone to know. We say it's to help find you, but is it? Do you really need to know everything about a person to find them in the woods?

Maybe you do. Maybe you do.

The days slipped by and everyone decided that they weren't going to be found. No one wanted to say it, but the days they'd been missing were too many, the clues too few. They were both gone, probably forever. That was going to be a huge blow, likely one we'd never recover from. Small towns don't get over those kinds of losses. They integrate them and memorialize them on street names and schools, and children are kept in cages so that they don't end up with similar fates.

It would be a curiosity that would drive traffic to the park, bringing in ghouls, amateur detectives looking for clues. It was the worst thing that could happen. Never, even in my angriest moments, did I want it to end like this.

And then Chris reappeared—cut, dehydrated, ten pounds thinner.

And he drew a map.

CHAPTER 32

IT'S ALL COMING BACK TO ME

Now

B en slips away at the revelation that Kevin would want to harm him, and eventually, I fall asleep.

And now it's morning.

I used to love mornings. So quiet and still. A fresh day where I could chart a new path. Where I didn't have to think about what I'd done wrong, or how to fix it.

In my old life, in New York, it was the only time I knew I was safe, because Kevin never woke up angry. He greeted each new day like it would be different. Like he didn't have anything to apologize for. He was sweet and affectionate, and when I loved him, long past when I should've stopped, it was in the mornings.

But there aren't going to be any more mornings with Kevin.

I was ready for that. I was ready for all of it. Or I thought I was, and the decisions I made, the things in my life that led me here—I have to accept them. Like I'm in recovery for my life. I accept the things I cannot change. I surrender. I am powerless.

"Cassie?"

It's Eric, standing over my cot, his eyes heavy, his body weary. He hasn't shaved or slept it looks like, and I feel a flash of guilt that I have anything to do with his current state. But I quash it. He's the least of my injuries, if not my worries.

I prop myself up and pull my hair back, twisting it at my neck. "Good morning, Eric."

"Did you get some sleep?"

"Yes, I guess I did."

"Good."

I swing my legs off the bed, my bare feet hitting the cold floor. A woodpecker starts to hit the side of the building, a rapid-fire clatter.

"Did you want to talk to me?"

"Yes, but . . . the lawyer's here. From town."

"The lawyer?"

"Jenny arranged it?"

Had I agreed to that yesterday, or had I simply let her suggestion wash off me? Maybe she remembers enough of the questioning we received after everything that happened with Cameron to look past my ambivalence and overrule me.

"I think so."

"I can't . . . I can't afford that."

"You'll have to discuss that with him."

"Oh, okay." I stand up and hug myself. It's cold in here, though the sunlight feels strong through the window. I feel an odd separation from time. Like it's not possible to determine how and what day or week I'm in.

Yesterday—it *was* yesterday—I was in that field, trying to figure out how to get back to civilization, and now I'm waiting to meet a lawyer. I'm going to be questioned. I'm going to be put under a microscope and tested. How closely they look is out of my control. I can only continue to play my part.

"Did you want a moment alone with him?" Eric asks.

"Yes, I . . . Thank you. Can I take a shower first?"

"Of course. Ben brought some clothes for you."

"He did?" I look around for him, but I'm alone in this room with three cots, a staging area for rescues. There's a small bag on the bed next to me, the clothes that Ben must've brought. This act of kindness makes me want to cry.

"I'll just leave you, then."

"Thank you."

He nods and turns to leave. I watch the set of his shoulders, the exhaustion, but also the decision. He's made up his mind about me, it feels like. Maybe it's just my imagination, but somehow, I don't think so.

"Eric?"

"Yes?"

"I'll explain everything."

He glances at me over his shoulder. "Speak to the lawyer, Cassie. You don't want to say anything you might regret."

CHAPTER 33
A PLOT, THICKENING

Then

August

'm at the turnoff. A few miles from here, I'll find what I'm looking for.

It's late, it'll be dark soon, and I need my energy for what's coming. So instead of pressing on, I make camp. I eat two protein bars and down a canteen of water. Then I find a stream and filter and treat my water for tomorrow. I put up my tent and crawl into my sleeping bag and lie back against the hard earth wondering if I'll be able to sleep.

Everyone must be wondering where I am. Ben, Jenny, Mia, Gareth, Bri. Is someone going to tell my mother I'm missing? Should I risk trying to send a message? No. I'm still not sure how Kevin found me. If he knows my number, then I need to keep it off unless it's an absolute emergency.

I close my eyes and start to count down from a thousand, and eventually I fall asleep.

In the morning, I wake up with the sun, my heart thrumming in my chest. I wash myself in the stream and change my clothes. I make myself breakfast and drink some water. I rearrange my pack, going over my supplies. If I need to come back this way, I'm fine in the short term. I can be out here for a couple of days, but no longer.

But it's too early for me to press on. I want to wait an hour or two. The forest is quiet this morning; too early even for most of the animals, though the birds are greeting the day with their usual song. I sit on my pack and hug my knees to my body.

Ten years ago, they'd sent a Huey for a flyover straightaway but hadn't seen anything. Then the weather deteriorated—rain and wind forecasted for days, too dangerous to fly in. They needed people to find her, triangulate her location and then send in help. The team had mostly been pulled to the valley for a missing family. But Jenny and I were there. We volunteered to go.

Jenny and I suited up in rain gear and packed our bags. We marched silently through the wet woods. The weather was out of place for that time of year, but that fit the general mood. Chris had barely made it out alive, and Cameron was hurt. She was out of food. We needed to get there quickly, but it was hard hiking in the rain, the trail slick, the mud caked on our boots. We got to this turnoff, and it was dark and stormy, thunderclaps shuddering in the sky. It was getting dangerous, and increasing the casualties was a bad idea. We decided to make camp and hope for better weather in the morning.

We put together a shelter and changed into dry clothes and then, suddenly, like a faucet being turned off, the rain stopped. It was Jenny's idea to make a fire—we were both cold to the bone, and given the heavy rain, the danger seemed low. We found rocks to make a fire ring and enough dried-out logs. We huddled as close to it as we could, steam rising from our clothes, studying the map with a flashlight, memorizing it. Three miles from where we were, maybe four. If we had the map right. If Chris did.

"It's upside down," I said to Jenny, turning it the other way around. "We need to go west."

"No, it's east." She plucked it from my hand and turned it. It was rudimentary but clear enough to follow.

"Maybe we should split up tomorrow morning," I said. "Each of us take one way and meet in the middle."

"We should stick together."

"We need to go fast, though. And if the weather's better, they can fly in tomorrow."

"Okay, good idea. Let me call that in."

She went to the tent. I could hear her rummaging around as I stared at Chris's handwriting. His hands had been shaking so badly from hunger and exhaustion when he drew the map that it was hardly recognizable. It had been a shock to see him so thin, so exhausted, so happy to see me. "You'll save her," he said. "Promise?"

"Shit!" Jenny said from the tent.

"What?"

"The radio," she poked her head out. "It got wet. It's not working."

"Fuck."

"What about yours?"

I patted myself down, shocked to find my harness empty. "I don't have it."

"What?"

I thought back to the last time I used it, earlier when we stopped for water. We'd radioed in our position, gotten an update on Chris. He was recovering, but it was still touch and go. "I must've put it down when we stopped the last time."

"That was miles ago."

We looked at each other in panic. This was bad. If we found

Cameron, we'd need a way to signal to them to come find us, and without our radios . . .

"We'll use a flare," I said. "It will be okay. They'll be up in the air in the morning for sure."

"Okay, but then if we don't have radios, we have to stay together. It's too dangerous otherwise."

"Yes, okay," I said. "I agree."

"This is a shit show," Jenny said.

"I'm sorry."

"It's not your fault."

It felt like it was, though. If Chris had never kissed me, would Cameron and Chris even have gone on this hike? Maybe the connection was remote, but that was the problem with mistakes. You never know which ones will have lasting consequences.

Ten years later, I sigh and pack up my things, then check my bearings. I don't have to wonder which way to go this time. It's four miles due west. There isn't a real trail, but the forest isn't thick and it's not hard to find my way. Others have been here before me, and when I get closer to the water, I slow down to listen. It's the same silence there was earlier, almost overwhelming. It feels like I can hear every crackle of every branch, even the insects walking on the leaves. I walk to the water's edge. It sparkles in the sunlight, and then a fish jumps straight up in the air and splashes down into the water like it's a breaching whale.

I crouch and put my hands in. It's cool and feels good on my hands, which are swollen from the altitude and extra weight on my back. I bring a handful up to splash my face, rubbing the water through to my neck. Part of me wants to strip down and dive in. But I'm just delaying the inevitable.

While I stay here, I haven't reached the end yet. Once I round the lake, there won't be any going back. And then I hear it behind me. Footsteps.

I rise slowly.

"You made it."

I turn around and there she is, hands on hips, her eyes boring into mine.

Petal.

She's standing on top of a rock, glaring down at me. She's shorn her hair and dyed it a deep chestnut that transforms her from someone who stands out to someone who blends in. But it's still her, those same eyes, unblinking. That strange confidence underneath.

"Why did you send me that message?" *It's time*, her text had said.

"Time to go," she says.

"No, you should've waited a few weeks, like we planned."

She shrugs and my hands go cold. Not just from the water, but from the ice in her eyes.

"You got my diary and turned it in?" she asks.

"Yes. Ben and I went to the cave. Everything's at forensics now."

"Good."

"What if they find . . ."

"They won't."

"How can you be sure?"

She gives that shrug again and I want to scream. To let out a month's worth of frustration into the ether. But I can't. I can't let anyone know where I am, because someone is looking for me now, someone is searching for me for sure.

"They arrested Sandy. They found the outstanding warrants."

"Excellent."

I release a slow breath. "She was a mess when you disappeared."

"She came to you?"

"She told us you were missing. She didn't . . . She never said anything about the money."

"I knew she wouldn't. Stupid cow."

"What did you do to Jim in that cave?"

"You really want to know?"

I feel queasy, thinking back to the smell, the contents of the dry bag. "No."

"Didn't think so. You always were the squeamish one."

"I did what I was supposed to do." I look around. "Where's Jada?"

"At our campsite." She points over her shoulder toward the woods.

"How's she doing?"

"Why don't you ask her yourself?" She turns and starts to walk along the edge of the lake. I rush after her and grab her arm. It's strong like rope. "Petal, wait."

"What?" She tugs her arm away and gives me another glance of her dead, cold eyes.

"Kevin. He's here."

A slow smile creeps onto her face. I shudder as I watch it form because it's terrifying.

"Good," she says, then stalks away.

CHAPTER 34
THE PACT

Then

August

After I unstick my feet from the ground, I follow Petal along the edge of the lake and then away from it, up a hill to a stand of thick cover that makes it impossible to see through from the air.

I should know.

When Jenny and I finally made it here ten years ago, after having lost most of a day on the other side of the lake because I let Jenny decide which side of the map was the right way up, calling fruitlessly for Cameron, pulling back bushes and getting slapped in the face by low tree limbs, the first thing I thought was that no one would see the flare when we sent it up, even if we found her. But then Jenny called Cameron's name in a desperate whisper, her voice hoarse from yelling, and we heard a faint reply. We looked at each other, stricken, and rushed to the source of the sound.

It wasn't Cameron.

It was a raven, black, large, sitting in a small clearing, beckoning us, it felt like. Telling us that our search was finally over.

Jenny started to cry, her legs giving out. She fell to the ground on her knees as I scanned the clearing, looking for something, anything. And that's when I saw it—a hiking shoe, lying at an off angle on the edge of the clearing, next to a thicket of bushes. I walked toward it slowly, not wanting to know if it was attached to someone or lying there on its own. As I inched closer, I saw the rock, sharp but not large, and the blood, rusting in the sun. Someone had fallen against it and hit their head, then crawled away. That was the flash in my mind, like a scene I'd witnessed. Like something I'd done or dreamed about. But this wasn't a dream, it was a nightmare.

I only wanted to wake up. I couldn't, though. Instead, I had to move closer. I had to kneel in the grass like Jenny was doing behind me, still crying, paralyzed by exhaustion and fear. I breathed in and out slowly and gathered my courage.

I knelt down and pulled the bushes away, and there was Cameron, a gash in her head, her eyes a fixed stare up at the sky. Dead, she was *dead*, there wasn't any debating it.

I threw up, heaving everything out of my body all at once. I'm not sure how long it took me to stop. When I was done, my stomach felt raw, cleaned out. I sat back on my heels and looked at Jenny.

Her face was streaked with tears. "We're too late."

"I know."

"It's my fault," she said. "My fault. The map. If I'd listened to you—"

"No, don't do that to yourself. We don't know. We don't know when that happened. When she fell . . ."

Her body shook. "We could've saved her if we hadn't lost the day. If we hadn't gone the wrong way."

"No, Jenny."

"Yes, yes. I . . . I touched her and she's still warm. That means . . ."

I thought I might throw up again even though there was nothing left inside me. I closed my eyes and breathed in and out slowly. "You shouldn't have done that."

"I had to check. I had to see if she was breathing, if she had a pulse."

I wrapped my arms around my body, feeling desperate and raw. Despite all my training, I hadn't thought to do that. It had been so evident that Cameron was dead that I didn't try to make sure. Was it because I wanted it that way? Was there something wrong with me? I'd spent the summer saving people, searching for them, tending to their wounds. I spent the last couple of weeks looking for *her*, and when the task was done, I didn't even stop to ensure that she wasn't with us anymore.

But she *was* dead, and there wasn't anything I could do about that. All I could hope to do now was to bring her body back safely, so her family could mourn, so the town could have closure.

I pushed myself up and walked to the center of the clearing where our packs lay abandoned. "We should put up the flares," I said to Jenny. "We can send them from here."

Jenny looked at me, in tension between her confident self and the person who'd fallen apart.

"Jenny. I need your help."

She shook herself, and the transformation was complete. "Yes. The flares. They're in my pack. And I'll check the radio again. Maybe it's working now."

"Good idea."

She opened her pack and found the flares, wrapped in plastic, protected from the elements. She handed the package to me, and I took out the flare gun and the flares, getting them ready to launch. She pulled out the radio and sat it on a rock. It still wasn't working properly, only emitting static, but that was better than the day before.

"Ready?" I held the gun up, pointing it at the sky.

"Yes." Jenny placed her hands over her ears.

I extended my arm as far as possible and turned my head away. I pulled the trigger, the *BAM!* louder than I remembered, then watched it arc up into the sky. I opened a second flare, and drove it into the ground at my feet, the sparks spraying in a circle, an unmistakable sign from above. We had two left. One more to put in the air and another for the ground if we needed them, because it would take a while for anyone to get to us.

Jenny closed up her pack and sat down on it, watching the sky. I wanted to sit too, but I was restless. I started pacing the perimeter of the clearing, looking for something, though I wasn't sure what.

On the far side, I found it. Where Chris had left her. Their packs, their tent, their sleeping bags. In front of the tent on the ground, there was a small notebook. I recognized it immediately. It was Cameron's climbing log, where she kept her stats, noting the details of every climb she completed.

I picked it up and flipped through it, seeing her precise handwriting, the dates of climbs gone by. And then I came to the entries from their time here. Dated, a few notations. How their food was running out. How her ankle hurt. The day they decided Chris would leave and she would stay. The next day, where she felt *so alone*. The day after, where she was *so scared*. The day Chris arrived back at the SAR site, she was still alive, but getting weaker. Then yesterday. *I don't know how much longer I can hold on. I'm so thirsty.*

The last entry was from that morning. It was written while we were wasting time on the other side of the lake with the map upside down.

I need to try to get to water. I think I can make it.

That was it. The next page was blank.

I stared at the notebook. She never made it to the water, but she *was* alive only hours before we found her. Jenny was right. If we hadn't made that mistake with the map, then we would've gotten here in time. She never would've risked walking on her bum ankle, never hit her head, never died.

This page was the evidence that, in the end, her death was our fault.

Mine. Because I knew which way to read the map, and I could've insisted. I could've fought with Jenny to come the right way, but instead, I didn't. I let her lead me around the wrong side of the lake, wasting time. Wasting life.

But no one could know that. I had to protect myself, and Jenny too.

So I tore the piece of paper out of the diary and crumpled it in my hand. I'd find a place to burn it later.

And now, here I am, back at the scene of my original crime. The first time I changed the evidence, hid myself, told one story where another was the truth. This time has been worse, even if it's something I agreed to. And this place, this almost circle of grass surrounded by thick trees—it felt like the beginning of everything. Somehow, I knew that it would be where everything ended, too.

But it's only a place. I shouldn't let it have such a hold on me. I should pay more attention to the people it contains. They've always been the problem.

When we get to the campsite, it's just as I remember it, only smaller. Like memories from childhood, those places we keep close in our minds, that shrink as we get older. There's a tent nestled in the trees, blending in with the cover above, green like summer grass. In the middle is a fire ring, the ash cold. And standing behind it, looking tired and thinner, is Jada. She's wearing a pair of fleece pants and a matching pullover. Her head is covered with a small knit cap, but I can see she's cut all her hair away, leaving it shaved close like she might've done if she was ill. It suits her, but it makes her look different, too. Older.

"You," she says, her voice flat. "Is it time?"

"It is," Petal says, touching her shoulder briefly, then letting her hand fall when Jada flinches.

"I thought we had a few more weeks." Jada gives me a thin smile. "I've lost track."

"It's August," I say as I set my pack on the ground, relieved to take the weight off. "A couple of days in."

"Oh. What's . . . I don't have my phone."

"I know. You left it in the Airstream, remember?"

She bites her lip. It's chapped. "Of course I do. Are they still looking for me?"

"No. The official search stopped a few weeks ago."

"That's good."

"Nothing about this is good."

"You know what I mean."

"It all started up again when Petal left. The searchers, the media."

"We knew that was a risk."

I grit my teeth. "This all got way more attention than it should have. Because of those stupid posts about Smokey."

"How was I supposed to know they'd blow up?"

"You were supposed to be keeping a low profile. You shouldn't have been posting at all."

"Is this helpful?" Petal says. "It didn't make a difference in the end."

"You're not the one who had to be out there every day. All that stuff in the press . . ."

"They only cared that I was missing because I was young and pretty."

"What about your mother? She's so worried about you."

Jada's face hardens. "She'll get over it."

"And Jim's family . . ."

"I'm supposed to care about them? They're the reason he was like that. His father . . . He's been beating Jim's mom his whole life. Jim thought that was normal."

"We showed him, though," Petal says, laughing now. "We showed him."

Jada nods. "It's funny how, after everything, he was so trusting. He didn't even notice that we'd gone down the wrong trail. He never even saw it coming."

"He never saw *me* coming," Petal says, her voice a monotone, her hands flexing then tightening in a slow, strangling motion.

"You strangled him? What happened to making it look like an accident?"

"We can't control everything."

"But if they find him—"

"I told you, they're never going to find him." She tips her head back. "And it's too late to back out now, Cassie."

"I'm not saying I want to back out. I'm just saying that . . . We didn't think this through. We didn't think about the other people who'd get hurt. We only thought about ourselves—"

"No," Petal says. "*You* didn't think this through. You didn't want to know the details, only your part. That's what *you* asked for. So don't worry about it."

"That's ridiculous. Of course I'm going to worry about it. This is my life too. We all need to get out of this. And they know about the website. Your posts in the abused women's forum. LifeisLife."

"So what?" Petal says.

"Wait." Jada pales. "*My* posts?"

"Not that I know of. Petal's posts are the only ones I've heard about." I look at Petal. "You made a mistake. Making those comments on Jada's Instagram account. Why did you do that?"

She doesn't blink under my gaze. "Just having a bit of fun."

"Yeah, well, great. That's great. Fun. *Fun?* Now they know. They know how we all met. Or they're about to find out. They'll find out."

Petal takes a step toward me, her hands out. "Calm down, Cassie."

I back away. I don't want her touching me. Petal's not who I thought she was. Not some semi-innocent girl caught up in a bad situation, but twisted in a way that's worse than the rest of us. "Don't tell me what to do."

Her voice is calm. "You don't have anything to worry about."

"How can you know?"

"Because I erased your posts. Jada's, too."

My mind is reeling. "What? How did you . . ."

"I've been hacking since I was fifteen. It was easy."

She's been what? *What?* "Who . . . Who are you?"

Petal gives me a haunted laugh. "Were you looking for poor little Petal? Always dragged this way and that by everyone? Abandoned by her mother. Mistreated by her father. Led around by Sandy. Poor Petal. She's too nice, too daffy, too silly, too anything you please to make decisions for herself."

"I never said that."

"But you thought it, didn't you? Did you think all this was *your* plan? Is that what you thought? That *you* were in charge?"

I take in a shaky breath. "I thought we were all in this together."

I look at Jada. She hasn't said anything in a few minutes, but none of this is coming as a surprise to her. Only me. I'm the one left out.

But why? Why did they even approach me in the first place?

A year ago, after Kevin slapped me across the face because

he thought I smiled at a waiter, I crept into the living room and wrapped myself in a blanket on the couch, turned on the fire, and picked up my laptop. I didn't have a plan, but I went in search of something. Someone I could confide in. None of the women I lunched with would understand what Kevin had done. How he was always keeping me on my toes, undermining me, making me second-guess myself and my worth. How his anger was escalating and becoming more focused on me. First he threw things. Then he punched a wall. Then he grabbed my arm and shook me. Then that first slap. Each time it felt like he was testing me, seeing how far he could go, what would make me leave. And when I accepted his tearful apologies, I was just confirming that I'd stay no matter what.

How could I explain to the very nice Upper West Side women in their expensive yoga wear why I stayed? I couldn't even explain it to myself. And their husbands were all friends with Kevin. If one of them told . . . I shuddered at the thought. Appearances were everything to Kevin. If there was any hint someone knew what he was doing to me, I didn't know what would happen.

So I googled. And before long I found it—an anonymous forum for abused women called SHELTER ME. It summed up how I felt exactly, and the women in there were so welcoming and exactly like me. Not in their everyday life, but inside, where it counted.

Things were easier after that. Kevin was still a menace in my life, but I didn't feel so alone. I understood why I was trapped. Why I couldn't make myself leave. How many times it would take me to try before it worked. All the statistics and stories that boiled down to falling in love with the wrong man and learning the truth about him too late.

There were hundreds of regular posters, coming and going, but Jada was the one I connected with first. I'd spent several months lurking, reading other women's posts, tallying up the similarities between my life and theirs. It was like I was making a checklist for abuse. Did I have enough points to qualify? He wasn't *that* bad. He'd never put me in the hospital or broken anything. He'd only hit me a few times, and there were stretches where things were normal. Happy even, though those seemed to be shorter, and it always felt like I was waiting, feeling his patience grow thin, until it was like tissue paper.

That's how Jada described it.

It's going to happen soon, Jada said, writing about how she could feel another beating from Jim coming. *I can see him thinning out. It's like his skin becomes translucent. One moment it's thick, and the next it's like tissue paper. So easy to tear. You can barely touch it without it coming apart.*

That was exactly how I felt about Kevin, only Jada said it so much better than I could ever manage. I liked her post, and then I reached out to her in a private message. I told her that her words were beautiful and asked if she could get help. If she had someone to tell.

My mother doesn't believe me, she'd written.

What do you mean?

She LOVES Jim. More than me, it feels like sometimes. Any time I try to say something about him, to tell her the truth . . . It's like he seduced her, even before me.

But surely if she knew who he was . . .

She cares too much about what Jim means. The life he can give me. His family. His dad's a jerk, a bully, even she can see that, but with Jim . . . I don't know. It's like those Netflix shows. Like all those shows about serial killers. Ted Bundy, all those guys. You know how they always have girlfriends? Not just before anyone knows who they are, but after? People don't want to believe what's right in front of them. How else could men get away with this for so long?

So you'll just put up with it forever?

She hadn't answered that question. But soon after, she added me to a different private thread. And that's when I met Petal.

She's like us, Jada told me by way of introduction. *She helps me.*

It didn't take me long to find out how. Petal's mind was like a spinning top, and she had a way of weaving fantasies, showing a way out, a way forward. She was trapped too, she said. Her father had been abusive, and now her girlfriend was. But in her imagination, she could escape. We all could.

That's how it started. Three women connecting across the country in anonymity. Providing support, solace, a lack of judgment. *When we escape*, that's what our fantasy was called. *When we escape, we'll* . . . fill in whatever blank you wanted. *Be happy, find love, live without fear, make better romantic choices.*

I don't remember who turned it from a *when* to a *what if.*

What if we didn't just escape but paid them back for what they did to us?

What if we hurt them like they hurt us?

What if they weren't around to hurt anyone else again, ever?

What if we made them disappear?

What if we gave them what they deserved?

Was it Jada? Was it Petal?

Was it me?

"We *are* all in this together, Cassie," Jada says, and now she has a smile on her face and she's holding out her hands to me.

She's seductive too. She and Petal seduced me down a path, this path. But they didn't have to try that hard. I was, without much persuading, willing to let them decide how their abusers were going to be punished, and to do my part in all of it.

Jim had to die—that's what Jada decided. He'd been abusing her for years, all through college. And she'd met his high school girlfriend once. She'd tried to warn Jada, to tell her what Jim was like. If he was hurting girls since he was a teenager, he was irredeemable. It was his life or hers, she'd said. Because it was only a matter of time before he killed her.

I'll help you, Petal had said, and they'd started to plan. Eventually, I chimed in with suggestions, a location. Somewhere, I crossed the Rubicon between fantasy and reality. I agreed to help.

What about Sandy? I'd asked.

The thing she's most afraid of is jail, Petal had said, and explained about the warrants. How she'd been working up the courage to turn her in. *But this is so much better*, Petal said, outlining her plan to make it so Sandy would get arrested after she disappeared. The clues she'd leave behind, the diary.

She talked down every objection. Or Jada did. Sometimes I didn't even recognize myself, even though all I had to do was keep my mouth shut. Act like I didn't know them when we met. Pretend I didn't know where they were when they disappeared. At the end of the summer, I'd help them escape from the park and from their lives, once and for all.

I didn't have to do the dirty work. I just had to keep the secret. I was good at that. The less I knew the better, Petal said, though I already knew too much.

But I should've asked more questions. I should've gotten all the facts. Because there were things I didn't know. Things they'd kept from me.

Like Kevin.

"Come, sit down," Jada says. "We'll fill you in on everything, and then we can make a plan."

"You think escape is still possible?"

"Of course it is."

"How can I trust you?"

"What do you mean?"

"Kevin . . . we were supposed to leave him out of it."

That's what I'd said when asked. That I only wanted to leave Kevin. That was enough for me. I didn't need anything more. He would let me go, once I did it. It would be too humiliating otherwise, to drag me back. People might ask questions. That was enough, I was certain. But that hadn't happened. Kevin's here, in Yosemite. Those messages I'd been receiving. It all connected back to Jada and Petal. It had to.

"That was never realistic," Petal says.

"What do you mean?"

"He can't get away with it, Cassie. We can't let him."

"That's *my* decision to make."

"No, we're all in this together. Our fates are intertwined. You didn't have enough at stake. We had to make sure."

"I have everything on the line."

She shakes her head. "Not the way we do. But it's okay. I've covered your tracks. It'll be all his fault."

"What are you talking about?"

"He's been threatening you, hasn't he? Telling you he was going to find you?"

The shock of what she's saying passes through me. I've been so very stupid. "You were the one sending the texts?"

"Of course."

"Why would you do that?"

"It'll be your excuse, don't you see?"

I'm filled with dread. "My excuse for what?"

"You'll find out, soon enough."

"What did you do, Petal? What's your plan for Kevin?"

She shrugs again, then looks over my shoulder. "Why don't you ask him yourself?"

CHAPTER 35

BACK TO THE FUTURE

Then

August

There's a rustling behind me, and I turn around with a sick sense of knowledge. It's Kevin standing there, holding some kind of GPS device in his hand, a blinking beep of light visible.

I know immediately that the blinking light is me.

My hand goes to my neck, to the medallion we all decided to wear to keep track of one another, with a microchip buried within. It's how I knew where to find them on the GPS device I'd brought with me. That it was safe to go there with Ben.

But of course, it means that they can track me too. Apparently, anyone can.

"Cassandra," Kevin says. He's wearing black cargo pants and a light gray T-shirt. A baseball hat, his hair longer than usual against his neck. He looks older, jowly, like he's been eating too much—drinking too.

I square my shoulders, fighting for courage I do not have. "It's Cassie."

His eyes narrow. Kevin is tissue paper today, tired, worn-out from the twenty-mile hike, his new boots dusty, his lips cracked. He looks past me at Petal and Jada.

"Who are they?" he asks, pointing.

"It doesn't matter."

"Answer me, Cassandra."

"You can't give me orders anymore."

He takes a step toward me, and I back up, then shuffle to where Petal and Jada are. Kevin won't do anything with two witnesses. There's safety in numbers.

Kevin squints at them, trying to puzzle them out. He settles on Jada. "You're that girl who's missing."

"I'm not," she says, but he's not listening.

"You," he says, pointing at Petal, "you're missing too. I saw it on the news."

Petal just stares at him, expressionless.

Kevin raises the GPS. "Are you the one who sent me this?"

She nods slightly.

I grip Petal's arm. "What the fuck, Petal?"

"I only gave it to him once I saw you had a big enough head start."

"Why?" I ask, but I know why. I know what she's going to say.

"Because he needs to be brought to justice."

"What are you talking about?" Kevin snarls, his hands balling into fists, the GPS tumbling to the ground. "What are you doing here? What. The. Fuck. Is. Going. On?"

The force of his anger hits me. I've seen him like this before when his violence landed on me.

"He's dangerous," I say to Jada. "Back up."

"Stop talking about me like that. I'm not dangerous. I'm your husband."

"They know, Kevin. They know all about you. They're the ones who helped me escape."

"You didn't escape. You ran away."

"What's the difference?"

He takes a step toward me. His dark eyes flash like fire, and my body tightens to receive the blow I know is coming.

"Do you know what it's been like? Having to explain to all our friends where you are? Having to answer their questions? Their suspicions?"

"You expect me to feel sorry for you? This is *your* fault, Kevin."

"All I did was take care of you. Give you everything you ever needed. I don't deserve this."

"And I did? You were supposed to take care of me, not hurt me."

"I never hurt you."

"What are you talking about?"

His hand raises then lowers as Petal moves away from me and toward him. He's never hit me in front of someone else. If there were a witness, he couldn't tell himself that it wasn't true. "You promised," he says. "You promised you'd stay with me forever. How could you? How could you leave me like that?"

I get a flash of our wedding. How happy I was that day. I carried tulips and wore a white flowing dress, and even though the wedding was small, just us and two witnesses and then a nice lunch afterwards, I felt loved and protected. I felt like I finally had what I'd been looking for all those years in Mammoth: a family.

Then that got snatched away and all I was left with was fear and disappointment. When I first realized how trapped I was, I was stunned. How could this happen to *me*? The girl everyone always thought was too headstrong—that girl was afraid of her own shadow? No, no. It had to be a joke. This couldn't be happening.

But it was. It was, and forever was a trap.

"And you promised you'd protect me. That you'd honor and cherish me. What about that, Kevin? What about that?"

"Come on, Cassandra. Please. We can go to therapy. We can work it out. I love you."

"You don't, though."

"Of course I do. Hey." He takes a step toward me again, and I take one back.

Behind him I can see Petal dropping down, fiddling with something at her feet.

"Hey," Kevin says. "You know I love you. I've loved you from that first moment when we met in the airport. I saw you across the room and I knew. That's my wife. That's who I've been looking for. And every day since then we've been together. I know there have been some rocky times, that I have problems with my anger sometimes. I'm working on that. But I need you. I need you, Cass, to help me." He holds his hands out to me in a plea.

His eyes are filled with tears, and a small part of me wants to go to him. To fall into the fantasy that he's created for me time and again, that it will be different this time, that it will be all right, that it will all work out.

But it's come too far for that now. Too far for so many things.

"No," I say, holding up my hand. "Stop."

"What?"

"Petal, how did you get him here, to Yosemite?"

"I called him a few days ago," Petal says from behind him.

"That was you?" Kevin asks.

"What did you say?"

Kevin answers. "She said you were in Yosemite. And then she told me to download an encrypted messaging app, and she sent me photos. Said I could come and get you if I wanted."

"Photos? What photos?" I ask Petal, half-hidden by Kevin but standing now.

"You were with a man."

"Ben?"

"Is *that* his name?"

Petal doesn't answer me or him; instead she says, "The messages disappear after you view them. Don't worry."

"How did you do this?"

"I hiked to where I could get a signal. That's how I sent you that message yesterday. When he told me he was in Yosemite."

"You sent him the GPS?"

"Yes, but I told him to get rid of the packaging. You did that, right, Kevin?"

Kevin looks back and forth between us. "Yes, I threw it out. You said you wouldn't turn on the signal until I did it."

"Good boy."

I turn over the information in my mind, trying to make sense of it all. To understand what Petal's done. "You didn't know where I was until Petal called you?"

"I knew you'd been in Reno. Because of the iPhone tracking."

"Find My iPhone."

"Yes."

"I disabled that."

"No you didn't."

But yes, I had. "Did you go to Reno?"

His shoulders slump. "No, I . . . I thought about it, but I didn't know how to find you. The tracker didn't move. So I knew the phone was off or you'd left it behind. I kept checking it, but it never changed."

"You weren't in Mammoth? A couple of weeks ago in a ski shop?"

"What? No."

I don't know if I can believe him, but why would he lie? It *was* just my mind playing tricks on me. The stress of seeing Chris, the fear those messages had put into me.

Or was it Petal fucking with me like she was fucking with me with the texts?

I look for her, but she's moved again, and now she's half-hidden behind him, next to where I set my pack down. Jada's off to the left, watching us, her body tensed.

"Did you tell anyone you were coming here?" I ask Kevin.

"She told me not to. She said if I wanted to get you back, to come and tell no one. She told me she'd help me bring you home."

"And when you texted her that you were in Yosemite, the tracker turned on?"

"Not immediately. I had to wait a couple of hours. And then she sent me a map. Told me to hike to a campsite and stay over-night. Said she'd send more instructions in the morning."

"This morning?"

"Yeah, I got the text and I checked the GPS, and there was a signal to follow."

"Jesus, Petal," I say.

Petal stands up slowly, her hands down. "What?"

"What if he'd caught up to me? What if he'd found me in the night?"

"I knew where you were the whole time. I could turn off his GPS anytime I wanted."

I shake my head slowly. "Don't do this."

"Too late for that."

Kevin turns around as Petal raises her hands. She has the gun that was in my pack. My gun. The gun she'd put in the post office box in Bishop, just in case, she'd said. *Just in case what?* I'd asked, but I hadn't gotten a satisfying answer to my question. I'd followed along, though, open to her suggestion, as I'd been to too many others.

"Step back," Petal says to Kevin, waving the gun expertly.

"You don't want to do that," he says, menace in his voice.

"Do not test me," Petal says. "You don't know who I am or what I might do." Petal waves the gun again. "And in case you're thinking, *This girl doesn't know how to shoot a gun*, you'd be wrong about that. My daddy taught me when I was a little thing. So back up."

Kevin's body tenses, but he does as she says, backing up until he's next to me.

"Petal, don't," I say.

"He knows my name and Jada's. He knows we're here."

"Because *you* told him to come here."

"I did it for you."

"I never asked you to do any of this."

"Didn't you, though?" She rolls the gun lazily toward Kevin, and he must see something shift in her eyes. He holds his hands up and takes a step back. "You should do it."

"What?" I say. "No. I'm not going to do that." I step toward Kevin now, feeling a need to protect him even though my brain is yelling at me to run. "There must be another way."

"There isn't," Jada says. "We made the decision, and there's no going back."

"Cassie—" Kevin says, his voice a plea.

"Shut your goddamn mouth." Petal raises the gun again, like they do on TV, slightly cocked to the side, pushing it toward him.

I'm half in front of Kevin. Maybe if Petal can't see him, if she can only see me, she won't do it. "We have to find another way, Petal. We have to find something else . . ."

Petal stares at me, hesitating, the gun lowering ever so slightly, and that's when he does it. Kevin, that stupid fucking man, starts to charge her, pushing me out of the way in the process with so much force that I trip, stumble, and tumble toward the ground.

"Kevin!" I scream right before I feel the back of my head slam into a rock.

And then, *BOOM! BOOM!*

Everything speeds up and slows down all at once as Kevin pinwheels through the air, then falls to the ground at my feet.

Dead.

CHAPTER 36
JUST THE FACTS

Two hours after Eric tells me the lawyer is here, I've spoken to him, taken a shower, and now I'm in Eric's office with Captain Cole, the recorder on the desk in front of us.

The lawyer's name is Matt Smith—he's young, barely out of law school, and he seemed nervous when I met him. His advice is to say nothing and invoke my Fifth Amendment rights, but I told him I wasn't going to do that. If I plead the Fifth, that would be admitting I'd done something wrong. I want to speak my piece and free myself. If that doesn't work, then so be it. He tells me that if I insist on talking, I should keep the details to a minimum. "Less is more," he says. "Let them fill in the blanks. Stick as close to the truth as possible. If you don't remember, don't guess. If you're not sure, say so."

I let that sink in, and then I sit down and the questioning starts. I take them through the preliminary information, some of which I've already covered—my marriage, why I decided to leave Kevin, enough details so they understand why I left the way I did. I show them the messages, the threats he made that I read and photographed in Reno, and the others I received along the way that Petal sent, acting like him. I tell them about the Instagram post by Jada, how someone recognized me and tagged others who knew me in New York. That message on the post—*Should we tell the husband?* Maybe someone did. Then there was the article about Cameron's disappearance, the one that used the last name Adams. That I'd turned on my phone in Reno, and maybe Kevin had traced it there. How he used to track me through Find My iPhone.

There were enough things swirling out there that if someone wanted to find me, they could. I wasn't in a witness protection program—I just wanted to put some distance between us. But he had money, maybe he had help finding me. Maybe it was him in town that day or maybe it wasn't. I was under stress. I couldn't explain everything, I only knew that he found me, out there in the woods, where I'd gone to hide.

"But why there?" Eric asks, stroking his beard. "Why did you go to that location?"

"I wasn't thinking straight."

"It must be more than that. That's where you found Cameron, isn't it?"

Less is more, Matt said. Keep things as close to the truth as possible. "I thought I'd be safe there. It was so remote. I was panicking. I needed a few days to think."

All those months ago, talking through our plan, trying to decide where they could hide out. *I know a place*, I'd written. *It's hard to get to. Almost no one goes there.*

Sounds perfect, Petal had written.

"But Kevin found you?"

"Yes."

"How?"

I reach inside my shirt and pull out the medallion. "This."

"What is that?"

I run my fingers along it. Petal had said at some point, *We'll all wear one. That way we can keep tabs on one another.*

Why would we need to do that? I'd asked.

Just in case we need to adjust the plan along the way. We might not always be able to communicate.

Where would we even get such a thing?

Leave that to me, Petal said. *Leave it all to me.*

It had arrived at my apartment a week later with a daisy decal, the petals trailing away, which I put on the back of my phone to remind me of the plan, the goal, what I was doing now. It was a disk on a chain with a GPS tracker embedded. I'd hidden the separate GPS device at the back of my closet with my climbing gear. Kevin had noticed the medallion one night when we were in bed, and it had made him jealous, thinking it was a man that might've given it to me. I told him it was from my mother, a peace offering, that she might be coming to visit. He'd lost interest quickly then.

"He gave it to me. Kevin. For our anniversary. I don't know where he got it. I thought it was a sweet gesture. But when he found me, he was holding a GPS device. It must have a GPS chip inside it." I take it off and put it on the desk. I'm free of it now.

"Why didn't he use it before to locate you?"

"I . . ." I stop, feeling panicked. I hadn't thought about that.

After the terrible shots, when Petal and Jada had held me back from trying to see if there was something I could do to save Kevin, they'd started packing up, getting ready to leave, making sure they didn't leave a trace.

It was never the plan for me to go with them. They were going to dissolve into the wilderness and emerge somewhere else, separate, and lead different lives. Petal had learned about new identities and life on the run with Sandy. All that stuff in her diary about just finding out that she was a criminal—that was made-up. A fake out. She knew all along about Sandy and her past. It was part of what drew her to Sandy in the first place.

Petal had been matter-of-fact to me after she'd shot him, efficient, saying that Kevin had been charging her, that he was dangerous, that *she had no choice*, even though it was her intention to kill him all along. She drew him there to tangle me up, to make it impossible for me to escape, maybe even to have a scapegoat. She wouldn't say, and there wasn't anything she *could* say that would make me trust her.

As for Jada, she was too far under Petal's spell to defy her. Or maybe they'd planned it together, leaving me out as the weak link. What did it matter? I had to think of myself now. They'd already made their escape, not even bothering to check that I was all right, that the blow to the back of my head from the rock I fell on wouldn't turn fatal.

But Petal had some last words of advice. If I wasn't coming with them, my story was going to have to be that he'd found me and tried to hurt me, and I did the only thing I could. She'd tucked the phone she'd used to text me into his pocket after wiping it down thoroughly, then she'd taken off her tracker and held out her hand to Jada and me, indicating we should do the same.

I'll get rid of these, she said.

I reached for mine and started to take it off, but then I stopped. No, I said. *I'll keep it.*

Bad idea, Jada said.

How else did Kevin find me?

Petal had looked satisfied as she took Jada's necklace, and I can't help but think now, what did she see around the corner that I didn't? The thread I left to pull?

"I don't know why he didn't use it before," I say. If you don't know, don't guess, that's what Matt the lawyer said. "Maybe it doesn't work unless you're within range? Maybe he was waiting to come find me. He didn't say. I wouldn't want to speculate."

"Well, now we can't ask him," Officer Cole says, and Matt reaches for my arm to keep me from speaking.

"What are you implying?" Matt says. Despite his youth, his voice is deep, commanding. I wonder how he ended up practicing law in Mammoth.

"There are a lot of questions that need answering," she says.

"And my client has agreed to answer all of them. Against my advice, I might add."

Eric sighs. "Shall we continue?"

"Of course." Matt drops his hand and I hug myself with my arms. How much longer is this going to go on? An hour? Two? I can't think of time. I just have to listen to the questions and answer them as best I can.

"Where did you get the gun?" Eric asks.

"Kevin had it with him. I don't know where he got it."

"All right. Take us through the shooting again."

I do what he asks. How I got to the clearing and stopped. How there wasn't any sign of anyone, but traces of old visits. People did that—visited the scenes of famous disappearances. Or maybe it was just hikers passing through, nothing new. A makeshift firepit. The grass a bit trampled, but it had been a dry summer. The wrapper from a protein bar swirling in the breeze. It all hit me. How stupid I'd been, running away like that. How I could just tell the authorities about Kevin. How I *was* the authorities.

I sat down to take my phone out and call in my location, to let people know that I was okay, and Kevin startled me. He'd threatened me. He wanted me to go back to New York with him and he wouldn't take no for an answer. Then he took out the gun and said he'd make me go. It all went hazy after that. I tried to run, and he caught me. We struggled. The gun dropped to the ground and then I did, hitting my head. I picked up his gun, and then he was running at me again, yelling, trying to get it from me, and I shot it. *BOOM! BOOM!*

"Two shots?"

"Maybe it was three?"

After Petal and Jada had left, following the route out that we'd planned to use in September, I'd realized that I didn't have any gun residue on my hands. It was something they'd test for—GSR—I knew from watching too many episodes of Dick Wolf shows. So I picked up the gun and I shot it one more time, praying there wasn't anyone near enough to hear the shot. I aimed at the woods, because an errant bullet could be explained in a way that an extra bullet in his chest after he was already dead could not. But they hadn't tested my hands, not yet. Instead, they'd let me take a shower. Did that matter?

"Which was it?"

"I . . . I don't know. I had no choice." My voice breaks and there are genuine tears on my face. "I had no choice."

"I think my client has said enough," Matt says.

"We'll need her to be available if we have further questions."

"Of course."

I wipe my tears away with the back of my hand. "I'm not going anywhere," I say.

At least not yet.

Now I'm back at the SAR site and I don't know what to do. There's a month left of summer. People will still come to the park and make mistakes and need to be rescued. Can I stay and do that? After everything, will they even want me to?

I open the door to my tent and bring my pack inside. I sit on the edge of my bed and stare at the wall, the way the light filters in. It was only three days ago that I left here, and so much has changed. The questions I pushed away all summer have answers now. Well, maybe not all. Maybe not enough.

But there's only one question I want to know the answer to.

Will we get away with it?

Good Riddance

Transcript of YouTube Video by CriminalMind

2.0M views · 1 day ago

CriminalMind:

Jim got what he deserved. I said what I said.

CHAPTER 37
MALIBU

September

A month goes by.

I tell my story again and again, each time with less detail as I've been instructed to by Matt. An identical story raises suspicions. Memory fades more quickly than we think; it changes, it mutates. Everything we think we know about victims from movies and *Dateline NBC* is wrong. It's not a movie that plays in your head, unchangeable. It's a dream. A nightmare. Some things come into focus and others retreat, and sometimes it's all jumbled up and makes no sense at all.

So that's what I do while I wait for news of Jada and Petal. While I expect them to be found, they aren't. Jim's autopsy is inconclusive, the contents of those dry bags from the cave are caught in some backlog that might never be cleared, and the news vans leave one by one until they're but a memory.

Kevin's autopsy confirms two shots to his face. They find my phone with the threatening texts. Petal erased all of my messages with her before she left, making sure they weren't findable. They gain access to his iPhone account and find that old ping on my phone in Reno and see that he'd been tracking me when I was in

New York. His assistant confirms that he'd been acting oddly all summer, our old friends say the same. One of them mentions that they'd noticed some bruises on me a while ago, that she'd had her suspicions about Kevin. That he was mean, dismissive of women. She could believe it, she'd said. She could believe *me*.

They find the gun in the clearing, three bullets missing. They find the stone I hit my head on, with a small patch of blood. The earth is too dry to tell if there are signs of a struggle, but Kevin's GPS shows he turned it on in Tuolumne, and that the signal it was showing came from the medallion I wore.

Chris confirms that we were together when I saw Kevin in Yosemite. My reaction. How I ran from him without an explanation. *She was shit scared*, he says. *And acting irrationally. I'm not surprised she ran.*

Ben tells them what I told him about Kevin. How he hurt me, that I ran, that I was scared of him.

I stay with my mother while the news vans circle Yosemite and eventually her house. It's strained between us—ten years of not talking doesn't get erased in one month. We're so different, she and I, that I don't know how to heal us. She asks more questions than the police, and I have no answers. I'm still full of questions.

Chief among them—where are Jada and Petal? Our initial plan was to get to where Petal had left a secondhand car she'd bought when she first got to Lee Vining. She'd stashed it off a side road that was reachable from the park, so it was ready and waiting. From there, we'd drive to Los Angeles and separate, getting lost in that enormous city. It was supposed to happen on the day after Labor Day. Petal and Jada had been hiking supplies to a cache in the woods right up to Jada's disappearance. If they ran out, they'd signal me and I'd find a way to bring them food. But they'd have access to plenty of water, and there were fish in the lake.

We didn't tell each other where we were going to go beyond

Los Angeles. No communication. That's how it was going to work. We'd say goodbye and that would be it, we'd be on our own. Petal had gotten new IDs for her and Jada, but I didn't need one. If everything went according to plan, no one would ever know that we knew one another.

And to date, that's how it's worked. I try to resist reading about myself, but sometimes late at night when I can't sleep, I take a peek. I'm quickly overwhelmed with the hashtags and hot takes. I'm a hero; I'm a villain. I should be arrested; I should be celebrated. A million possibilities without any resolution. Everyone has an opinion, and everyone feels free to share it.

But still, I notice the things no one figures out.

—My posts on SHELTER ME are gone, Jada's too.

—That Kevin never bought a gun.

—Why he waited so long to search for me.

—How he found me in the first place.

—Where he "bought" the medallion.

—The fact that two abusive men died in the park that summer.

There could be answers for all of it. It's too easy, for example, to get an unregistered gun in this country. I wasn't that hard to find. Who knows what tips someone over, especially a man like Kevin.

And as for Jim? He and Kevin had no connection. Abusive men aren't exceptional. And Jim's body was too far gone, too ravaged by animals, for the coroner to come to any conclusion about how he died. Maybe Sandy killed him and Jada too. Maybe she did a better job of hiding Jada's body. Maybe that's why Petal left, what Petal was going to tell the authorities the day before she disappeared, and then she made a different choice to take the money and run. Or maybe Sandy had killed Petal, too, and one day her bones would appear, bleached, cleaned, hard to identify.

Only Sandy could explain, and Sandy wasn't talking.

Ben's not talking either. Not to me, though I try once or twice to reach out. I'm guilty, he thinks. Maybe Kevin's death wasn't an accident. These are the charges I lay at my own feet. And since I can't acquit myself, I leave him be.

Dates on the calendar peel away, the trees lighten, the air cools. Labor Day weekend in the park goes by without me.

I make a short appearance at the closing party, where we all gather at the T-SAR site, and Bri hugs me long enough for it to get awkward, like it's a final goodbye.

The police have finally told me I'm free to go, though they want me to stay in touch. I give them my new cell number and promise not to change it. To check in once a month, like I'm on parole, though I haven't been charged with anything. The news vans pulled out weeks ago, and I'm leaving too.

I sleep one last night in my tent before gathering my things and tucking them all back into the pack I arrived with. As planned, I was careful with my money and I have enough saved from the summer to settle somewhere for a few months and figure out what I want to do. And then there's Kevin's money that I'm going to inherit if I can bring myself to take it. I haven't started the process yet—I don't even know how much Kevin left me in his will, just that I'm his heir. He made some big show of us getting wills soon after we got married, but part of Kevin's control was that he never told me how much we had or where it was. He just gave me credit and bank cards to use, to monitor me and my spending.

Jenny agrees to drive me out of the park and suggests we stop at the Mobil for one last . . . her voice trails off like my thoughts have one too many times.

Time is a circle, a wave, something that buries me and lifts me up all at once.

We get our tacos and margaritas and sit outside at a table looking at Mono Lake.

"Does it all seem too hard to believe?" Jenny asks. Her light blue eyes have turned dark, moody.

"What's that?"

"Everything that happened. Then, now."

"I don't think life follows a predictable path."

"Is that your way of telling me to fuck off?"

I half laugh. "You always did have a way of putting things."

"Friend hat?" she asks.

"Friend hat." ·

She hesitates. "Did I have it wrong all this time? Was it *you* who screwed up the map?"

"Does it matter?"

"I think it might."

I play with the wrapper from my tacos. "We weren't the reason they were out there, Jenny, or why they got lost. We didn't tell Chris to leave her. All we did was try to save her. And I feel guilty every day about that, but it's not our fault. We did our best."

"And the map?"

"Don't torture yourself. Maybe it was me, maybe it was you, maybe it was both of us."

That's part of the truth. Jenny made a mistake with that map, but I let her. *I let her.*

"And Jada, Jim, Petal? Your husband . . . That's all a coincidence?"

I keep my breathing even and calm. "How could it be anything but?"

"I keep trying to puzzle it out, but I can't get there."

"Because there isn't anything to find. And Kevin . . ." My throat closes up and I look away, indicating that I can't talk about it.

We stay in silence for a moment, and when I turn back to Jenny, she nods, then stares at her drink. "I had to ask."

"I understand."

"Are you mad?"

"No, of course not." I smile at her as best I can. "I'd ask the same questions."

"Where will you go now?"

"Maybe back to New York. Now that Kevin's gone . . . There's some money."

"Will you stay in touch?"

"I'll try."

"And Ben?"

"What about him?"

"Friend hat, remember?"

"Right." I take a long drink, then squeeze the bridge of my nose as my brain freezes. "It's all too complicated. Kevin. What I did. Who'd want to be with me?"

"Did you ask him?"

"He made it perfectly clear that he didn't want anything to do with me."

"What's he doing here, then?" Jenny asks, glancing over into the parking lot where Ben's standing in front of his truck, a dark puffy pulled up tight to his neck.

My heart rises like a schoolgirl's. "Did you tell him I'd be here?"

"Maybe."

"What does he want?"

"Why don't you go find out?"

Ben waves at me. My own hand raises in response, but I still hesitate. If I rise and walk across the parking lot, what will it mean? I can never tell him the truth. I don't even know for sure that I'm out of danger. If Petal and Jada get caught, then this house of cards we've built will come tumbling down.

But I find myself standing, walking down the concrete path until I'm in front of him, our breaths clouding around us as the sun sets behind him, casting him in shadow.

"I thought you might need a lift," Ben says.

"Where?"

"Malibu? It's beautiful, this time of year."

"You want me to go to Malibu with you?"

"I thought it might be a good place for you to rest, and maybe for us to see if we can be something real outside of this place."

That sounds nice, Malibu. White sand beaches and slow rolling waves that I could try to learn to surf on. Hanging out with Ben sounds nice, too. Like something a normal girl would do in a normal life. Spend a summer, meet a guy, ride his pickup truck into the sunset.

Can I do that? Can I take my broken, black heart and heal it?

"Are you sure?" I ask.

Ben smiles. "No, but we'll never find out if we don't try."

"And what about everything that happened with Kevin. You're okay with that?"

"I'm sorry I didn't take him seriously enough. That I wasn't there for you."

"That wasn't your fault."

"I feel sorry just the same."

I meet his eyes. "I'm sorry too."

He pulls in a slow breath. "So, will you?" He holds out his hand like he's asking me to dance.

Malibu. Not the place I was aiming for, but does that matter?

I close my eyes for a moment, thinking of the ocean, how it sucks at your toes when you stand on the shore, how the waves surprise you, wetting your calves, the pants you thought safe.

Life is risk.

I did all of this, all of these terrible things, to have the life I'd been cheated out of when I made the wrong choice and married Kevin. To plunge into the ocean even if the red flag warnings were fluttering in the wind. Even if the undertow was too strong to withstand.

Even if the outcome was unknown.

Because you can't plan for everything. You can only put both feet in and hope for the best.

"Yes," I say as my new phone beeps in my pocket. Some old, buried instinct makes me take it out, expecting a message from my mother, some new grievance about me leaving again.

But that's not what it is. Instead, it's something that makes me suck in my breath.

A text from a blocked number, but I know who it's from.

I'll be watching you, it says.

Petal.

"Everything okay?"

I reach up and search for the medallion I wore for so long. It's gone, in an evidence locker somewhere, but the feeling of being watched remains.

"Cassie?"

I slip my phone back into my pocket and do my best to smile at Ben. "It's nothing. Spam."

I look out past him at Mono Lake. Is she watching me right now?

No, she's not stupid enough to be here, so close to Yosemite.

But I believe her. She's watching, somehow, from somewhere.

Maybe forever.

October

It's fun, isn't it, making people do things?

Making people think one thing about you and then using that to make them dance like a puppet? Or one of those creepy marionettes they scare children with?

To be the one holding the strings and the one dancing, too.

I've always been able to do that, ever since I was little.

The kids in the playground. My teachers, who'd shake their heads and then laugh and let me get away with it. All those young girls Daddy hired to look after me once Mama left.

Mama was the only one who saw through me. The only one I couldn't make do exactly what I wanted. The only one I couldn't make stay.

Daddy was an easy mark. He felt so guilty about Mama that he'd give me whatever I wanted. He let me DO whatever I wanted. Stay out all night, steal things, drink, drop out of school. Oh, he'd talk tough in front of others, make it all seem like I was out of control, but that wasn't true. I was just having fun. Being carefree. Being like Mama.

A free spirit.

That's what he always called her, and that's what I was too.

Free.

I always knew that one day I'd fly the nest, find out what my true power was. But money's a trap they don't tell you about. America makes it seem like if you just work hard enough you can get whatever you want. But that's not true. The system's rigged, and if you don't realize that and grab whatever you can to get yourself outside of it, then you'll sink like most people do.

I was waiting for my opportunity. Waiting for my moment to seize.

And then I met her. Sandy. She stopped for gas at the station while I was filling up my car, and I just knew. SHE was my ticket to ride right out of town. And I was right. She was an easy mark, too, not even hiding that bulging money belt at her waist. I pretended I didn't know how to open the cover on my gas tank, and that was all it took.

And the funniest thing was—she thought SHE was seducing ME.

Like I had to be with some old woman to get off. Like I didn't have my pick of Wellfleet and Provincetown and anywhere else I wanted to go.

Fuck, she was stupid.

Stupid, but useful.

She'd been in bed with some bad people and had learned some tricks. Where to get a new identity. How to travel incognito. How to jump-start a car. How to listen in on the police. With my hacking skills, we really could've been something. Lit the world on fire and taken it for ourselves.

But she didn't want to crime anymore, she said. She wanted to settle down, RETIRE, lead a normal life.

RETIREMENT? Are you kidding me? She might've been old and ready to settle down, but I was just getting started.

I had it all planned out. I was going to take her money and run once she was stupid enough to show me where she hid it. I would've left her in the dust and never thought about it again. But then she had to go and hit me, slap me HARD right across the face when we had some stupid argument after I lifted this dumb guy's wallet in a bar. That was HER mistake.

I knew women like that. Women who stayed. Women who got HIT. Like Daddy did to Mama before she ran away. Which is why she ran away.

Those women are some of the easiest to manipulate. All you have to do is be nice to them and they'll tell you everything, give you anything.

They're weak like that, and I'm not weak.

If Sandy thought I was going to stay with her and let her do that to me, she had another thing coming.

But it gave me an idea, that watchful expression Sandy had on her face after she slapped me, waiting to see how I'd react. She'd done this before, she was telling me. She was testing me. So I tricked her. I started to cry, to play poor Petal, like I'd been doing for months, and right then I decided—I was going to get her back. Back for the slap, and every other woman who'd been hit. And then she'd see.

I'd been on that forum before. SHELTER ME. I used it to find random hookups when I was bored and needed money. I'd find a likely prospect and then I'd figure out who they really were and see if it was worth my time. That site's security is shit.

I met Jada like that. She was pretty, but she didn't have money. There was something about her, though. I felt sorry for her, I guess. That Jim was a nasty piece of garbage who was only going to get worse. He really was going to kill her one day if she didn't get out.

I liked to think about it. Killing Jim and finding a way to blame Sandy for it. It made me smile at night while she was snoring next to me. Sandy hated jail and never wanted to go back there. She talked about it all the time.

She talked so fucking much.

And then, like a miracle, like a UNICORN, Cassie started posting in the forum. Cassie, who had a rich husband. Cassie, who nothing bad had happened to, just a couple slaps and a husband who had an unhealthy interest in where she was. Whatever.

WHATEVER.

I sent Jada in first to see what she was like, to gather intel, to see if I could get that money her husband had. Jada was the Trojan Horse, and she played her part perfectly. When I rode in, Cassie was ready to spill everything.

But he kept that money buttoned up tight. Kevin Adams. He wasn't a moron like Jim or Sandy. Cassie was smart, too, but naïve. Still thought people were mostly good. She was just as easy to crack open as the others. I did it just like people who hit do: testing, testing, seeing what she'd go along with, where she'd buck. Didn't take her long until she was agreeing that Jim should die for what he'd done, that Sandy should pay, too.

She was the one who made me think it could happen. All that talk of Yosemite and how remote it was. How you could get lost there for weeks and no one would find you. I found all that stuff about Cameron and Chris pretty easily and saw the possibilities. How we could lure Jim and Sandy there. How we could get away with it and plant the seeds for Sandy's downfall.

The only problem was that Cassie didn't want to bring Kevin into it.

But I couldn't do that, could I? Leave her mostly innocent? Leave her in a position to tell?

I'm not stupid.

So there were two plans. The one Cassie knew about and the one I was conducting on the side. And it worked. She did what I wanted, and Kevin did too.

I got Sandy's money, and even if they don't blame her for Jim's death, she's going to be in jail for a long time. But if the stupid police do their job, then there's enough evidence to convict her for Jim. Her clothes and feces in the dry bags. Jim's blood on the wall.

Maybe she'll try to blame me, but I don't think so. Sandy doesn't trust the authorities to do right by her. That's why she ran out on her plea deal in Florida. She never was going to cooperate. She just used that as an excuse to get enough time to get away.

Besides, who'd believe her? Why would nice Petal, innocent Petal, diary Petal do something like that? She wouldn't, that's what. But Sandy, with her criminal record and history of violence and fighting with Jim and being jealous—she could snap. She could do something horrible to Jim and Jada, too.

I dropped Jada off somewhere in Venice. Her eyes lit up when she saw *the ocean. I wonder if anyone will recognize her now that she's cut off her hair? If she'll be able to keep quiet and abandon her old life?*

If she knows what's good for her she'll stay hidden. And if she's caught, she's going to say that Sandy kidnapped her and she escaped. That she kept running until she knew she was safe. We worked it all out.

She won't tell the truth. She'd be implicating herself in cold-blooded murder.

But just in case, I'll be keeping an eye on her. Oh yes.

As for Cassie, she hasn't seen the last of me yet. She's going to collect that money, her inheritance from Kevin. She won't be able to resist. And when she does, then I'm going to get my fair share.

In the meantime, I'll be in the last place anyone would think to look.

No one's going to find me.

There's no point in putting up one of those missing posters.

HAVE YOU SEEN HER?

No.

This is the TRUE diary of Petal Fernandez, and she's already gone.

ACKNOWLEDGMENTS

OMG, I wrote another book! And you're reading it—thank *you*!

Don't know how I keep doing it, but let's do it at least once more, right? Right?

A little over a year ago, I decided to make a change in my professional life, and so the first person I'd like to thank is Stephanie Kip Rostan, my *new* agent, though it already seems like we've worked together forever. Thanks so much for listening to what I want to happen and helping make it a reality. This is our first book together, but I already know it won't be our last.

To my editors, Kaitlin Olson, Laurie Grassi, Brittany Lavery, and Adrienne Kerr. There was a lot of you on this one and each of you brought something important to the book. Thanks especially to Kaitlin for telling me what I knew but hadn't yet pushed myself to do—write a more sinister ending!

To the marketing, publicity, and publishing teams at Atria and Simon & Schuster Canada—thank you for giving me the opportunity and for putting the book out there. A special shout-out to Kevin Hanson at S&S Canada—for taking a chance on me six books ago and letting me do my thing since then.

To my copy editor, Stacey Sakal, and the cover designer, thank you for making the inside and outside look fantastic and without errors.

To Rich Green and Ellen Goldsmith-Vein at Gotham for all the Hollywood connections.

To the usual suspects and some new ones too: My life besties— Tasha, Candice, Sara, Christie, and Tanya. Sandra (for tennis analysis and laughs), Elyssa Friedland (book bestie and fellow cult aficionado), Carol Mason (for Santa Monica and long phone calls), Rachel Stuhler (our movie WILL get made this year), Liz Fenton (are you driving to work? Call me!), my Ghosts with the Most screenwriters' group, Amy Jo Johnson, and Shawn Klomparens.

To my family—Mom, Dad, Cam, and Mike; my nephews Owen, Willian, Liam, and Anders; and my niece, Charlotte. Someday soon you might read this. Trippy. And to the Prices.

To my husband, David—by the time anyone reads this we'll have been together for 28.5 years. I literally cannot imagine my life without you.

And finally to Cam and Scott. This book is a work of fiction, but it was inspired by their amazing time as search and rescue workers in Yosemite and the stories they've told me over the years about the lives they saved. Thanks for sharing Yosemite with me.

As Cam says, they get credit for all the details I got right and are blameless for the mistakes and creative license.

ABOUT THE AUTHOR

CATHERINE McKENZIE was born and raised in Montreal, Canada. A graduate of McGill University in history and law, Catherine practiced law for twenty years before leaving to write full time. An avid runner, skier, and tennis player, she's the author of numerous bestsellers, including *I'll Never Tell* and *The Good Liar*. Her works have been translated into multiple languages, and *I'll Never Tell* and *Please Join Us* have been optioned for development into television series. Visit her at www.catherinemckenzie .com or follow her on Twitter @CEMcKenzie1 or Facebook and Instagram @CatherineMcKenzieAuthor.